"Luisa Perkins spins an eerie web with her haunting tale of a displaced spirit told in tight, lyrical prose."

—Melanie Jacobson, author of
The List and *Not My Type*

"In Luisa Perkins's new novel, *Dispirited*, a teenage girl discovers that a young boy's spirit can shake loose of his body, and she sets out on a daring quest to restore everything to its proper place. Its storytelling is propulsive, taut—without a single unnecessary word—vivid, romantic, and fascinating."

—Glen Nelson
Director, Mormon Artists Group

For Ireene —

DISPIRITED

With love —

A novel by

Luisa M. Perkins

ZARAHEMLA BOOKS

Provo, Utah

ISBN 978-0-9843603-6-9

Published by:
Zarahemla Books
869 East 2680 North
Provo, UT 84604
info@zarahemlabooks.com
ZarahemlaBooks.com

your arms stuck high overhead. He remembers panicking once like that when he was little, then Mama easing the shirt up and over his shoulders. That's the release he needs—he feels his collarbone and neck come free and then *sfiff*—he's loose.

Really? He's out? He looks around and gets dizzy. Gravity no longer anchors him. Little movements spiral him uncontrollably.

Run to ground, Blake. Go on home.

With a jolt, Blake realizes he's back in his body. But if he's gotten out once, he can do it again.

And soon he does. Soon he can get out of himself with the slightest of efforts. Up and out. He wanders around the townhouse, looking for his mother in all the old hiding places. Walls stop him for a long time, but only because he thinks they can.

One night he's practicing his spirals, rolling around and around and then stopping suddenly. He throws his arms out as a counterbalance—and one arm goes through the window. The closed and barred window. Blake only pauses for a minute before imagining his hand outside pulling the rest of him through. Then, he realizes, he can fly.

He floats up over East 78th Street into the still winter night. He feels the cold only as the slightest whisper of a breeze, even though he knows it must be below freezing. Using the grid of streets below as a guide, Blake flies farther and higher. The sleeping city spreads beneath him like a great, jeweled blanket. He steers himself gradually downtown.

Night birds notice Blake. So do squirrels in trees and feral cats wending their way through Central Park. He can see all of them in fine detail, as if through a magnifying glass with no distortion. All the animals look up and look at him, one by one. They don't seem surprised, or even shy.

Can people see him, too? He wonders. He drifts above Central Park South, then turns left and travels down low on Broadway, where there are plenty of people walking the street despite the late hour and the cold. No one seems to see him. Is that because they can't, or because, being New Yorkers, they choose not to? Blake isn't sure, but the diversion of making faces at preoccupied grown-ups pales quickly. It's much more fun to be up high. Blake leaves the sidewalk for the open air.

The city looks glorious from up above. He stops high atop the Manhattan Bridge to look around. He sits on the edge of the western tower and notices that he is wearing pajamas.

Pajamas? Does a ghost need pajamas?

Because that's what he is, Blake suspects. Isn't it that way in all the stories? Ghosts are people separated from their bodies. But what *is* this that's left when the body is gone? This weightless, sometimes visible self, free and light—this is the *real* Blake. Isn't it?

Can he change how he looks? He imagines himself in last year's Halloween costume, and he is wearing it instantly, torn pants, fake hook, eye patch, and all. In a blink he changes into his church clothes, then his bathing suit, then nothing at all. But that's embarrassing. Even though he's alone, he's outside. His pajamas will do just fine.

Looking out across Brooklyn, Blake notices that the sky is getting lighter. Not much, but enough to worry him. The winter nights are long, and it's impossible to know how long he's been out. What if Dad comes in to get him up for school, and he's not there? His body is there, of course, but this part of him that is out flying around is also the part that wakes and talks and laughs. He flies home faster than thought and immediately finds himself outside their townhouse. It takes a bit of courage to jump back through the window glass, but once that's done, he's back safe in his room.

Blake hovers at the ceiling for a bit, looking down at himself. *I'm just a small boy*, he thinks, and suddenly remembers that he was supposed to be looking for his mother. In all the exciting nights he's been learning and perfecting his new skill, he has forgotten why he had wanted to learn it in the first place. How could he forget Mama? The shame of it overcomes him, and he glides down gently to his body. Tomorrow night he'll fly out and look for her, he promises himself, maybe even find her.

He closes his eyes and prepares to settle in, as he has in the past—a sinking in, like lowering yourself into a hot bath, like pulling on your most comfortable jeans.

Except he's not sinking. He opens his eyes and reaches out to touch his own hand, to pass through the flesh and put it on again. It is solid. It won't let him pass. He tries harder, but cannot penetrate his skin. A little panicked, Blake reaches over and puts his hand through the wall next to the bed. No problem. As easy as moving through air. He moves around the room, swiping his limbs through the dresser, the bookshelves, the floor. Nothing in the room stops him. He comes back to the bed and touches his cheek, tentatively. It is as hard and cool as stone. He shrinks back, because it suddenly doesn't feel like his own skin anymore.

Just then, Blake's body opens its eyes and smiles up at him. Not a nice smile, Blake realizes with a nasty shock. Blake's body laughs, and it's not his laugh at all. Blake sees now that nothing about his body is quite right. It's as if he has twinned himself somehow, or as if his mirror image has come to independent life. His body won't stop laughing. Blake reaches out, tries to cover his body's mouth to muffle that terrible sound—and his body slaps his hand away, sending him spinning across the room.

"You can't come in," Blake's body whispers. "I live here now, and you can't come in."

CHAPTER TWO

HOUSEWARMING

"WHAT DO YOU SEE?" hissed a small, cold voice. Cathy flinched, stopping her toothbrush mid-stroke. The white movie-star lights in her new bathroom dimmed to dark gold, while the shadows in the mirror beyond Cathy's reflection lengthened and gained substance. A cavern yawned behind her, stretching into black nothingness. Its depths made her light-headed, but she couldn't look away.

"What do you see?" the voice repeated. A faint buzzing in her ears grew to an unbearable whine. The blackness in the mirror sucked her down and in, farther and darker, inch by inch. Wrenching her gaze from the mirror, Cathy dropped her toothbrush into the marble sink and whirled around. She blinked and stared down at her five-year-old sister standing in the doorway.

"Huh?" Cathy asked, realizing her mouth was still full of toothpaste. Avoiding the mirror, she turned, bent over the sink, and rinsed out her mouth.

"What did you see?" asked Mae.

"Nothing, Mae. I didn't see anything." Cathy slid past her sister and sat down on her bed. She wiped her lips with the back of her hand and leaned her forehead against the cool brass bedstead. Mae came to her side and leaned on her knee. Cathy tried to smile.

"Need something, Maybe-Baby?" she asked.

"I was just wondering what you were up to. I thought I'd check on you."

Now Cathy grinned, and her shock lessened a bit. Mae cracked her up sometimes.

"I'm fine! Don't I look fine?"

Mae wrinkled her forehead and squinted her eyes. "No," she re-torted. "Maybe you need some fresh air."

"You're right. Maybe I do. In fact, I think I'll go for a walk—do a little exploring. Do you want to come with?"

"Nah, no thanks. I'm gonna go play in my new room some more. It's so awesome!" Mae raced out of the bedroom.

Cathy groped around under her bed for her flip-flops, then pulled her long brown hair into a ponytail without the help of a mirror. What had just happened in the bathroom? Whatever it was, she wanted to get away and sort it out. She shivered at the memory and left.

As she walked down the driveway, Cathy gazed up at the new house. Everyone else oohed and ahhed over how fancy it was, but Cathy thought it was the ugliest thing she'd ever seen. Way too big for the lot it was on. Skinny white vinyl siding. Windows that pretended to be paned, but were really just big sheets of glass with plastic grilles stuck to the inside frames. The worst part was that every house on the block looked exactly like this one. The whole neighborhood was like a bunch of inbred cousins at a family re-union.

Of course, she hadn't told anybody all this, because who was there to tell? Her best friend Jessica had abandoned her for orches-tra camp all the way out in California. Jess wouldn't be back in New York until the end of the summer, and who knew how their friend-ship would change now that they weren't living just a few blocks apart anymore?

Cathy could see her sisters jumping on the thick cushion of Fawn's window seat. Fawn and Mae were thrilled about their bed-rooms (pastel carpeting, wallpaper borders with princesses on them), the big refrigerator (water and ice dispensers on the outside), and the new cedar swing set in the back yard. Cathy had been shocked at how easily the girls had made the transition from Manhattan to this backward town with the weird Indian name. Fawn and Mae were only eight and five, but still—totally disloyal. Didn't they miss the city at all? Even if they did, they were too little to see Cathy's point of view.

On the sidewalk, the thick heat of August engulfed her. She walked fast anyway, wanting to get out of the subdivision as quickly as possible. Tall maples lined the main road into town; she slowed down once she reached their shade. Gradually, the metallic hiss of cicadas soothed her jumpy nerves and the humidity wrapped her in a heavy blanket of calm. Bushes along the sidewalk bent under the weight of what looked like ripe raspberries. Could they be edible? That seemed too good to be true. She decided to walk down to the gas station for a soda and see if they had a map of the area. Maybe there was a park nearby with trails.

Cathy considered her other options for someone to talk to. Her mom was normally a great listener, but not this time. Any complaints Cathy made to her would be taken the wrong way. The whole stupid house thing was part of a bigger problem. Athena Wright was now Athena Harford; she'd gotten remarried just weeks before. Cathy didn't feel ignored, not exactly. It was just that her mom and Malcolm were floating around in a bubble and didn't seem to notice that not everybody was as happy as they were.

Her mother was usually so smart, but intellect had failed her when she had met Malcolm. What did she see in him? So he was a "famous" Shakespeare scholar. So he apparently adored Cathy's mother and did everything he could to make her feel loved and special. That didn't make up for the fact that he was pale and awkward and boring and nothing at all like Cathy's dead father. There was no way he was worming his way into Cathy's heart and trying to take over where he had no business. Cathy hoped she had made that clear.

As she walked, Cathy kicked pinecones into the culvert that ran along the sidewalk and kept thinking over her choices. Maybe she could talk to Blake. Since the wedding, he'd been deferential to his new stepmother, gallant in a show-off way with Fawn and Mae, and polite (but not exactly warm) to Cathy herself. He seemed to get along great with his dad. It was no wonder. Blake was tall, athletic, apparently some kind of braniac, and played the piano like no teenager Cathy had ever heard.

Would he understand? They were almost the same age. They'd both been uprooted and moved from the city they'd lived in all their lives. Cathy didn't know whether she could trust him, though. He'd said something at their parents' wedding reception that had been bothering her for weeks. They had been standing in the receiving line—he in his custom-made tux, she in a lilac silk dress. An old friend of Malcolm's had paused to chat with Blake.

"You'll both be seniors in the fall, eh?" The man had nodded at Cathy and smiled. "You even look a bit alike. I'll bet the kids at your new school will think you two are twins."

Blake had looked at Cathy sideways and laughed politely. "Somehow, I doubt it," he'd answered dryly.

Just a little comment, just a little slip of his mask, but it had lodged in her memory like an irritating grain of sand. She had been bristling to ask him what he had meant by that from the second he had said it, but had been too confused to know how. Now she feared that if she brought it up, he would have forgotten all about it. He'd think she was totally neurotic for even mentioning it.

Lame. Another thing she couldn't tell anybody. And now this bizarre episode while she was brushing her teeth. Had she really heard a voice in the bathroom, or had it just been Mae? And that thing with the mirror turning into a dark cave—was she going nuts? Maybe she had just gotten light-headed for a minute. Cathy shivered again.

She reached the mini-mart attached to the gas station and went inside. The air conditioner was cranked up high. The clerk behind the counter hummed a tuneless counterpoint to its roar. Cathy grabbed a soda and browsed the snack aisle. As she turned to go to the register, she bumped into someone. Her soda bottle crashed on the floor, spraying sticky orange liquid all over her legs.

Metal crutches clattered down. Cathy slipped in the soda and sat down hard in the mess. Whoever she'd run into was still scrambling above her. He grabbed a shelf loaded with potato chips to keep from falling. For a moment, he seemed safe. Then the shelf ripped loose from its pegboard, and the guy fell into Cathy's lap.

She flung her arms over her head as mylar bags rained down on them.

Shouting in light-speed Spanish, the clerk came charging around the counter and slipped in the soda as well. Cathy leaned back against the candy shelves and laughed. It was like something out of an old movie. The guy on her lap turned around to look at her, then pulled himself off of her and started laughing as well. The clerk glared at them both and started picking up bags of chips, muttering under his breath all the while.

Cathy stuck out an orange-spattered hand. The guy reached around and clasped it hard. Cathy realized that he must be about her own age. She smiled into his tilting blue eyes.

"Hi, I'm Cathy Wright."

"Way to make a first impression, Cathy. Richard Mallory—call me Rich." His grip on her hand tightened.

"Yikes, you're strong." Cathy wiggled her fingers. Rich dropped her hand at once.

"Sorry. It's all the weight lifting I do." Rich pointed to his sticky crutches. Cathy realized they weren't the kind you got when you sprained your ankle; these were made for permanent use. Rich used his arms to shift his weight off of his twisted legs.

"Amyloplasia. It's not contagious," he said.

Cathy pointed to her own legs. "Klutziness. I don't think it's contagious, but that hasn't been confirmed." Cathy felt her face go hot and got to her feet. Had she just made the most tasteless joke of all time? But Rich laughed.

"Thanks. Most people look away and pretend they don't notice I'm not normal. You're refreshing—like a nice, cold, orangey drink."

Cathy went down the aisle, ripped open a package of wet wipes, and passed some over to Rich. They mopped the worst of the mess off of themselves and the floor.

"You pay for those," the clerk interjected, pointing at the wipes and chips.

"I'll pay for them," Cathy and Rich both said. They smiled at each other.

"Jinx. You owe me a soda," said Cathy, "Actually two. One for jinx, and one for bumping into me."

"Bumping into *you*? You did the bumping," Rich countered.

"Fine. Let's split all this, grab a couple more drinks, and call it even."

"Done."

Cathy finished the floor while her new acquaintance scrubbed off his crutches. The clerk rang up the cost of the accident. "$22.37," he announced, clearly afraid they would balk. Cathy pulled some crumpled bills out of her pocket and started smoothing, sorting, and counting. She looked up after getting eleven dollars together to realize that Rich had already paid the clerk.

"Here," she said, holding the money out to Rich. He shook his head and turned toward the door.

"Sorry, my hands are full," he said over his shoulder. "Just keep it for now. I'll hit you up for it later." Cathy shoved the money back into her pocket, grabbed the bag of sodas, and followed him out the door to the parking lot.

"Which way are you going?" Rich asked.

Cathy pointed the way she had come. "We just moved to Silverado Estates, but I was hoping to not go home for awhile."

"Silverado? Which house?"

"303 Turley Lane."

"Well, howdy, neighbor! I live at 306."

"Really?" Cathy frowned. Number 306 was across the street from her house. "I haven't seen anybody at that house. I didn't think anyone lived there yet."

"We moved in at the beginning of the summer, but we've been at the shore for the last two weeks."

"Well, that's why, then. We moved in two weeks ago."

"Gotcha. Okay. Escape from Silverado. If you don't mind company, I can give you a tour." He raised his eyebrows. Cathy nodded and smiled. "We could walk downtown to Main Street, or up to Waverly Lake. It's more of a pond than a lake, but it's pretty up there. What's your pleasure?"

"Ooh, the lake. Pond. Whatever. Do you think it'll be cooler there?"

"Definitely." Rich pried his crutches out of the hot, sticky asphalt. "And we can pick berries on the way." He pulled a plastic bag out of his backpack and handed it to her.

Rich's speed on his crutches surprised Cathy. She hurried along next to him. A truck came up the road and slowed as it approached them. Someone rolled down a window and yelled and waved at Rich. He smiled and nodded back.

"Do you know people here already, or is everyone in this town just freakishly friendly?" Cathy asked.

"Both. I was born and raised right here in Kashkawan—our old house is down on Chestnut, off of Main. By the school. Have you been over that way yet?"

"Nope."

Rich stopped at a berry bush, leaned hard on one crutch, and started picking fruit. Cathy held out the bag and Rich tossed the fruit in.

"You *can* eat those?" she asked. "Wow. I just assumed they were poisonous, or something. It's not the kind of thing they plant on the streets in Manhattan." She popped a berry into her mouth. Warm, sweet juice exploded on her tongue. She closed her eyes in bliss.

Rich hopped up the sidewalk, picking as he went. "So that's where you're from?"

"Yeah. This seems like a different country. Kashkawan is cute and all, but I hate our house."

"Seriously? How come? I love ours. We've never had central air before. And it's a lot easier for me to get around."

Cathy felt ashamed of her ingratitude. Rich was right. The new house *was* extremely comfortable. "I don't know. Maybe I'm blaming everything on the house. My mom just got remarried, so I have a new stepfather and a stepbrother. And I have to spend my senior year at a brand new school where I don't know anybody."

Rich stopped and pushed his straw-blond hair out of his eyes. "Poor babe," he grinned. "But you know me now. Although I'll only be a junior this year. I hope you'll still talk to me."

"Of course!" Then Cathy realized Rich was teasing, and she rolled her eyes. "What's the school like?" she asked after eating a handful of berries. "You must know everyone if you've lived here forever."

"It's small, but fine. I guess. I don't have anything to compare it to. Sports are very big, which you might guess is not really my thing."

"Right. So what do you do?"

"Read, listen to music. Computer games. Obscure stuff like that. What about you?"

Cathy laughed. "About the same."

Rich turned left onto a dusty unpaved road. The shade was deeper here, the cicadas louder. The trees grew so thick that soon the noise from the road faded away. The rutted clay road traveled gradually upward. After going around a bend, Cathy and Rich came to a fork in the road. A sweet reek filled the air, a smell that almost shimmered in the heat. Rich nodded toward the left fork.

"That way's the town dump—obviously," he said. "We've got to go uphill a ways here to the right, and then we'll be at the lake. Are you up for it, or have I worn you out?"

"I love to walk. Did you know New Yorkers walk an average of five miles a day?"

"Good to know. But there won't be any taxis coming along to bail you out if you get tired."

"I think I can handle it."

Waverly Lake was tiny, but gorgeous. Just the sight of it, placid and blue in the summer heat, made Cathy feel cooler. And Rich was right: it wasn't as muggy up here. A long, wide beach lay before them. The sand must have been trucked in. Rich had to slow down once his crutches hit its shifting surface. Cathy cut her pace to match his, looking around as she walked. Tall sugar maples and oaks came right down to the water's surface on either side of the beach. Far away, a woodpecker worked busily. The sound of its drill accented the peace that settled over Cathy.

They sat down at a picnic table near the water's edge, backs to the table on the side facing the water. Cathy kicked off her flip-flops and passed Rich a soda. "You win," she said. "I love it here. I'm starting to get why my mother felt so drawn to this area when we were looking for a house." She sipped her drink and considered the view. "Is this a reservoir, or has it always been here?"

"It's been here forever—or at least as long as Kashkawan has been settled. This all used to be the property of the Voorhees family. They got thousands of acres in a New Amsterdam land grant and built a big house near here back in the mid-1600s."

"Aren't you the historian."

"You'll be one, too, soon enough. We've got legends aplenty here in Kashkawan."

"My mother will love that," Cathy said. "She did her dissertation on American Folklore. And she has Dutch ancestry, so she's really excited about living here—'exploring our heritage,' and all."

"But you don't share her enthusiasm," observed Rich. "I get that."

Cathy shook her head. "No offense. I'm just not drawn to the Hudson Highlands the way my mom is. I'd rather read about Rip Van Winkle and Ichabod Crane from the safety and comfort of a bench in Central Park."

Rich's laugh echoed from the opposite shore.

"Cool!" cried Cathy at the sound, and hooted like a loon. Her voice came back to them, faint and empty sounding. It sounded like the cry of someone lost, and gave Cathy goose bumps, reminding her why she'd wanted to escape the house in the first place. She shivered and rubbed her upper arms, trying to chase her unreasoning fear away.

"You can't be cold," said Rich.

"No—I got spooked at the house this morning. I'm just trying to shrug it off."

"Why? What happened?"

Cathy hesitated. She'd known Rich less than an hour. Right now, he was the closest thing to a friend she had. No way was she going to risk alienating him by telling him about her earlier freak-out in the bathroom. Now, sitting in the peaceful sunlight, Cathy realized that she must have imagined the entire thing, because what she thought she had experienced was impossible. She let out a breath and smiled.

"Really, it's nothing," she said. "Hey, I should probably get home. The only person I told I was leaving was my five-year-old sister. Walk back with me?"

"Sure." Rich stood up and put the empty soda bottles into his backpack. "I hope coming up here won't get you into any trouble."

"Oh, no, it's fine. I'd love to do it again another time—I mean, if you want."

"Absolutely." He started across the sand, planting his crutches and swinging his twisted legs between them. "Don't forget the berries."

"Got 'em," she replied. "Goodbye, lake!" she called out across the water.

"... ache," her lonely voice came back. Suddenly, Cathy felt small and incredibly isolated. She turned and hurried up the beach after Rich.

CHAPTER THREE

DISPOSSESSION

BLAKE DOESN'T SEE others of his kind very often. Isn't that strange? With so many people in the world dying every day, he would have thought the air would be thick with beings like him. Maybe Aunt Edie had been wrong. Maybe his mama's spirit was someplace else entirely, not anywhere in this world. Maybe when your body died, it was a whole different situation, and your spirit had to leave the earth completely.

But how would it do that? And where is heaven? And how was his body stolen from him? Who has taken it over? Is he trapped forever, here on the outside of where he should be?

He doesn't know the answers to any of these questions, and it's getting harder even to remember that he has questions. He finds himself forgetting things: what his favorite books are, what his mother looked like. If he works hard, he can recall details like these, but with every day that passes, they become more slippery. Memories fall away from him like stones into a dark chasm where he is unable to follow.

He shadows his body constantly, but from a distance. Whenever he gets too close, and his body knows it won't be seen, it chases him and hisses vicious threats at him. Hatred flows from it in palpable waves. How could it harm him? He has no idea, but he's sure it can. As frightening as this is, he can't stay away; his body pulls at him like a magnet. At night, he rests on the roof of the apartment building across the street from his own. During the day, he waits in the small park near his school. On weekends, he trails his father and his body to museums and to concerts, to baseball games and to church.

Once in a while, if he's feeling brave, he'll float through his father's window and curl up at the foot of his bed like a cat to rest. He knows that he can't be seen by anyone but his body, but his father feels his presence in some subtle way. Malcolm's sleep becomes restless. He moans and says Blake's mama's name out loud as he dreams. This gives Blake a wrenching feeling of homesickness, a yearning that is the strongest thing he experiences while existing here on the outside.

When he does encounter other spirits once in awhile, he asks them for advice. Has the same thing happened to them? Do they have plans for regaining control of what's been taken from them?

But trying to talk to them is useless. They seem disoriented, confused—like children who have just been startled awake, or like the crazy people he has seen on TV once or twice. Why are they here? They don't know—they don't seem even to understand what he is asking. They wave him away like a distraction, or a reminder of things they'd rather not acknowledge. He does notice that they, too, are compelled to follow certain bodies around, flesh-and-blood people that seem to resemble these bewildered, otherworldly echoes and shadows.

Sometimes he sees other beings that are something else entirely. Tall and gaunt, with hollow, staring eyes—these ignore him and focus their attention on his body. They seem to sense that there is something different about it, the way wolves know which deer is weak and ready for the taking. Perhaps they are somehow related to the creature that has stolen his life. Perhaps they want to take Blake's body for themselves. These beings can travel unseen and pass through walls the way he can, but otherwise they seem just as solid as real people.

Is *he* real anymore? He wonders sometimes. He wonders what will become of him. He wonders whether he'll ever taste a grilled cheese sandwich or a chocolate bar again, and whether the sharp and persistent memories of tastes will stay with him when everything else has vanished. He wonders where God is, and what He thinks about all this. He has a lot of time to wonder these things.

Day and night. Spring and fall. After awhile, he finds it almost impossible to hold onto his sense of self. The details seem as insubstantial as this thing that he's become. Sometimes he can't remember his name. One day, in a burst of clarity, he imagines himself dressed in his favorite T-shirt and jeans, the clothes that he always chose first in the afternoons once he could change out of his school uniform. This outfit feels most like the person he once was, the boy he barely remembers. He keeps his spirit dressed like this and not in pajamas anymore in the hope that he can hang on.

No matter the passage of time, he still needs to be close to his body. He watches it grow as the seasons pass. He follows it down the streets with his father, its stride gradually lengthening over the years. He watches it play catch or a pick-up game of lacrosse in the park with friends. He sees it at his desk at his window doing his homework. Through all these changes, he himself stays the same. Perhaps he'll be nine years old forever. He doesn't know; he doesn't know anything anymore.

CHAPTER FOUR

CLOSE ENCOUNTER

CATHY HAD BEEN PUSHING Mae on the swing for so long her arms were starting to ache. "Pump your legs, Mae, pump!" she said for about the forty-seventh time. "It's so much more fun when you do it yourself." She stopped pushing and sat down on the next swing over. It was too low to the ground. Malcolm had hung it for Fawn, who was a good foot shorter than Cathy was. She pumped awkwardly, legs going back and forth at an angle to escape dragging on the lawn, but she was still able to get the swing going. She worked to match the motion of Mae's swing.

"See, Maybe? Come on: out and back, out and back. You can do it," Cathy said. Mae kicked her legs a few times, but gave up after a minute, her swing slowly losing momentum.

"Push me again, please?" Mae begged. She opened her root-beer-brown eyes wide and stuck out her lower lip. Mae had known since she was about two years old that this face worked miracles. Cathy had to turn away to keep from laughing outright and letting her win.

Fawn's best grown-up voice came from the tented roof fort of the swing set. "Maybe-Baby, you're starting kindergarten tomorrow. Cathy won't be at school to push you. You're almost five. You really should practice pumping, or the other kids'll think you really *are* a baby. Believe me; I *know* what that's like."

"You should listen to Fawn," said Cathy, suppressing another smile. "She knows what she's talking about. She was in kindergarten just three short years ago."

Mae jumped off the swing and pranced around the lawn. "Kindy-garden, kindy-garden," she chanted. "I can't wait!"

Cathy wished she could borrow some of her sister's enthusiasm. She dreaded the next day. She fantasized about not going to school—just taking the GED exam instead and staying home for a year before college. If she did that, she could read all day long and not have to worry about any of the nonsense that passed for social interaction between teenagers. No tests, no stress over what to wear every day, no stupid Prom. It sounded like heaven. Her mother and Malcolm would never go for that, though, even if she offered to do extra chores every day. Stupid Malcolm. She could probably talk her mother into it if it weren't for him. As it was, there was no way she was getting out of her senior year.

Academically, she'd be fine. It was the people that worried her. What would she have in common with anyone here? These kids had all known each other forever. Their friendships had been set in stone for years. Besides, Rich had made it sound like it was a huge jock school. She only did team sports when forced. Maybe she could get away with taking tennis or swimming. Were those even options, though? Since she was a late transfer, she wouldn't get her schedule until the next morning when she reported to the guidance counselor's office.

At least there was Rich. They probably wouldn't have any classes together, but he had been great company over the past few weeks. They had similar taste in music and books, which counted for a lot. The best part about him, though, was how easy he was to be around. He never seemed to feel like he had anything to prove, so Cathy could relax around him as if they'd been friends for years.

Blake appeared to be unfazed by any of the transitions that were stressing Cathy out. He was such a robot. At first, Cathy had assumed his serenity was an act, but now she wondered whether it was just years of habit gained at that stuck-up, Upper East Side prep school he'd attended. He seemed so buttoned down, with no comic relief whatsoever.

Cathy stood, reached up, and peeked in through one of the tent flaps. Fawn presided over a tea party for her entire international doll collection. She had at least ten of them, all in multi-colored native costumes. Fawn's spread of pretend food, china tea ware, and assembled guests looked like a United Nations picnic in miniature.

"What about you, Fawn? Are you looking forward to school?"

Her sister nodded, smoothing her dark brown hair back behind her ears. Her green eyes were characteristically serious. "Oh, of course. I'm sure there will be some nice kids there. And we get to ride the bus. I've always wanted to ride the bus." Fawn passed a plate of plastic scones around to her immobile companions.

"True," Cathy agreed gravely, though she secretly wished they all could just walk the half-mile into town. Instead, the bus would pick them up at the entrance to Silverado Estates, which would probably be good once the weather turned cold. "The bus is a plus."

"That rhymes!" squealed Mae, and changed her chant. "The bus is a plus! The bus is a plus!"

Cathy watched her sister dance, then let her eyes drift around the back yard. Despite their lack of taste where the house was concerned, at least the builders had left the property alone. Huge oak and tulip trees stood around the perimeter of the sod that Malcolm had paid to have planted weeks before. High up, their leaves rustled in a slight breeze that was imperceptible down below. Several huge granite rocks thrust up out of the ground. One rock in particular had caught Cathy's eye from the day they had moved in. Sitting in the shade of a large maple tree, it looked a little bit like a camel at rest. Now seemed like as good a time as any to try climbing it.

Cathy examined both ends of the camel and decided to try going up the left side. Here, the rock sloped much more gradually. Her sneakers should be up to the task. Once she got moving, it was a pretty easy climb. The rough, lichen-covered surface gave her plenty of traction and she scrambled to the top in a matter of seconds. The hump was flatter on top than it had looked from the ground. It lay nearly level with the forest floor behind; the rock itself acted almost like the face of a little cliff. She surveyed the world from her new vantage point.

"Now *this* is the spot for a tea party," she said under her breath.

She looked toward the house, but the maple tree's dense foliage blocked everything but the corner where Blake's bedroom window was. In fact, Blake now sat at his desk, probably emailing one of his Manhattan friends. He was either at the computer or at the piano for hours at a time. Cathy wondered again whether Blake was nervous about school at all. If so, it certainly didn't seem like he was going to confide in her.

A cloud passed in front of the sun. For a moment, it cut the glare so that Cathy could see much better through the window. What would Blake think if he knew she was watching him right now? It probably wouldn't go over very well, she decided.

"This is my rock."

Cathy whirled, her stomach lurching. For a split second, it had sounded like the same voice she'd heard in her bathroom weeks before. She almost cried with relief when she saw a boy standing on the leaves behind her. He looked about Fawn's age, but taller and painfully thin. He had long, brown hair and dark eyes with purple shadows under them.

"You scared me!" Cathy cried. Her heart was going a mile a minute. He was only a kid, though. He probably hadn't meant to startle her. Cathy forced herself to calm down. She adopted the jovial tone she automatically used with her sisters and their friends. "And I'm sorry, but I'm pretty sure this is *our* rock." She pointed behind her in the direction of the house. "We just moved here a few weeks ago. I bet we can share the rock with you, though. It's really nice up here, right? Do you live nearby?"

The boy nodded. "I didn't think you could see me."

"Oh, I didn't see you at first, not when I climbed up here. This is a great hiding spot. But I hope you haven't been playing Peeping Tom."

The boy slowly shook his head in emphatic denial after a pause. Cathy wasn't sure, but it seemed like he was just telling her what she wanted to hear. It was weird—he looked familiar, somehow. She frowned, trying to figure out how she knew him. Maybe she'd seen him around the subdivision without realizing it.

"Hey, what's your name? I've got a sister about your age. Are you going into third grade?"

The boy shook his head again. Then he glanced over Cathy's shoulder and froze in terror. His face grew even paler; he looked like he might burst into tears. "I've got to go," he whispered. He turned and ran into the woods, his big, dirty T-shirt flapping silently behind him. He moved so lightly over the leaves that he made almost no sound. He reminded Cathy of someone out of *The Leatherstocking Tales*. What had scared the boy so badly? She turned around again and got her own shock. Blake stood at his window, looking directly at her. His face, usually so carefully neutral, was full of rage and hatred. As bizarre as that was, she saw something else even more frightening in his expression. Cathy recognized it, but it didn't make any sense. Why on earth would Blake be *gloating?*

"Girls!" came her mother's voice from the back door. "Come in for lunch."

Mae ran squealing toward the house. Fawn climbed down from the fort and followed more sedately. Cathy didn't move, her eyes still locked with those of her stepbrother. He glanced away first. Cathy faintly heard her mother's voice calling Blake from the bottom of the stairs inside the house. He turned and left his room without looking back.

Cathy sank down and sat on the rock. Even on this hot summer day, it chilled her bare legs. The cold helped steady her nerves. What was Blake's deal? He had obviously recognized the boy. But what could the kid have done to make Blake so angry? He'd seemed harmless, pathetic even. She'd have to ask Rich whether he knew the boy. Maybe he could help her figure this out.

"Cathy? Are you out there?"

Though she would have preferred to avoid seeing Blake at the moment, Cathy clambered down the rock at the sound of her mother's voice. Her mother, though usually very reasonable, didn't like to be kept waiting at mealtimes.

Everyone sat waiting for her at the kitchen table. Cathy hurried to wash her hands and slid into her seat.

"Mae, it's your day to say the blessing," her mother said. Fawn started to groan, but broke it off at a stern look from Athena.

Cathy bowed her head with everyone else as Mae began the prayer. Mae always had a lot to say to God, covering topics as diverse as the New York Mets' current standings, the weather, and the health of her pet turtle, Trivet. Normally, Cathy found Mae's conversations with Heaven very entertaining, but right now she wished her little sister had a fast forward button. She wanted to bolt down her sandwich and get over to Rich's house as quickly as possible.

The hair on the back of her neck stood up; Cathy felt certain Blake was looking at her. She opened her eyes. Sure enough, his eyes bored into hers from across the table. Her mouth went dry. She had never felt less like eating.

Then she got mad. Was Blake trying to scare her? Why? What had she done to him? Well, she wasn't going to be bullied by him. She would get to the bottom of whatever this whole thing was and tell Blake to get over it. She cocked an eyebrow at him and pointedly closed her eyes just in time for the chorus of amens. Then she picked up her sandwich and gave her mother a big smile.

"I love chicken salad, Mom. Thanks." Cathy took a huge bite and chewed as fast as she could. Blake sat in silence and ate his own food without looking at anyone.

"You're welcome, honey," replied her mother. "What are you up to this afternoon?"

"I'm going to go hang out at Rich's. Maybe we'll walk up to Waverly Lake again."

"Can I go?" asked Mae. Cathy tried to think of a tactful way to turn her down, but her mother stepped in instead.

"No, Mae; you *may* not. You need to help me organize all your school supplies, remember? We're going to put labels on everything and pack up your backpack."

"Yessss!" said Mae, blowing breadcrumbs everywhere.

"Yuck, Mae!" Fawn rolled her eyes and brushed off her arm. "You totally spit on me."

"Did not!"

"Yes, you did!"

Cathy took advantage of her mother's distraction over the brewing squabble. After gulping down her milk, she wrapped up the rest of her sandwich in her napkin, shoved it in her pocket, and cleared her place. She had gotten to the front hall and opened the front door when Blake's hand on her shoulder stopped her.

"What were you doing up on that rock?" he hissed into her ear. Cathy yanked herself out of his grasp and turned on him. "What were you doing," he repeated with gritted teeth, "Spying on me?"

Cathy glanced toward the kitchen. Her mother was still mediating between Fawn and Mae. "Of course not!" she whispered. "Why would I? Anyway, there was nothing to see except a stupid guy obsessed with his computer. Why do you even care? What's wrong with you?"

Blake's face went red with suppressed fury. "The only thing wrong with me is *you*. You're always running around outside like this is the Garden of Eden or something. Just because we're out in the middle of nowhere doesn't mean it's safe to do that. You need to watch yourself. And keep away from that idiot boy you were talking to."

"Why? Who is he? How do you know him?"

Blake grabbed her arm and steered her outside onto the front porch. He shut the door with quiet care and let her go. He glared at her for a few seconds. Then he closed his eyes and took a deep breath.

"Look, I don't know who he is—just some loser from this inbred little town. He's always up on that rock looking in my window. I finally went out and chased him away last night. He creeps me out, and I don't want him around you or the little girls, or Athena, for that matter. There's something wrong with him, and I don't want you to get hurt."

Blake's admission deflated Cathy's anger. "Oh. He seemed harmless to me." She mentally reviewed her encounter with the kid; there *had* been something a little strange about him. Was it more than a coincidence that'd he'd frightened her so badly at first? "He's been up there at night?" she asked. "Just watching you? That's bizarre. Did you tell Malcolm about it?"

"No. It didn't seem worth mentioning at first. I figured he was just some weird neighbor kid. Which is probably what he is. And as far as Dad goes—he's happy for the first time in as long as I can remember. I don't want to bring him down, you know?"

"Yeah, of course; I know exactly what you mean. I call it 'the honeymoon bubble.'"

Blake flashed a grin at her, and Cathy barely caught herself from gasping at the transformation. How could someone go from quiet good looks to devastating handsomeness with one smile?

Gross. She mentally stomped on that spark; what could be more disgusting than being attracted to your own stepbrother?

"You know, right now you're actually acting like a brother instead of an android," she kidded. "That's a real step forward in our relationship." She grew serious again. "But now I want to find out who that kid is, and why he's hanging around here so much."

"Can you let me handle it?" Blake put up a hand to forestall her protests. "I know you're a big girl and all. But it seems like *I'm* his focus. I can take care of it. And when I figure out what's going on, I promise I'll give you all the details."

Cathy considered his request. It went against her independent nature to let it go, but maybe she should surrender in the name of this newfound family unity. She squared her shoulders and stuck out her hand.

"Truce. I won't run off alone for a while—at least without telling someone where I'm going. But you have to be careful, too. And swear that you'll fill me in on that kid's story. And we have to go to Malcolm if anything weirder happens."

"Deal." Blake took her hand and shook it, then shocked Cathy by pulling her into a hug. "We're a family now, and I'm not going to let anything happen to that," he murmured in her ear. Cathy patted his back politely until he let her go. "See you later," he said finally, and went into the house.

Cathy stared after him, feeling a little like Alice down the rabbit hole. "Curiouser and curiouser," she breathed, and started down the front steps. She couldn't wait to see what Rich thought about all this.

CHAPTER FIVE

UNEARTHED

"ARE YOU KIDDING ME?" Cathy came out of the doors of the high school just as her bus left the parking lot. Her locker had been sticking. By the time she'd gotten it shut and shoved everything she needed into her backpack, the halls had completely emptied out. She had hoped, though, that someone would hold the bus for her.

She could call her mom for a ride, but decided against it and sent her a quick text instead. The walk home would give her some quiet time, some space to think. She knew it was a paradox, but sometimes this little town seemed so much more crowded than New York had ever felt to her. She sometimes felt a little claustrophobic. Maybe it was just all the trees obscuring her view of the sky. She started down the school's long drive toward Main Street.

Kashkawan School was a far cry from LaGuardia High on West 65th Street. There, her grade alone had had more students than this entire school. It was very pretty, Cathy conceded, poised high on a hill like a sedate old lady looking out over the Hudson River.

The student body seemed the same way: tidy, cooperative—and very vanilla. School had been in session for a week, and everyone had been polite so far. But 'polite' and 'welcoming' weren't exactly the same thing. Cathy was an outsider. Just coming into a room, she felt like she was interrupting conversations that had been going on for years. The girls definitely exuded a sense of domain, and she was a lowly squatter.

Not like Blake. He had made friends with an ease that she envied. Maybe boys had an easier time letting someone new join an established circle. Were they nicer than girls, or just less territorial? Cathy couldn't decide.

Life as the new kid with the popular stepbrother stank, but Cathy would be much worse off if it weren't for Rich. He sat with her on the bus every day and had introduced her around. They didn't have any classes in common except for Advanced French, but every day they had eaten lunch together and had done homework at each other's houses after school. Rich was probably wondering where she was right now.

Cathy looked around and realized she'd walked most of the way home, but suddenly felt very reluctant to show up there just yet. Why not go up to the lake again? Solitude would be very welcome at the moment, she decided. She walked past the entrance to Silverado Estates and took the dusty turn-off.

The road seemed different than it had when she and Rich had come up here: quieter, and darker somehow despite the harsh sunlight. Fewer cicadas, maybe—Cathy would not miss their mind-numbing racket once summer was over and done with.

There was something more, though. It felt as if the woods were holding their breath, like the hider in a game of hide-and-seek when the seeker is close by. Cathy slowed down gradually, looking around. Was this even the right road? She stopped where it forked.

Was it the *same* fork? On a hot day like this, the presence of the dump should be announcing itself to her nose. But no smell of garbage was coming from the road on the left. No, she had come the wrong way. She must have overshot the correct road, and this one must run roughly parallel to it. She calculated for a moment. If that were true, then she should take the left-hand fork, which would probably join up with the road to the lake. If not, well—she could always turn around and go back the way she had come.

Cathy turned left and walked for a while. This road wasn't going to join up with anything else anytime soon. It was dwindling and losing its identity. Encroached on and tamed by thick grass, it became less a road and more an old country lane with each step. The woods seemed less wild as well.

She came around a bend and stopped. Someone had deliberately planted these trees. Vast, ancient sycamores marched down either side of the curving path, their enormous trunks patched white and green, wrinkled and slubbed with the scars of age. They reminded Cathy of the plane trees in Riverside Park back in Manhattan, and her stomach fluttered with homesickness at the thought.

The silence thickened as she started moving again. She let out a nervous giggle, which came out muffled sounding, as if she'd laughed into a pillow. But actually, she liked it here. She took off her heavy backpack and swung it from hand to hand as she continued on. One more turn of the path, and she paused again, forgetting to breathe for a few seconds.

Before her was the most beautiful house she'd ever seen. It stood three stories high, with little windows peeking out from under the deep eaves of the roof. The smooth, butter-colored walls—limestone, maybe—seemed both to absorb and to magnify the summer light. Great pillars held up a deep, long porch mostly obscured on both sides by huge holly trees. Right in the center of the house was a large wood door, black with age. As imposing as it was, the entire house seemed merely to be a frame for that door.

Cathy noticed the strangest thing of all about this place. No driveway ran in front of the house. The path on which she stood led right up to the broad front steps.

"Spooky," Cathy whispered. But it wasn't, actually. Not at all. The house looked abandoned, but there was no threat here. In fact, Cathy felt safe for the first time since her run-in with that boy on the rock days before. Alone, yet out of harm's way. It felt like a weight had tumbled off her back.

She walked up the path, up the steps, and up to the door. The thick coolness of the stone porch's air poured over her like a waterfall. She knocked, her knuckles making almost no sound on the thick slab of wood. She reached out for the tarnished bronze doorknob, but pulled her hand away before touching it, suddenly shy. This place felt like a gift, and she didn't want to unwrap it all at once. She turned and looked back the way she had come. She had her privacy—that was certain. She might as well make use of it.

She sat down on the top step and pulled her water bottle out of her backpack. She would get out her homework in a minute, but first she wanted to rest and savor the feel of this place. She leaned sideways against an intricately carved stone baluster and stretched her legs down the steps before her. She took a long drink and sighed. Her feet were hot, so she kicked her sneakers off into the grass, then thumbed her socks off and tossed them after. She wiggled her toes, now deliciously free. It felt cooler up here than it had been in town, but it was still plenty muggy. She let her gaze wander about the weedy garden on either side of the path and the overgrown hedge that lined it. A sound coming from inside the house snapped her attention back.

Low and insistent, with a steady rhythm, it sounded like a heartbeat, or what the pulse of a giant might be like. Cathy turned slowly. The stone under her hands was no longer cool—it felt almost blood warm. She crawled toward the front door and crouched next to it. Closing her eyes, she gently laid her ear against the black, weathered wood. The beat was definitely louder now. Was it a signal to her, a code she should be able to interpret? She reached up and gripped the doorknob, trying to turn it ever so slightly. The knob didn't give at all, but the house's pulse seemed to quicken and grow more insistent.

Cathy gazed down the length of the dim porch. It darkened and stretched before her for what looked like miles. She felt like a mouse or an ant, insignificant and very vulnerable. "Who are you?" she whispered back, not really wanting to get an answer.

The pulse quickened again before stopping abruptly. The porch became a porch again, not a dank and unending tunnel. Cathy sat for a moment by the door, her mouth hanging open. Suddenly, this place didn't seem so peaceful, and she wanted to get home as quickly as possible. She jumped down the steps, grabbed her shoes and socks, and put them on as fast as she could. Too late, she remembered her promise to Blake. "Serves me right for going off alone," she muttered. She grabbed her backpack and ran all the way down the path as fast as she could.

She had a stitch in her side by the time she reached Route 403. She walked the rest of the way to Silverado Estates, sweating and trying to catch her breath. She decided to go straight to Rich's instead of stopping at home. She had to sort out the events of this afternoon in her mind before she saw Blake again. To avoid being seen by anyone at her house, she went through Rich's side gate and around to his back door. Thankfully, he was there. He got up from his kitchen table and opened the sliding glass door at her knock.

"You're a little worse for wear," he observed, smiling. "What happened? Did you get detention, or something?"

"No, my stupid locker was sticking again, and I just barely missed the bus. May I come in?"

"Oh, yeah, of course." Rich moved aside to let her pass. "I'm just plowing through the homework. Have a seat. Can I get you anything—orange soda, perhaps?"

Cathy laughed. She had a true friend in Rich, she realized. Suddenly, the world didn't seem quite so threatening. "Okay, that joke is getting a bit stale," she said. "But I'd love some water." She sat down and let her backpack fall to the floor. Rich slid over to the fridge using one crutch and got her a tall glass of ice water. She drank it gratefully and set the glass down with a sigh.

Rich joined her at the table. "If you barely missed the bus, it shouldn't have taken you that long to get home. Even I don't walk that slowly."

"You walk faster than most people I know," Cathy countered. "And I didn't walk straight home. I decided to go up to the lake, but I got lost trying to find it. I must have taken the wrong turn-off, because I never even found the dump.

"But I wanted to ask you about what I *did* find. What do you know about an abandoned stone house in the middle of the woods not very far from here? It's really more than a house—it's a mansion, and it's in perfect shape, but you can tell it's been empty for a long time. There are rows of huge old sycamore trees out in front of it."

Rich frowned. "I have no idea what you're talking about. It's close to here?"

"Yeah. Like I said, I thought I'd taken the road to the lake."

"Huh. That doesn't make any sense. I guess we could look it up on the Web."

"Oh, good idea. Let's find some satellite photos of Kashkawan."

Rich opened up his laptop and started typing. Cathy scooted around to the chair next to him so that she could watch.

"Okay, we're lucky," he said. "These images are really recent, because Silverado Estates is showing up. Here's my house, and there's yours. Let's scroll over west . . . there's the dump, slightly more attractive from the air than up close and personal . . . there's Waverly Lake . . ." Rich sat back, looking at the screen. "Are you sure you didn't get yourself turned around?"

"I guess it's possible," Cathy said. She retraced her steps in her mind. "No, actually, I don't think so. I didn't cross Route 403 at all going there or coming home. I came out, turned right, and walked east until I got to Turley Lane."

"But look, Cathy." Rich pointed to the screen. "There's Turley. There's Lake Road. And then there's not another turn-off on our side of 403 until it hits Route 9."

"Rich. You have to believe me. It was there." Cathy put her arms on the table and rested her forehead on them.

"Okay, okay. I believe you. But what's the big deal about this house, anyway? What happened to you?"

Cathy's arms muffled her voice. "I can't tell you. You'll think I'm insane."

"You? Insane? Nah," he scoffed. "Try me. Come on. You can't tease me like that! I'll never get my homework done, let alone get to sleep tonight. I'll be obsessed with wondering what happened."

Cathy considered. It wasn't fair to leave him hanging. If she hadn't wanted to confide in him, she should have gone straight home and kept all this craziness to herself. She tried to think of something she could make up to tell him instead of the truth, but her mind was a blank. Besides, Rich would see right through her. He was too smart to try to fool.

"Okay," she said. "But you have to swear two things. You have to believe that I'm not making this up, and you can't tell anyone about this. Nobody. Swear," she commanded.

"I swear. But I can't hear you very well with your face all covered up like that."

Cathy sat up and brushed her hair off her damp face. "Weird stuff has been happening to me ever since we moved here. Do you remember the day we met? The reason that I was out for a walk in the first place was because something had freaked me out in the new house.

"I was brushing my teeth, and I kid you not: I heard a voice ask me what I saw in the mirror. A real voice, out loud. The lights went all dim and strange for a minute, and I got dizzy, but then everything was back to normal. Nothing like it has happened since, but I still really don't like to spend a lot of time in my bathroom. And I can't sleep with the bathroom door open, either.

"Then, the day before school started—do you remember when I told you about that boy I saw in the woods?"

"Yeah—I didn't know who he was. But you didn't give me a ton of details."

"Blake says he hasn't been back since that day, but I've been looking for that kid at school and all over Kashkawan. I haven't seen him anywhere."

"Well, like I told you before, maybe he's a homeschooler. There are lots of those around here."

"I guess. But there was something definitely off about him. And Blake doesn't like him at all. If I thought he was spying on me, I wouldn't like him, either.

"But even that whole thing isn't as bizarre as what happened to me today. I thought I was heading toward the lake, but the dump wasn't there. Then I thought I'd passed it, and I tried to cut across it to find Lake Road, but I found this mansion instead. It was really pretty and not scary at all—like my own personal haven. Plus it was nice and cool and quiet there, so I decided to do my homework on the porch." She paused. Rich raised his eyebrows at her.

Cathy looked at her friend, trying to guess what his reaction was going to be.

"And . . ." Rich prompted.

"The house had a heartbeat." Cathy paused, then made herself continue before she could turn chicken. "I was sitting there, and all of a sudden, I could feel this pulse. I put my ear to the door—it was unmistakable. I tried to open the door, and when I did, it was just like that day with my bathroom mirror. Everything got all dim and strange, and then everything snapped back to normal."

"Well, all right. Everything's normal now. No problem."

Cathy glared at Rich. He didn't seem to be kidding, but there was no way to be sure. "Are you mocking me? Because I swear, Rich, I can't even believe I'm telling you all this. If you are making fun of me, I'm going to kill you, and I'll be cheerful about it. This isn't funny to me. I know I sound like a complete lunatic. But I'm telling you, it's true."

Rich stared back at her for a while. He opened and closed his mouth a few times. Cathy waited, hoping that he'd find some way to discern that she wasn't crazy and that she wasn't playing some elaborate practical joke.

Finally, he said, "Cathy, you're my friend. I've only known you a few weeks, but you're pretty much my *best* friend, as pathetic as that sounds. You're the first person in years, outside of my family, who hasn't kept me at a distance like some Special Ed case. Instead, you look past my legs and see *me*. So I think you're a pretty perceptive person. Who knows how far that perception may extend?

"What you're telling me is unbelievable, yes. But I believe that *you* believe it, no matter how crazy it sounds. Can that be good enough for now?"

Cathy closed her eyes to keep the tears back, frustrated with herself and the whole situation. "Yes. Of course it can. Thank you. I wouldn't believe any of this if I hadn't been there myself. I can't ask any more of you than that."

Rich laid his hand on her shoulder. "Why don't we go out and see whether we can retrace your steps? It's not that far, right? Then you can show me exactly what you found. Maybe that house isn't on the satellite photos because the trees are too dense around it, or something. Come on, let's go."

Cathy barely kept herself from sobbing with relief. She sighed heavily instead and nodded. "Okay, that would be great. Thank you. Maybe when you see the house, you'll recognize it. Either way, I'm counting on you as Kashkawan's unofficial historian to get to the bottom of this."

"As far as the house itself goes, yeah. But you're on your own with research into buildings with heartbeats. I have no idea how to help you there." Rich got up and grabbed his crutches. "Just leave your backpack here. You can pick it up when we get back. Or better yet, stay for dinner and let me copy your French homework—that will repay me quite nicely."

"Deal. Let me just text my mom." Cathy smiled shakily and stood. "I promise, it's not far at all."

A little way down Route 403, Cathy slowed down. "This must be it," she said, pointing at the side road. "I ran most of the way to your house."

"I hate to say it, but that's Lake Road."

"Okay, fine. Just walk with me up there. Maybe there's a fork you haven't been down before."

"Sure, no problem. Lead on."

They walked up the road a few hundred yards. Before they'd gotten far, they got wind of the dump, its oppressive stink as thick and heavy as a boiled wool blanket.

"This can't be right. I didn't go anywhere near the dump before. If I had been, I would have smelled it," Cathy murmured. "Let's go back to 403."

Once there, they walked all the way to Route 9 before Cathy gave up in disgust.

"It's not here," she wailed up to the sky. "I do not understand this!" She stared unseeing at the thick woods across the road.

Rich took a bandanna out of his jeans pocket and wiped his forehead. Then he swabbed down the handgrips and cuffs of his crutches. "I don't know what to tell you," he said after a few moments. "But why don't we go back to my house and regroup? We're not solving anything out here on the road."

Cathy looked at him. After a moment, she nodded in defeat. "Okay." She looked around one last time, then hung her head and followed her friend home.

CHAPTER SIX

THINGS PAST

MALCOLM'S DREAM IS always the same. He's slow dancing with Gail in the living room of their dark apartment. Moonlight streams through the windows, limning every surface with silver. Sarah Vaughan is moaning over a lost lover, and the sound of Clifford Brown's trumpet weaves itself around her voice, trying in vain to comfort her. Gail and Malcolm have played this song hundreds of times; they never tire of it. The silk Oriental rug under their bare feet can't quite muffle the creaks of the scarred old oak floor underneath as they dance in slow, intimate circles.

Oh, Gail feels so good in his arms. Every familiar curve of her is nestled into his body. The lush figure she has acquired since giving birth doesn't thrill her, but Malcolm can't get enough of it. Gail rests her beautiful head on his shoulder. She hasn't yet lost her hair. He murmurs into its dark curls, loving the smell of it, singing along to the music softly. The moment is perfect.

From down the hall comes an infant's wail. Blake has been a colicky baby. At ten months old, he's only now starting to sleep for more than a few hours at night. Gail automatically breaks their embrace at his cry, smiling up at Malcolm with those luminous eyes that stole his heart the minute he met her. "I'll be right back," she whispers, and goes to comfort Blake.

She disappears down the hall, but the crying goes on and on. After a few minutes, Malcolm goes to see whether he can do anything to help. But when he opens the door to Blake's room, no one is there. Now he realizes that the sobs are coming from behind him, in the master bedroom. Maybe Gail has taken the baby in there. When he turns the doorknob, the crying breaks off suddenly. He eases the door open, relieved that she's gotten the baby settled down for the moment.

Gail is in bed with her back to him, he sees. She must be lying down and nursing Blake. He tiptoes around to his side of the bed and eases himself under the covers as noiselessly as possible. Gail looks as if she's already fallen asleep. The familiar planes of her face are peaceful and relaxed. He reaches out and caresses her hair.

"Daddy."

It doesn't matter how many times Malcolm has had this dream— he's always surprised at the sound of his name from behind him. He turns over and sees nine-year-old Blake standing at the side of his bed.

"Daddy," his son repeats, "I'm cold." And Malcolm knows he's telling the truth. His slight frame is shivering underneath his thin pajamas.

"It's warm under your covers, Blake," Malcolm whispers. "Go back to bed."

"Tuck me in?"

Malcolm sighs. As big a boy as he is, Blake rarely makes it through the night without waking at least once. He has many gifts, but effortless sleep is not one of them. Malcolm wants to stay in bed with Gail, but he can't resist the pleading in his son's eyes. "Sure," he whispers. "Let's not wake up your mother."

He gets up and glances back at the bed. His heart breaks for the millionth time. Of course Gail isn't there. Cancer took her away from them five years ago. He puts his arm around Blake and walks out to the hall with him.

The door to Blake's room is locked. Malcolm jiggles the faceted glass doorknob and hits the door with his fist in frustration. This can't be right. The doors in this old apartment have never had locks, not even the bathroom doors. He's irritated with Blake for a moment and frowns down at the boy in the grey half-light. "Blake, what have you done?"

"I don't know," answers Blake in a small voice. Then he bursts
into tears. "I don't know, Daddy, but I'm so cold." He sinks down
to the carpet, hugs his knees, and rocks back and forth. Malcolm
fiddles with the doorknob for a few more seconds. But then he gives
up, kneels down, and puts his arms around his boy to try to warm
him. They rock together on the floor until Malcolm wakes up, his
heart cold and heavy once more.

CHAPTER SEVEN

LOVE'S LABORS

A VOICE IN A MIRROR. A creepy kid stalking his neighbor. And best of all, a mysterious house with a heartbeat. Rich tried to process the whole crazy story Cathy had told him yesterday. Why did he even take her seriously? What kept him from just calling Athena Harford and recommending that she get her daughter some psychiatric help? It wasn't like him to entertain the possibility of supernatural happenings. Rich had prided himself all his life on living by logic, by science, by empirical proof.

The earth orbits the sun; therefore the seasons change. Rich's mother has an immune system sensitive to pine pollen; therefore her body produces too much histamine every spring, causing hay fever. People are afraid of getting too close to abnormality and deformity; therefore, Rich has never had real friends.

But Cathy had come into Rich's life in the middle of the summer and proved that last theorem wrong. It wasn't that she ignored his amyloplasia the way some people tried—and failed—to do. She had acknowledged it head on within seconds of meeting him, then simply set it aside as unimportant. It was a gift Rich had never expected to get in a million years.

Because of that gift, Rich now enjoyed a freedom he'd never had before: the freedom to be truly himself with someone other than his parents. He was sure Cathy had no idea of the balm she was to his soul, how their conversations about Poe and Tolkien and Flannery O'Connor had kept him awake at night savoring the feeling of being understood on a deeper level than ever before. To keep all that, Rich found he might be willing to suspend his usually healthy skepticism for a while.

Rich set his back against one of the heavy oak doors of the Kashkawan Library, pushed, then braced his crutches and quickly swung himself through the opening. Yes, Cathy's story the afternoon before had been unbelievable, but Rich had decided to take her at her word. Today she had gone home on the bus to babysit Mae while Mrs. Harford took Fawn to a dentist's appointment, so Rich had promised Cathy he'd try and find information on any local house that matched her description.

"You'd do that for me?" She had squeezed his upper arm as she asked, relief softening the urgency in her face. He had nodded, his throat too dry to speak for the moment.

"Thank you," she had said. "I know I can figure this out with your help."

The look in her beautiful hazel eyes had made Rich feel a little light-headed. Cathy clearly had no idea of her effect on him. Rich knew that allowing himself to fall in love with her was probably a really stupid idea. She was smart, beautiful, and normal. He was a cripple. *Differently abled*, he reminded himself sarcastically. He was having a hard time caring about whether or not he was being stupid, though—or whether he was pushing his luck by hoping for some-thing more than a friendship. He was enjoying the feeling of being needed too much for that.

The ancient librarian looked at him over the top of her glasses and smiled when he stopped at the front desk. The afternoon sun-light streaming through the windows transformed her short white hair into a nimbus. Stooped, pink-cheeked, and frail—Mrs. Green-lese still looked exactly the same as she had when Rich was little. Rich guessed that was an advantage of being really old.

"Richard Mallory! I haven't seen you here since school started," she said. "How may I help you today?"

Rich had his story ready. The librarian was the sharpest, most perceptive person he knew. "Hey there, Mrs. Greenlese. I'm doing a report at school—another local history project. I thought it would

be cool to do some research on some of the old houses around Kashkawan, like the Davenport place across the street, or the Voorhees
mansion up on Cat Rock Hill. Where should I look first?"

"Ah." The old woman adjusted her glasses and pushed herself up
from her desk. She scuffed her heavy black shoes slowly across the
old plank floors toward the Reference Room, beckoning over her
shoulder without looking back for Rich to follow her. She spoke as
she walked, not bothering to keep her voice down. Rich could hear
a couple of little kids down in the Children's Room, but other than
that, the library was deserted.

"Well, we have *The Philipse County Journal* on microfiche back
to its beginnings over 150 years ago. But you know that. You've
looked through those before." Mrs. Greenlese unlocked the door of
the Reference Room and held it open for Rich. "*The Journal* probably wouldn't have details on the Davenport house, since that place
was built right after the Revolutionary War, but we do have several
volumes of Thomas and Isaac Davenport's journals. There's probably
some information in those. But the new Voorhees mansion—I'm
certain that would have been covered in the paper. The Voorhees
family threw a huge housewarming party when the new house was
opened. It was the event of the season. That was in about 1870, I
believe." She sat down and opened the microfiche index.

Rich chuckled as he sat down next to her. "That's the *new* Voorhees mansion up there? But wait—the Voorheeses were some of
the first Dutch settlers in this area. Didn't they come to Kashkawan
in the 1600s? Where did they live before the Cat Rock house was
built?"

Mrs. Greenlese looked up at Rich. "Well, when they first settled
up here, they lived in log houses, like everyone else. After a couple of
generations, though, they'd made quite a fortune trapping and trad-
ing. They built a huge stone mansion near Waverly Lake in the early
1700s and lived there for over a hundred years. It burned down in
1859. The family moved down to their new townhouse in Manhattan and didn't get around to rebuilding up here until after the Civil
War, and by then they'd decided that the Cat Rock views would be
more suitable to a family of their prominence."

Rich could see the humor in the librarian's watery blue eyes. "The views *from* Cat Rock, or the views *of* Cat Rock?"

"Exactly," she answered, turning back and scanning through the index. "Yes, here we are. The fire occurred in November of 1859, and the new house . . ." she turned the page. "The Cat Rock house was finished in May of 1871. You can get the fiches out of that file there and look at them yourself in the reader. If you decide to make print-outs, just bring me your money when you're done. The copies are 25 cents each now, I'm afraid."

"It's still a bargain, Mrs. Greenlese. Thanks."

The librarian got up and shuffled to the door. She turned and squinted at Rich. "I know I can trust you to be in here unsupervised. And to put the fiches away in order." She waited for his answer, bushy white eyebrows raised.

"Oh, yeah, of course. Thanks."

She shut the door softly behind her. Rich knew that the Voorhees records wouldn't do him any good. He had only mentioned the Cat Rock mansion as part of his cover story. The house Cathy had come upon in the woods couldn't have been the old mansion, since it had burnt down. But would a stone house have burnt down completely? Even if it hadn't, surely Cathy would have mentioned that the house she'd found was a ruin. No, it couldn't be the right place.

On an impulse, Rich decided to look up the story about the fire anyway. Maybe neighbors would have been mentioned. That might give him some clues to finding a house near Waverly Lake that could prove Cathy's story true. He found the correct fiche and inserted it into the reader. The fire had been the paper's lead story that week, and a detailed sketch depicting the mansion in flames was the front page's centerpiece. He scanned the story for names. Sure enough, three families from the surrounding area had come to the Voorhees family's rescue: the Lamoreaux, the Couenhovens, and the Peecks. Rich printed out a copy of the front page and took it over to the computer on the other side of the room.

"Yes," he whispered a few minutes later. A search of the library's catalog had turned up two books that were indexed to those three names: *Kashkawan: Its First Three Hundred Years* and *A Pictorial History of Philipse County.* Miraculously, neither was on the restricted list. Rich decided he'd check them out and take them over to Cathy's house. They could look through them together. Rich's heart warmed at the thought.

Down, boy, he cautioned himself. It would simply be more efficient for Cathy to look through the illustrations herself than for him to sit here and guess. He printed out the call numbers for the books and took them out to the main stacks.

A few minutes later, he gave the books and a quarter to Mrs. Greenlese at the front desk. "Oh yes, very good choices," she murmured as she scanned his card and the books' barcodes. "These should give you everything you need for your report. If not, you could try the Philipse County Historical Society. They have a lot of old photographs and drawings." She smiled and handed the books to him. He stuffed them, along with the printout of the newspaper story, into his backpack.

Rich stood on Cathy's porch for a few seconds before he rang the doorbell. His heart pounded, and it wasn't because of the half-mile walk from town. He took a couple of deep breaths and tried to focus on being cool and calm. Just as he reached for the bell, Mae flung the door open, startling him badly.

"Hello!" she warbled, hopping up and down on one foot and looking up at him with round eyes. "Do you want Cathy?"

"Hi—yes," he answered, flustered all over again. He looked up as he heard footsteps coming down the center stairs.

"Mae, you know you're not supposed to answer the door," Cathy scolded as she reached the entryway.

"I didn't answer, because he didn't knock," Mae answered, clearly confident in her reasoning. Rich bit back a smile, but Cathy put her hands on her hips and cocked her head at her little sister.

"Well, how did you know Rich was at the door, if he didn't knock or ring the bell?"

"I heard his sticks on the steps."

"They're called crutches, Mae."

"Okay. But I knew it was your friend, because the sticks sound different than feet."

Rich laughed. Cathy looked at him and rolled her eyes. "Sorry," she muttered.

"I don't mind. She's great." He grinned at the little girl. Mae smiled back, then stuck her tongue out at him and scampered upstairs giggling.

"Come on in," Cathy said. "I hoped you would come by. Did you have any luck at the library?" She closed the door behind him and led the way into the living room. She turned on a lamp and sat down on a fat white sofa.

"I think so," he answered. "I found the names of some people who used to live near Waverly Lake, and I checked out some books about them. I thought it would make sense for you to look at them, since you could recognize the house if you saw it." He sat down next to her on the couch, set his crutches aside, and unzipped his backpack.

"Wow, thanks, Rich! I'm excited to see them. Can you stay for a bit?"

"Yeah, I don't have a ton of homework. I'm anxious to see whether these books help at all," he said as he handed them to her.

She leafed through both books slowly, looking at illustrations and maps and daguerreotypes. Rich looked over her shoulder, pointing out the names he'd found. But she shook her head at each picture of a house.

Rich sat back, disappointed. His hunch about the Voorhees family's neighbors seemed to have amounted to nothing. Then Cathy turned a page and gasped.

"This is it!" she cried, pointing to an engraving.

"Cool!" Rich leaned over to look at the caption. His heart sank. "That can't be it, Cathy," he said.

"No, I'm sure of it. Do you see those funny little windows up

under the roof? And those holly trees? This has to be it ..." her voice
trailed off as she scanned the text on the facing page. "See?" she said,
nearly bouncing on the couch cushions in her excitement. This is the
Voorhees mansion, and it's right by Waverly Lake! It has a name. Of
course. All real mansions have names, right? *Hulsthuys:* That must be
Dutch. It says 'Holly Place' is the English translation. Oh, let's go
over there as soon as my mom gets home! Or maybe Blake will get
home from cross country practice first. I know we'll be able to find
it. Let me see if there's a map of the property—"

"But Cathy . . ." Rich interrupted. He stopped, not sure what
to say.

"What is it?" Cathy turned to face him, her eyes sparkling and
her cheeks flushed.

Rich was suddenly very aware of the length of Cathy's thigh
pressed against his as he sat next to her. He hadn't realized how
close they had gotten while looking through the books. His heart
thumped hard in his chest. It sounded so loud he was afraid she'd
be able to hear it. He wanted to kiss her so badly, it was almost a
physical hurt. He held her gaze for a second, wondering if he dared.

No. Logic and reason beat back impulse and hope. He looked
down abruptly and fished through his backpack until he found the
microfiche printout. He held it face down on his lap for a moment.
He looked at her again and could see her confusion.

"When you saw this house yesterday, did it look like it had been
in a fire? A really big fire a long time ago?"

"No." Cathy furrowed her brow as she thought. "No, the windows had glass in them, and the stone was this beautiful butter color,
like those old English houses you see in Jane Austen movies. I could
tell it was an old house, but it was in perfect condition. Why?" she
asked, glancing down at the paper he was holding. "What is that?"

Damn. If he had kissed her, he would have been able to put this
off for a few more minutes. Rich hesitated before handing it to her.
"I don't know what you saw, Cathy. But the house in that picture
doesn't exist anymore."

CHAPTER EIGHT

CONTRETEMPS

CATHY STARED AT RICH. "I don't understand," she whispered. She looked at the printout he'd given her. She blinked back tears and read through the article twice. Then she looked up, shaking her head in confusion. "I *know* this is the house I saw."

Rich took the open book off her lap and turned a few pages. "Cathy, the story of the fire is right here, too. This is not the house we're looking for. And see?" He showed her a map of the Voorhees property. "Look, here's where Holly House was." He pointed to the site and looked at her.

"Holly *Place*," she corrected.

"Whatever. You're missing the point. Do you see? Here's where the house was, and here's Waverly Lake." Rich waited, looking at her with expectation in his eyes.

"I know. That makes sense. That looks like exactly the way I went yesterday."

"But it can't be," he said, emphasizing each word. "That's where the dump is now. You know that. I showed it to you on the computer yesterday. You haven't seen it in person, but I know you've smelled it."

Rich was right. Cathy could feel her face turning red. "You think I'm crazy," she said.

"No! I don't, I promise. But I'm having a really hard time with this. You have to understand, Cathy. You're insisting that something that's impossible is reality. That's pretty much what crazy people do. I'm doing my best, here."

Cathy clenched her jaw and looked at the carpet. It galled her to be patronized by her best friend. Rich took her hand in his and tugged on it until she looked at him again.

"Hey. Please don't be mad at me," he said.

"I'm not mad at you. I'm just frustrated," she said, her voice quavering. She really didn't want to start crying right now, but she felt like she was going to break down any second.

Rich seemed to understand. He squeezed her hand. "Look, I should probably go. Finish looking through those books. There has to be a logical explanation for this. Maybe we missed something the first time. Tomorrow is Saturday. We could go out in the morning and look for the house again." He paused. "That is, if you still want to be my friend."

Rich's tilted blue eyes were full of anxiety. He really was very good looking, Cathy noticed absently.

"Of course I want to be your friend. I just can't believe you still want to be mine."

"Oh, I never let silly little things like hallucinations and delusions stand in the way of relationships," he said. He let go of her hand and punched her lightly on the shoulder. "That was a joke."

"That was a *bad* joke," she amended, but smiled in spite of herself.

Rich slung his backpack on and picked up his crutches. "Call me tomorrow," he said.

"Okay." Cathy walked him to the door. On the porch, he turned and started to say something, but he closed his mouth instead.

"What is it?" she asked. He shook his head.

"It's nothing. I'll talk to you later."

"All right. I'll call you. And Rich?" She put her hand on his shoulder. "Thanks for going out of your way and getting me that stuff. You're terrific." She leaned in and kissed him softly on the cheek. "Thanks," she repeated.

"Any time," he said, turning away quickly and navigating the front steps with practiced care. Cathy watched him head down the driveway and across the street to his house, then turned and went into the house.

"Call *me* Ishmael," Cathy murmured a few hours later. So much for pretending her life was normal. She couldn't settle into her reading, which was unusual for her. Most of the time when she read, she could close out the entire world around her and get so involved in the environment of the book that her mom would literally have to shake her to get her attention. Whatever the genre—science fiction, history, mystery—the delicious escape, that sense of being elsewhere, was the same.

She'd hit a snag with *Moby Dick,* though; she was trying her best to get into it, because she knew her mother thought it was the best American novel ever written. She had chosen it for her essay assignment in English, but now she regretted it. Melville just didn't hold her interest thus far. Resting her forearms on the book's open pages, she gazed out the window over her desk and watched the storm roll in.

The sky got darker and darker as the clouds obscured the setting sun. Thunder boomed through the hills of the Highlands. For the first time, Cathy understood why Washington Irving had compared the noise of a thunderstorm to the sound of giants bowling. It *did* sound like mammoth ninepins were crashing down the alley created by the Palisades. She had always loved thunderstorms in the City—it enhanced the sense of community inherent in the vast network of neighborhoods. New Yorkers treated any natural phenomenon as a reason to band together and prove that they couldn't be bullied.

Up here in Kashkawan, the storm felt much different, completely oblivious to any upstart human civilizations in its path. Silverado Estates in particular was a recent interloper, one that all of Nature, from the deer to the weather patterns, seemed to regard as a temporary nuisance at best. Cathy felt very exposed in their new, vinyl-coated house—like a target that perhaps the lightning could not resist.

Every Friday night was Date Night for the newly married Harfords. Mom and Malcolm had gone out to dinner, leaving Cathy and
Blake in charge. The little girls had gone to bed a while before; the
thunderclaps had disturbed them not at all, at least so far. Fawn, still
numb from her dentist's visit, hadn't begged to stay up the way she
usually did. The little girls had always been skilled at sleeping through
potential distractions, from wailing sirens to clanking old radiators;
Cathy envied their focus and dedication. She pressed her lips together, stared at the page, and tried to get back to what was happening on
the *Pequod*. Now that it was raining, it was really getting too dark to
read, but Cathy didn't feel like turning on the light yet.

Maybe she'd find Blake and tell him that she was going over to
Rich's house. Blake could handle things here now that the girls were
asleep. Then, instead of heading across the street, she could look for
that strange house again. She knew it had to be there. Why hadn't
she and Rich been able to find it?

The idea of going back didn't frighten her, now that she'd had
time to consider everything that had happened. Despite everything
Rich had shown her to the contrary, she still believed that there had
been some mistake, that the house she'd seen and the old Voorhees
mansion were one and the same. She pulled *A Pictorial History of
Philipse County* out from under *Moby Dick* and turned to the page
she'd marked. That *had* to be the place; she would recognize it anywhere in the world.

"Hey, how's it going?"

Cathy snapped the library book closed, set it aside, and turned
in her seat. Blake stood in her bedroom doorway, a poetry anthology
in his hand. What had he just said? Cathy stared at him, distracted
for the moment. Hadn't she shut the door when she had come in to
read?

Blake tossed her a grin and nodded toward *Moby Dick*. "How's
it going," he repeated.

"Oh," she said with a laugh. "It's *not* going. I can't concentrate.
Maybe we should trade. You could give this a try, and I could get
going on the English Romantics."

"No, thanks. I'm putting off the white whale as long as possible. Dad loves that book, but somehow I think it's got to be an acquired taste."

Be social; be nice, Cathy reminded herself. Blake had been perfectly friendly to her ever since their discussion on the porch about the spy boy. She nodded. "Yeah, Mom, too. I guess that's just one more thing they have in common. But I'm with you, I think." She leaned back in her chair. "This weather is just wigging me out a little. It's so different than the storms at home—I mean, back in the City—which is dumb, I guess. We're only an hour away."

"You felt safer—insulated somehow—in Manhattan."

"Yes, that's exactly it! Out here, I feel like there's nothing but us."

"Mmm." Blake raised his eyebrows. "Sounds like a recipe for trouble." His normally tan face was pale in the faint light, but his eyes seemed almost to glow.

It occurred to Cathy that her new stepbrother was still very much a stranger. Her heart hammered in her chest. "What do you mean?" she asked, raw suspicion in her voice.

"Whoa—nothing. I was just kidding around. Do you mind if I come in?"

Get a grip, Cathy told herself. This stuff with the mystery house had gotten her completely jumpy. "No, no. Of course not. Have a seat." Cathy gestured toward the bed.

Blake sat down and leaned forward against the footboard. "I miss the city," he sighed.

"Yeah, no kidding. Me too. What do you miss most?"

"My favorite pizza place, right around the corner from our old apartment. And being able to order in sushi whenever. But mostly, I miss the people."

"Your school friends?"

"Yeah, of course. But also the guys at the pizza place, the doormen—just all the neighborhood people. What about you?"

"Well, I miss the people, too. But I really miss the architecture. I never got tired of looking up and seeing all the detail work on the old buildings." Cathy thought for a moment. "And I love walking in the city at night and looking at all the lit windows of people's apartments. Those windows always seem magical to me. All these different people, living out their lives so close to one another, like a million different movies going on at once."

Cathy glanced at her stepbrother; was this sounding too far out to him?

Blake had a dazed, almost hungry look on his face. "I know exactly what you mean," he murmured.

"You do?"

"Oh, yeah." Blake leaned his elbows on his knees and looked at Cathy intently. "That's what I meant about missing the people. The stimulation of being around all that life—it's like being inside a power plant or something, you know, when the electricity makes the hair on your skin stand on end?"

Cathy nodded uncertainly. Blake went on.

"When Dad said we were moving out of the city, I had no idea it would be to such a godforsaken place. There's no life to it, right?"

For all her mental complaining about Kashkawan, Cathy now felt perversely defensive of it. "Well, it certainly is different. But it's starting to grow on me. In fact, I found a place close to here that felt—"

A flash of lightning accompanied by a huge peal of thunder interrupted Cathy. A second later, she heard a loud crash somewhere in the house. She and Blake both jumped to their feet.

"What was that?" she cried.

"It sounded like it came from down by my room."

They ran down the hall and into Blake's bedroom. A huge mass of sticks and leaves had thrust itself through his window; shattered glass lay everywhere, and papers whirled frantically in the wind coming through the hole.

"That must be the big maple tree," Blake said. "I'm going down to see whether the whole tree came down on the house, or just a branch." He brushed past Cathy, who turned to follow.

"I'll go with you," she said, but then heard Mae wailing in her bedroom. She turned around and headed toward her sisters' rooms instead.

"It's okay, Mae," she said, bursting through the door. But her little sister lay sound asleep, cuddling her bedraggled plush elephant and even snoring a little. She didn't even flinch at Cathy's entry. *Unbelievable.*

Cathy backed out quietly and shut the door. *It must have been Fawn,* she thought, and tried her room next. No, Fawn was still asleep as well. She stood in the hall, shaken. How could she have imagined someone crying? Lightning flashed again, and this time, the power went out.

Where was Blake? Cathy ran downstairs and through the living room, but stopped when she got to the sliding glass doors to the back yard. Only a branch had fallen off the maple tree, but it was an enormous one. The main trunk still sizzled where a giant wound gaped raw. The branch lay across the camel-shaped cliff rock and extended all the way to Blake's window; only the very end of it had touched the house. It had made a mess in Blake's room, but with all the trees around the property, the damage could have been much worse.

Cathy started to sigh with relief, but choked on her own breath as a movement caught her eye. Blake and the spy boy stood facing each other up on the rock. Blake loomed over the kid, obviously shouting, his face ugly with rage. The boy shrank back, but seemed determined to stand his ground this time. He wore that same huge T-shirt and grubby jeans, she noticed. He must have been sheltering under the maple's dense foliage since before the rain had started, because he wasn't soaked to the skin the way Blake was. Blake, for all his anger, seemed unwilling to touch the boy in any way. The kid was obviously weird, but what had gotten Blake so worked up? He looked a little carried away. She decided she should put a stop to it before things got out of hand. She opened the door and yelled into the driving rain.

"Hey!"

Both boys whirled to face her, Blake's face blank with shock, the kid's shining with delighted surprise and relief. The boy waved at her, then turned tail and ran off into the storm. Blake turned and looked as though he was going to try to follow him, but then charged down the side of the rock and up to the back porch instead.

"What are you doing, you idiot?" he shouted at her, his hair dripping into his eyes.

"What am *I* doing? What are *you* doing? You looked like you were going to kill that kid up there. What is it with you and him, Blake?"

"It's his fault that branch came down. He has got to stay away from this house."

"Are you out of your mind? He's a kid! That tree got hit by lightning. You can see the burn mark on the trunk. How could a little boy have caused that to happen?"

"It's none of your business," he snarled, and bumped her shoulder hard as he moved past her into the house. He stomped through the kitchen, dripping water and wet leaves everywhere.

"Oh, yes it is, you big jerk!" Cathy said, following him. "You asked me before to pretend I'd never seen that boy. You said that this was something you were going to take care of. But it didn't look like you did a very good job of that. You were totally out of control."

Blake turned on her at the foot of the stairs. "I would have gotten rid of him if you hadn't butted in. Why did you help him?" Blake paused, wiping his face with the back of his hand. "And he waved to you. Why would he do that? Have you seen him again and haven't told me about it? What are you hiding from me?"

"No! I didn't go looking for him, even though I wanted to. I trusted you. But now I'm not sure why I was so stupid, since you obviously have some sort of history with him. Why did you lie to me? Tell me what's going on!"

"Yes, what *is* going on?" Malcolm's mild voice came from behind her. Cathy and Blake both turned to find their parents standing by the door to the garage.

"Dad—I didn't hear the garage door open." Blake's voice trembled, and out of the corner of her eye, Cathy could see him shaking.

"The power is out, son. I had to open it the old fashioned way. Are you going to answer my question?"

"A branch got hit by lightning and came through my window, and Cathy and I were arguing about what to do next."

Cathy forced herself not to roll her eyes. It was a lame cover-up attempt.

But Malcolm seemed to accept it. Athena didn't seem so sure. "Are the girls all right?" she asked.

"They're fine," answered Cathy. "I checked on them just a couple of minutes ago. I guess they really *can* sleep through anything."

Athena directed her next question at Blake, who still dripped all over the carpet. "And what possessed you to go outside in the middle of a thunderstorm?"

"I just wanted to see how bad the damage was." Blake slowly recovered his usual polite smoothness. "I'm sorry. It probably wasn't the smartest thing to do."

"Well, go upstairs and get dried off and changed before you compound the issue by catching cold," she said. Cathy narrowed her eyes as she looked at her mother. Could she actually be buying his apology?

Blake obeyed Athena without so much as looking at Cathy.

"I'll go upstairs and start cleaning up," said Malcolm. He gave his wife a pained smile. "Of course this had to happen on a weekend. We won't be able to get a repair scheduled until Monday at the earliest." He followed Blake upstairs.

Athena held out her arms and Cathy rushed into them. "I'm

sorry this happened while we were away," Athena said quietly. "It's a lot of drama to ask you to handle."

"It's okay, Mom," Cathy answered. "I guess it could have been worse."

Athena pulled back from their hug and looked into her daughter's eyes. "Would you like some hot chocolate?"

Cathy nodded gratefully. "That sounds great."

In the kitchen, Cathy sat on a bar stool and watched while her mother lit a few candles, melted some chocolate, and heated milk. Athena's calm, efficient motions and the warm, flickering light soothed her. While she was whisking the chocolate into the milk, Athena pierced Cathy with the look she'd been dreading—the keen, "let's get to the bottom of the situation" look.

"What else is going on, Cathy?" her mother said in the deceptively casual tone she always used for interrogations. "What were you and Blake really fighting about?"

Cathy looked around behind her. She knew Blake would be furious with her for breaking his confidence, but right now, she felt no loyalty at all to him. She kept her voice down.

"Okay, there's this weird neighbor boy that Blake has seen in our yard a few times. He was outside just now, and Blake was trying to chase him off."

"I don't understand. A boy? Someone your age? Does Blake know him from school?"

"No, he's just a little kid, maybe Fawn's age. He seems harmless to me, although I don't know why he likes our yard so much."

"You've spoken to him?"

"Yeah, once."

"Where does he live?"

"I don't know. He doesn't ride our bus, but Rich says that a lot of homeschoolers live around here. I'm guessing he lives somewhere on the other side of the woods behind the back yard. I have no idea why Blake hates him so much."

"That doesn't sound like Blake at all. He seems to get along with everyone. He seemed pretty upset just now; I've never seen him lose his cool like that."

"I know. It's weird. Thanks," Cathy said as her mother handed her a mug of chocolate.

"It worries me that a young boy would have been out in this storm," Athena mused. "He could have been seriously hurt. I'll have to talk to Malcolm about this. Maybe Blake has confided in him."

"Okay, but Mom? If there's any way you could keep me out of it, I'd be grateful."

Athena smiled. "No one loves a rat fink, eh? I'll do my best, sweetie. Now, what else is on your mind?"

Cathy carefully looked her mother straight in the eye as she sipped her chocolate. "That's really it," she lied. "Other than Blake's freak-out, life is totally normal."

CHAPTER NINE

OUT OF ORDER

CATHY WOKE UP to find the moon shining through her window like a searchlight. The storm had moved on while she was sleeping, leaving no trace in the sky of its violent passage. What had awakened her? Her alarm clock flashed 2:23 a.m., which meant the power had come back on. Morning was hours away. She turned over, hoping to recapture the familiar lethargy that meant sleep was on its way. She settled her covers and shifted her pillow to a cool spot, but just as she laid her head down again, her eyes widened in shock.

Someone was in her room.

A figure crouched in the deepest shadows by her bathroom door. Her heart hammering in her throat, Cathy held her breath and strained to see clearly in the half-darkness. The moon had seemed so bright just seconds before; now its light seemed to obscure more than it exposed.

Should she cry for help? Who would hear her in time? She mentally catalogued everything within arm's reach that could be used as a weapon, and came up with exactly two less-than-satisfactory items: the clock and her tiny bedside lamp.

A car drove down Turley Lane, its headlights illuminating her room briefly as it passed by the house. The light reached into the corner. There was no one there.

Cathy exhaled. She flopped onto her back and stared at the ceiling. Adrenaline coursed through her system; there was no way she was getting back to sleep now. She got up and went to the bathroom in the dark, then decided that she'd get back in bed and see whether *Moby Dick* would prove useful as a sleep aid.

"Mom will freak if she finds me up," she muttered as she went to her desk for the book.

"Your mother loves you," said a small, tired voice.

Cathy spun around and dropped to her knees. Her bedroom door was still closed. How had someone gotten in?

"Who's there?" she hissed into the darkness. A figure stepped out of that same corner on the far side of the bed. In the moonlight, she could easily identify him. It was the spy boy.

Cathy's light summer nightshirt suddenly seemed completely inadequate. She reached out and snatched the duvet off her bed and wrapped it around her. Feeling a little more protected, she stood up.

"What are you doing in my house?" she demanded. "Why are you here?"

"I can't be anywhere else, not for long," the boy said. "My home is here. Only it isn't mine. Not any more."

"What are you talking about? No one's ever lived in this house before." Cathy paused. "Where are your parents?"

The boy looked toward Cathy's door. He hugged himself tightly and shuddered. "I don't know," he admitted. "I'm just so cold."

His huge dark eyes held her gaze, and Cathy suddenly felt so sad and overwhelmed that it made her knees weak. This boy couldn't hurt her; she towered over him and outweighed him by a good forty pounds. Curiosity now replaced fear. She had to get to the bottom of this once and for all.

"Take one of the blankets off the bed and wrap up, like I did," she directed.

The boy shook his head. "It won't help. But thank you. And thank you for helping me during the storm. You're so nice." A brief smile lit his features; suddenly he seemed very familiar. He looked a lot like—but then the fleeting connection was gone.

Shrouded in her duvet, Cathy shuffled to her bed, sat down, and turned on the lamp. She blinked in the sudden light. "Well, you're welcome, I guess. But I don't see how I helped you," she said. "All I did was yell."

"You distracted him. I couldn't have gotten away from him if you hadn't done that."

"Well, if I helped you, maybe you could return the favor and help me. Tell me the truth. What is the deal with you and Blake?"

"Blake," whispered the boy.

"Yes, Blake. My stepbrother. How do you know him?"

Misery filled his eyes. "He stole from me."

"Blake? Blake stole something from *you*? No offense, but what could you possibly have that he would want?"

"Everything," the boy snarled. Though he stood at least ten feet away from her, Cathy still reared back at his sudden venom.

This was ridiculous. This kid had broken into her house. Why was she even talking to him? She should yell for Malcolm. But would Blake get mad about that? Cathy still fumed over their earlier fight, but she didn't want to upset him further.

"Listen," she said, trying to figure out what to do. "You can't be here in the middle of the night. You can't just walk into someone else's house."

The boy stared at her as if she were speaking Greek. Cathy realized they were getting nowhere like this. She went to her dresser and pulled out a sweatshirt and some jeans, then huddled under her bedspread and pulled on the clothes over her nightshirt.

"What's your name?" she demanded as she gathered up the duvet and tossed it onto her mattress.

"B-b . . ." He hesitated. "Bunny," he said after a moment.

Cathy ducked under her bed to hide her smile and grab her sandals. "No, really."

"That's what my mom called me," the boy mumbled, his eyes filling with tears.

"Whoa, okay," Cathy said. "Bunny it is. I'm going to walk you home, Bunny. I know it's the weekend and all, but you should be in bed. Come on." She held out her hand, hoping he would take it, but he shied away. Cathy raised her arms in surrender. "Fine. I won't touch you. But we've got to go."

Bunny followed her downstairs and out of the house without a sound. A strong wind had blown away all the storm clouds and still kept the trees dancing. At the bottom of the driveway, Bunny turned and looked back at the house.

"Can't I stay?" he pleaded.

Cathy stared up at the black velvet sky and summoned patience. "Bunny, there's no way. You don't even know us. Let's get you home, and you can come visit another time. Now, which way do we go to get to your house?"

The boy shot her another measuring look, then started down the sidewalk toward Route 403. Cathy followed. Her skin started to crawl once Bunny turned left up   the road that led to the dump. "I don't think this is the right way," she said.

"Yes, it is," said Bunny. "I know where I'm going."

They walked until the ruts in the road smoothed out and gave way to grass. Crickets sang and frogs croaked in the dark woods, and a far-off owl hooted a couple of times. The leaves of the tall sycamores on either side of the path whispered and sighed in the wind. Cathy tried to take comfort in the normal night sounds and assured herself that nothing out of the ordinary was happening—because up ahead in the darkness was the house that shouldn't exist, a house called Holly Place that had burnt down 200 years before. She still hoped they'd just find the town landfill. But sure enough, soon she could see the mansion's stone walls, pale in the dappled moonlight.

"Of course you live here," Cathy said under her breath, but the boy heard her.

He turned around. "I only stay here sometimes."

"Because it's only here sometimes, right?"

Bunny furrowed his brow. "What?"

"Never mind." Cathy noticed that the dark circles under the boy's eyes weren't as deep as they had been just minutes ago in her room. He looked a little less flimsy, too. Whenever she had seen him before, he had seemed frail enough for the wind to knock him over. Now he looked stronger, somehow. Cathy looked beyond Bunny to the house. "Is there a side door you can sneak in?" she asked. "I don't want to wake anybody up."

"No one will hear me. Thanks for walking with me, but I'm fine now. I'll see you around." He walked across the lawn to the front porch. Cathy waited to make sure he actually went inside.

After mounting the steps, the boy turned around.

"I remember now." He smiled. "My mother called me Bunny, but my name's Blake. Blake Harford."

"That's not funny," Cathy said. She charged across the lawn and up the front steps of the house. She bent over and got right in the boy's face. "I don't know what you're up to, but it's got to stop," she said. "Otherwise, I'm going to have to tell your parents. And mine. And maybe call the police. You can't—" She stopped as the boy put out his hand and brushed her hair away from the side of her face.

Squirm.

His skin didn't feel like skin; it was hot and damp and somehow charged with electricity. Cathy drew back at once. Her cheek throbbed where he had touched her. She pressed her palm against the spot and stared.

Bunny hung his head and sighed. "I'm sorry. I shouldn't have done that."

"Who are you?"

"I told you, and you didn't believe me." He paused, seeming to consider, then spoke in a rush. "Would you come inside? I think I could show you, and maybe then you'll understand."

Cathy wanted to protest. What about his parents? What about the fact that this house shouldn't even be here? She looked at the front door and wondered what secrets lay behind its black bulk. Why not? She shouldn't even be here. She was already in major trouble if someone woke up and found her missing. And she couldn't deny that she was itching to go inside. She nodded at Bunny.

"All right."

He smiled at her again—that big, beaming grin he'd flashed when she'd yelled at Blake during the storm. She realized with a jolt that he looked just like her stepbrother. Now that she saw the resemblance, she couldn't believe that she hadn't recognized it before. He was different here than he'd been at her house, though. Less wan and more sure of himself. He had been changing since they got close to Holly Place.

He turned, went up the steps, and waited for her by the front door. She approached slowly and felt the low, subtle drums start under her feet once more.

"You'll have to open the door," Bunny said. "I can't."

Cathy opened her mouth to argue, then decided against it. Whatever his reason, hopefully she'd understand soon. She reached out and grasped the tarnished bronze doorknob. It felt blood warm, she noticed as she turned it. She leaned against the massive slab of wood and pushed. The door swung open silently, and soft, golden light spilled over her. She and Bunny stepped inside, and the door closed behind them without a sound.

She stood on the cut stone floor of a vast front hall. Several yards away, wide twin staircases spiraled majestically up to a second level. Fluted arches to either side framed closed double doors made of the same dark, carved wood as the front door. Wallpaper with an intricate pattern of vines, leaves, and fruit covered the walls above the paneled wainscoting.

The light, though, astonished Cathy. It poured through ranks of tall, paned windows. Countless dust motes danced in its beams as it flooded the room with warmth and grace. It was the heavy, liquid light of late summer afternoon. Cathy went to one of the windows and brushed her fingers against the silk fringe of the rich draperies as she looked outside. She saw the brilliant blue and green of an August day, when moments before, she'd been standing in the moonlight. Bunny came and stood beside her.

"Time is different here," he observed.

"No kidding."

"I found this house a few weeks ago. It's the only place I can be where I don't hurt. And I can remember things better while I'm here."

Cathy could see how that would be possible. She felt peaceful, yet alert and energized—the way she had when she had first come here. "I found it myself a couple of days ago," she said, "But when I brought a friend back, it had disappeared. And I don't see how it can be real. It was supposed to have burned down a long time ago. I guess no one else is here, right?"

"I guess that depends on what you mean by 'here.' And it's the realest place I've been in a long time." Bunny moved away and beckoned.

"Come into the traveling room. I think I can show you what I promised." He went to the arch to the left and waited for Cathy. "Follow me," he said, and walked through the doors.

Through the doors, Cathy thought. Without opening them first. She reached out and knocked on the carved, polished wood. Solid and ordinary, if you didn't count the warmth and slow pulse of it. She opened the door and went inside.

Night again, but this room didn't fit with the grand, gothic hall she'd just left. It looked . . . it looked like the bedroom of a New York City apartment. A boy's bedroom, she guessed by the *Star Wars* posters over the bed and the sports gear stacked next to the dresser. The pale orange light of the zinc street lamps outside cast long shadows across the bookcases and toy shelves lining the walls. She looked out the narrow, sashed windows on the opposite wall. Sure enough, a row of brownstones stood across the street, veiled by the upper branches of honey locust trees. Cathy could hear the faint sounds of traffic on a nearby avenue.

Bunny stood by the bed. He trembled as he looked down at the boy sleeping in it. She went to stand next to him and got yet another shock. The unconscious boy looked like his twin. Cathy whirled around, crossed the room, and took a framed photograph off the dresser. She moved to the window in order to see it better. Smiling up at her were Malcolm and the boy, who could only be Blake. Looking up, she realized she recognized the furniture and some of the books. She stood in Blake's old Manhattan bedroom.

She went back to Bunny's side. "That's you," she whispered.

The boy shook his head violently. "That's my body, but I'm not inside it anymore."

"Bunny, what happened?"

"I'll show you. It hurts, but if you see, maybe you can help me." He went to the bedroom door. "Wait over here, and I'll show you."

Cathy moved to the wall by the door. Bunny went through it and then reappeared after a second. "Look," he directed, and she turned around. The room had changed subtly. The trees outside the windows were now bare of leaves. A boy still lay in the bed, but he wasn't asleep. He stared up at the ceiling with great concentration. After a moment, a shadowy form floated up and out of the boy, who now had his eyes closed. Was it a spirit? Was the boy dead? But no: the boy's chest rose and fell as he breathed.

The spirit looked down at its body for a moment, then cartwheeled and somersaulted in midair. Cathy drew back, but Bunny whispered, "Don't worry. I can't see us."

"That's you." Cathy said. "Why are you out of your body?"

"So I could look for my mother. She died—like your father died, right?"

Cathy nodded.

"I wanted to find her, so I taught myself . . . this." He gestured toward the spirit. Cathy watched as it floated through the window and out of view.

"I didn't know how dangerous it was, though. I had no idea." Bunny raised his hand and turned it slowly clockwise. As he did, the sky outside sped up and changed, as if in a stop-motion film. Morning was coming.

A shadow moved over the window, and the spirit of a man flew through the glass and hovered over Blake's bed. Cathy flinched and gasped, her heart pounding. The man had a sickly, bruise-colored light around him. His eyes burned with malice and deep hunger. He grinned and caressed the sleeping boy's face with a gaunt hand. Then he gathered himself, dove toward Blake's body, and disappeared.

"No!" cried Cathy. She ran forward, but Bunny grabbed her arm. That same hot, swampy feeling flooded her skin where he touched her.

"It's okay," he said, but tears streamed down his face. "This is like a movie. We can't change it. Come with me. I can't watch myself find out what's happened." He let go of her and went out. Cathy followed him back to the front hall of the house.

Exhaustion overwhelmed her. She sank down onto the soft, thick Oriental carpet and buried her face in her hands. What was this place? Why was it here?

"I think because I need it," said Bunny softly.

Cathy looked up. "You can read minds, too?" she asked, unable to avoid a little sarcasm.

"A little. You were kind of shouting."

"Sorry. When did that . . ." Cathy didn't know what to call the dark entity that had stolen Blake's body. ". . . that *thing* do this?"

"I was nine. How old is my body now?"

"My age. Seventeen. You've been . . . out . . . for eight years?"

Bunny paled. "I guess so. I didn't realize it had been so long. It's hard to hold onto things—time, memories—unless I'm in this house. Here, for some reason, I'm myself again, but out in the world, it's slippery." His face darkened, and he paced back and forth in front of Cathy like an animal in a cage. "Do you see what I meant earlier? He stole everything from me—my body, my father, my life. And I don't know how to take them back. But I think, somehow . . ." He looked at her, his dark eyes burning. "I think you can help me."

Cathy's mouth felt like a desert. She cleared her throat with effort. "Bunny, what happened to you—it's really terrible. But I don't know how to help you. You need a priest or a shaman or an exorcist, or someone like that. I don't know anything about this kind of . . . whatever it is. What makes you think I could do something?"

Bunny looked around and gestured at the room. "This house does. The fact that you can see it and come in. I've never been anywhere like this, and I don't think that just anybody can come here. We're here for a reason."

Cathy looked at the boy. This all seemed totally crazy. A wave of fatigue hit her, and she shook her head. "I've got to go home. I'm too tired to think right now. Besides, if my mother finds me gone, she'll ground me for life, and then I'll be no help to you at all."

She got up and walked to the front door, then turned back to Bunny. "You'll be okay here by yourself?"

A faint smile flitted across the boy's face. "Yeah, sure. It's the next best thing to being home."

"Try to stay here, then. I don't want Blake . . . or whoever he is . . . to get agitated again."

"His name's Zared," said the boy.

"How do you know that? Have you ever talked to him?"

Bunny shook his head. "The house told me."

Cathy looked at the boy, thinking. "If the house can tell you his name, why can't it tell you how to get rid of him?"

He shook his head again, and his huge eyes welled up with tears. "I don't know," he whispered.

Great. She'd made him cry again, after all he'd been through. She wanted to hug him, but she couldn't stand the thought of that awful feeling she'd gotten when he'd touched her before. "Look, I'm really sorry, but I've got to go. I'll come back tomorrow," she promised.

Bunny nodded and managed half a smile. He got up and walked to the other set of double doors. "I'll be waiting," he said, and floated through solid wood again. Cathy turned and went out the massive front door the only way she knew how. The night air felt as still and warm as bath water, but she shivered as she hurried home.

Back in her room without incident, she slipped off her jeans and slid back into bed. She glanced at the still flashing alarm clock and groaned. 4:41 a.m. She probably had another four hours at most before Malcolm and Athena woke the family for Saturday chores. She forced her legs and shoulders to relax and took long, deep breaths through her nose until she felt herself sinking into oblivion.

CHAPTER TEN

NOT IN THE SKY

FINALLY. CATHY ESCAPED the house as soon as she could the next day. It was a lot later than she would have liked, though. Malcolm had hired a couple of men to cut up the enormous fallen branch and chip all its leaves and twigs, but it still took the family hours to clean up the rest of the mess from the storm. Of course, then there had been laundry to do and her creepy bathroom to clean, and she'd had to finish her stupid *Moby Dick* reading.

All the manual labor had left her plenty of time to think. Ghost boys, magic houses, and evil stepbrothers: seriously? Why was this happening to her? Suddenly, she craved the quiet safety of a normal high school day—months and months of normal days. Right now, a prosaic senior year at a boring high school in the middle of nowhere, with her biggest decision being which college to attend, sounded like the best thing ever. Was a normal life too much to ask for? When her mother had gotten remarried, Cathy had thought she would be able to set down the adult-sized burden of worry that she'd been carrying around since her father had died five years before. But now, her problems seemed bigger than ever.

With a pang of longing, Cathy wondered what her father would think about all this. Peter Wright had been unlike Malcolm in almost every way. A corporate lawyer, he was as gregarious and charming as Athena was poised and serene. What a beautiful couple they had been, both with dark hair and eyes. They had met in college and had planned to grow old together. Cathy's father's laugh had been loud and infectious, and he'd loved to tease and hug and dance with his three daughters, even tiny Mae, who had been barely a year old when he died.

He had been riding home from La Guardia Airport in a taxi-cab, returning from a week-long deposition trip to Los Angeles. No one knew what caused the massive automobile accident on the RFK Bridge that night, but it had killed six people and had taken Cathy's father away from them forever.

Malcolm was much quieter than Cathy's father had been. Cathy didn't get his sense of humor at all, but Athena seemed to love his corny jokes. He lived and breathed books and music as much as Cathy's mother did. Sometimes Cathy wondered whether they were too much alike—but they seemed to get along well, at least so far.

She wondered about the loss of Malcolm's first wife, though, and whether her stepfather had even the slightest clue that he had lost his son years ago as well. Blake wasn't Blake at all. Could you live with an impostor for that long and not notice anything?

How could she possibly help Bunny? That—evil spirit, or whatever it was—that had stolen his body—it had looked malevolent, and as if it knew exactly what it was doing. She hadn't known such things even existed, and she didn't see how an ordinary teenage girl could carry out a rescue on the scale that Bunny seemed to expect. Why did it have to be her? She did not want to take this on. But as her mother loved to say, wanting was not getting.

Now it was almost four in the afternoon, and she was supposed to be back for dinner at six. She didn't have a lot of time for visiting Holly Place, but she'd promised she'd come today. Her cell phone buzzed in her jeans pocket as she hurried down the driveway and along Turley Lane. Had her mother come up with one more chore that couldn't wait? No. Rich's number flashed on the phone's tiny screen.

"Hey," she said.

"*Hola*," came her friend's voice. "I just saw you walk by the house. Do you want company?"

Cathy hesitated. She really wanted to see Rich. But she had promised Bunny, and she couldn't risk not being able to find Holly Place again. There was no way Rich could come with her, and she couldn't blow Bunny off—not without risking having him show up in her room in the middle of the night again. "No, thanks," she said with regret. "I have something I have to do right now."

"Oh." Surprise and disappointment colored Rich's voice. "You're still mad at me about yesterday, right?"

"What? No!" Cathy closed her eyes for a moment in frustration. They had only been friends for a little while, but they already spent most of their free time together. She hated the idea of lying.

"Rich, I'm not mad. I just have to run an errand, and I don't have a ton of time, okay? We can hang out after dinner, if you want— maybe watch a movie, or something." She held her breath, hoping that her friend would be satisfied.

"Sure, all right," he said after a pause. "Call me when you're done eating, and we'll figure something out."

"Great. I'll see you later." Cathy closed her phone and stuck it back in her pocket. What was she going to say to Rich about this whole situation now that things had gotten so much more complicated? If only she could give him some proof that she wasn't nuts. How could she show him? Maybe it would just be easier to find some way to help Bunny and get rid of Zared as quickly as possible. Best friends shouldn't have secrets from one another.

She fretted about Rich all the way to Holly Place. As she turned the last corner of the path through the woods, she saw that Bunny sat on the porch steps waiting for her. She smiled and waved. He stood and bounded down the steps toward her and barely stopped himself from charging right into her. He definitely looked healthier than the first time she'd seen him, and his thin face was one big grin.

"You came back," he said.

"I said I would," answered Cathy.

"I know. I'm just used to being disappointed. You're the first person I've had any real conversations with in a long time. Come on in," Bunny said. "I think I need to show you the dreaming room. At least, that's what the house told me."

"You said that last night. The house really talks to you?"

"It doesn't exactly talk. I just kind of hear words in my mind, but they're really clear. Or I see things in the dreaming room."

"Dreaming room?" Cathy echoed. "The place you're supposed to show me now. Is it the same as the traveling room?"

"No, it's a lot different. I think I've figured out how they both work, pretty much. The traveling room will take you to anything in your past that you want to see. I've spent a lot of time there, actually. I can see my mom again, even if I can't talk to her.

"But in the dreaming room, I'm pretty sure you only see the present, or maybe a little bit back or forward in time. I don't know exactly. But I think you need to visit the room yourself, and see what it wants to show you. I think it will help you find a way to help me."

"Right." Cathy somehow didn't think that helping him was going to be quick or easy. What had she gotten herself into? She sighed. "Okay, lead on, Macduff." Cathy walked up the porch steps and looked around. There was no denying that it felt wonderful being here again. Peace wrapped her up like a fuzzy blanket.

"That's a misquotation," Bunny said.

"Huh?" Cathy paused with her hand on the doorknob.

"That line from *Macbeth* you just said. It's actually '*Lay* on, Macduff.' It's been misquoted for over a hundred years, though."

Cathy smirked. "Okay. Did the house tell you *that*, too?"

"No, my dad's an expert on Shakespeare. But you knew that."

Of course she did. Malcolm. Bunny knew him far better than Cathy did. More than anything else, that realization brought home the truth of everything she'd experienced with Bunny. This was all *real*. Cathy took a deep breath and let it out slowly. For the second time, she turned the blood-warm doorknob and entered the house that shouldn't be there.

She felt like she'd walked into a refrigerator. The high-ceilinged room was cold and still. The light was different, too. Cathy looked out the beautiful windows and saw a gray, wintry day. Snow loaded down the holly and bare sycamore branches and lay thick on the lawn outside. She shivered with more than a physical chill.

"Why is time different here, do you know?" she asked.

Bunny shrugged. "Everything else is different. Why wouldn't time be different, too?"

Cathy guessed that was a reasonable theory—or lack of one. She looked up the stairs. How many rooms were up there, and what were their purposes? This floor seemed to have just the two rooms off either side of the main hall. She couldn't see any other doors besides the two sets that stood across from one another. But there must be something else beyond the back wall behind the double staircase as well; the house would be too shallow, otherwise. And wouldn't there be windows as well? There was no door leading that way, though, at least not that Cathy could see.

"This way," said Bunny, interrupting her thoughts. He motioned her toward the doors he'd gone through the night before as she had left. Cathy nervously glanced back over her shoulder at the traveling room doors as she followed him. She knew what she had seen there had only been an illusion of sorts, but she couldn't help thinking about Zared and shuddering.

A rush of delicious aroma flooded out at her as she went inside. The smells of fresh bread and chocolate and fallen leaves and something she couldn't quite define swirled together and infused her senses with a pleasant lethargy. Bemused, she walked slowly into the room. It, like the hallway, had intricate wallpaper that stretched up to the high ceiling above dark wood wainscoting, but this wallpaper was an abstract damask in shades of brown. The pattern played tricks on her eyes, and she found she had to look away.

There was no furniture in the room, but a thick silk carpet in rich reds and golds lay on the floor. Cathy's feet sank into it almost to her ankles. Impulsively, she sat down and took off her shoes, then wiggled her toes through the luxuriant weave of the fibers. Heaven. She gazed up at the elaborate crystal chandelier that winked and sparkled overhead and realized she was sitting exactly in the center of the room. At the far end of the room, a huge fire blazed in a massive, carved marble fireplace. It was much warmer in here than in the front hall, though a gray winter landscape still appeared through every heavily draped window. She leaned back on her elbows and relaxed.

"What now?" she asked Bunny, who sat down cross-legged next to her.

"Wait and see," he replied.

"So cryptic," Cathy murmured. Gazing at the walls, she couldn't remember the last time she'd felt so comfortable, so perfectly at ease. The wallpaper design dragged at her attention. It was as if—

Cathy sat up with a start. She blinked and looked at the wall again. Her eyes hadn't deceived her. The patterns on the wallpaper *were* shifting. That egg-shaped paisley was morphing into someone's head and shoulders—

Blake's head and shoulders are visible above the piano as he plays his way through the third movement of Beethoven's "Tempest" Sonata. The notes roll and thunder forth from the piano, and Blake increases the tempo and volume until he is playing like a person possessed.

He is *possessed, Cathy realizes. This is Zared in Blake's body. Tears stream down his face, and his teeth are bared in a grin that speaks more of agony than of pleasure. It is as if he both loves and hates the music at the same time. After a few moments, he stops abruptly mid-measure and bends over to the book bag at his feet, rooting through the bottom of it until he finds what he wants—what looks like a small balloon filled with an off-white powder.*

Cathy gasps and covers her mouth, but her stepbrother doesn't seem to hear her. His fingers shaking, he unties the balloon. Then with infinite care he pours a tiny amount of the powder onto the webbing between his left thumb and forefinger. He lifts his hand to his face and snorts the powder up his nose, sniffs hard and long, and swallows. His eyes flutter closed in apparent ecstasy.

After a moment, he reties the balloon and shoves it once more deep into the bottom of his bag. Wiping his eyes and nose with the back of his hand, he straightens up and begins playing again exactly where he left off. Faster and louder, every note is perfect, yet tortured, until he finishes the movement with a final, crashing chord. He's changed the piece; it's not supposed to end with a bang. Leaning his elbows against the piano keys with a discordant jangle, he buries his face in his hands and starts to giggle. But he doesn't sound amused at all.

The wallpaper shifts. Blake/Zared is in his room at his computer. The light from the monitor illuminates his face, but his countenance is dark. Again, he's grinning while crying; again, he looks anything but happy. Cathy can't see the screen, but as she zooms in closer,

(how much closer can she get without him sensing her somehow?)

she can see the monitor's image reflected in her stepbrother's dilated pupils. It is of a woman with hard, dead eyes and a twisted, lipsticked smile. A woman wearing nothing but a bit of fur and lace, her body contorted at impossible angles. An object.

With a click of his mouse, Blake focuses on another image, this one even more lurid than the last. The color is high in his cheeks and sweat beads his forehead. His breathing is shallow; he looks ill. Cathy feels nauseated and wrenches herself away from the scene, forcing her eyes to refocus until she sees only wallpaper once more.

CHAPTER ELEVEN

OUT OF TIME AND HARSH

CATHY CURLED HERSELF into a ball and wept, grieving for Bunny and his long, forced exile. What was going to happen to him? And what about her family? Were they safe? She wished there were some way for her to scrub those images of Blake off of the movie screen in her mind. Too much information. She dried her eyes and sat up.

"Bunny," she said, turning, but the boy was no longer next to her. Cathy stood up and looked around. The chandelier still twinkled and the fire snapped brightly, but she found herself alone in the room.

Outside, the sky looked a little darker, but there were no shadows to mark the passing of time. She went to one of the windows. Running her hand along the silky nap of the crimson velvet drapes, she leaned her forehead against one of the panes. Its cold calmed her as she digested the ugly images she had just witnessed. She started to feel calmer as she watched as her breath fogged the glass. She looked out at the snow. No winter-braving animal had marred the perfect surface with its tracks. No dead, brown leaves had escaped the snow's gentle yet inevitable weight.

Cathy idly wondered whether she could open the window, and what would happen if she did. Would winter remain, or would time shift the way it did when she used the front door? She knew where she was, or sort of—where did the dump go when she was here? More than that, she wondered *when* she was.

Her stomach growled, and she realized she was very hungry. Her body knew how long she had been here; it must be dinner time, at least. She pulled her cell phone out, but its screen remained dark no matter how many times she touched the screen.

"Of *course* the house's magic doesn't extend to satellite coverage," she muttered, wasting her sarcasm on the empty air. She rushed over the thick carpets to the double doors. She was never late for dinner, and the thought of Blake wondering where she was threw her into a panic. What if he suspected she'd been with Bunny? Her stepbrother was far more dangerous than she could ever have imagined. Who knew what he was capable of, if he was taking drugs and downloading hardcore porn right there in their house?

"Bunny!" she called in the front hall. "I've got to go! I'll come back as soon as I can, okay? Bunny?"

Where could he have gone? But she couldn't stay and wait for a response. She ran out of Holly Place, slamming the thick door behind her.

Why had he left her alone in the dreaming room? Had he seen what she had seen? If so, then Cathy realized she shouldn't be surprised. The horror she'd experienced during the vision had been almost intolerable for her; how much worse it must be for Bunny to see what the usurper Zared was doing with the body he'd stolen.

A few hundred yards down the path, Cathy looked at her cell phone again. It worked fine now, and Cathy was even later than she had feared. It was almost eight o'clock, and dinner had been at six. Her mom was going to be angry. Worse, Blake would probably freak when he saw her again. *Crap.* If she was going to spend any more time at Holly Place, she was going to have to figure out how to judge the passage of time.

As she came up Turley Lane, her heart sank even lower. She had been hoping to sneak into the house somehow, but her mother and stepfather sat on the porch swing. She saw Athena's shoulders relax and her anxious gaze soften as she caught sight of Cathy. Now there was no putting off confrontation. As a bonus, Rich might be looking out his window, wondering when she was going to call. And what was her cover story, anyway? She had no idea how to explain her absence.

As she walked up the steps, it was Malcolm who spoke first. "Where have you been, Cathy?" He never seemed to raise his voice, but Cathy could tell he was mad.

Our first fight. Good. Maybe he'd be a little less boring if he got riled up. As she thought it, though, she realized that the last thing she needed right now was an angry stepfather getting in her way. She had to suck it up and bring things down a notch.

"I was . . . in town," she said.

"Doing what, may I ask?"

"I was . . . at the library, doing some research. And, uh, there was this little boy there. The boy I saw during the storm. He needed help, and I lost track of time." Cathy bit her lip and twisted her hands behind her back. She knew she usually stank at lying, and hoped she sounded more believable than she felt.

Athena squinted her eyes at Cathy the way she always did when an answer didn't satisfy her. "He needed help? With what?"

"Reading. He needed help with reading. He's not a very good reader." *Stop babbling, Cathy.* "He's a little socially awkward—I think that's why he and Blake got off on the wrong foot—but he's a good kid, and I felt sorry for him."

Malcolm seemed unconvinced. He had his arms folded, and he tapped the fingers of one hand against his elbow. "Why didn't you answer your phone? We tried to call you several times after you missed dinner. I was just about to go out driving and looking for you."

"Oh—I turned it off in the library. Sorry. I guess I should have put it on vibrate."

Athena still looked dubious. "It's not like you to be so irresponsible, Cathy. You're almost an adult, but you still need to live by our rules as long as you live in our house."

"You're right, Mom. I know. I am really, really sorry. It won't happen again. Malcolm, I apologize for worrying you. I think you know that I'm not usually like this."

"I know you're not, Cathy. That's why we were so worried." Malcolm furrowed his brow for a moment, sighed, and said, "Apology accepted. I guess you wouldn't be a normal teenager if you didn't blow it once in a while." He smiled, put his arm around his wife, and squeezed her shoulders. "All's well that ends well, right? And you must be hungry."

"Yeah," Cathy said with a laugh. "I'll just go make a sandwich for myself, if that's all right."

"I've got your dinner on a covered plate in the oven," said Athena. "Hopefully it hasn't gotten too dried out. Help yourself. Malcolm and I will stay out here for a while longer, I think."

Cathy couldn't believe her luck. She hugged her mother. "Sorry again," she whispered.

"I'm just glad you're safe," Athena murmured as Cathy pulled away. "Oh, by the way, the boy you helped. What was his name?"

"Bunny." It was out before she could think. Cathy tried not to wince and bit the inside of her cheek instead, wishing she could bite the word back. Bunny had told her that his mother had given him the pet name. *Busted.*

She looked at Malcolm out of the corner of her eye. Sure enough, his quiet face had gone gray, and he looked like he had seen a ghost. *Tell me about it, Stepdad.* "It's a nickname, of course," she said. "His real name is Robert."

"And he lives close by?"

"Yeah, in that trailer park off Route 403. I walked him to his driveway and then I came home as fast as I could."

Athena smiled. "Okay, hon. Go eat some dinner."

"Thanks, Mom." Cathy chanced another glance at Malcolm. He'd recovered somewhat, but was staring out across the yard and seemed oblivious to the rest of the conversation. Cathy took that as a sign that she should make her escape. One lie down, two to go. She dreaded seeing her stepbrother inside, and she had to figure out what she was going to tell Rich. But first, she had to eat.

In the kitchen, Cathy wolfed down her casserole and put her dishes in the dishwasher as quietly as she could. She could hear the soundtrack to her sisters' favorite video game coming from the den, punctuated by assorted whoops and laughs; they must be trying to squeeze in as much fun as possible before bedtime. She tiptoed past the doorway to the den, but just then the game's character died on-screen, and Mae somersaulted and flopped on the carpet in frustration. She caught sight of her older sister and jumped up.

"Cathy!" she said. "Mom and Malcolm were *soooo* worried about you. Are you grounded?"

"I don't think so," answered Cathy, glancing up the stairs and wondering how far their conversation would carry. She lowered her voice a little. "I just talked to them outside. I didn't do it on purpose, so I think everything's okay."

Sitting on the den couch, Fawn reset the video game and paused it. "Blake told us all he thought you should get grounded," she informed Cathy. "I'm glad Mom and Malcolm didn't listen to him, though."

"Where *is* Blake, upstairs?" Cathy asked. Now more than ever, she wanted to avoid him as long as possible.

"I think he's running," Fawn said. "Outside, not on the dreadmill."

"*Tread*mill, with a 'T,'" Cathy automatically corrected. She relaxed a little even as Blake's hypocrisy chafed her. *He* could go out running alone—at sundown, no less—with impunity, while she was supposed to stay close to the house? That hardly seemed fair. "Thanks," she said aloud. "I think I'll go take a bath, guys. I'll see you in the morning." She gave Mae a one-armed hug and climbed the back staircase.

As she walked past Blake's bedroom, she paused. If her stepbrother really was out running, that meant he didn't have his book bag with him. Maybe she should search it and see whether she could find any of the drugs she'd seen him taking. She didn't know whether she'd seen the recent past or the near future. What if she didn't find anything? What if she did? Should she chance it? She had no idea how long Blake had been out, or when he would be back.

Inspiration hit her. She went to the linen closet and got out the stick vacuum. She'd run it over his bedroom carpet one more time, checking for more broken window glass, and see whether his book bag was out in the open. If it wasn't, she'd find another time, when she was less likely to get caught. Looking around her, she opened Blake's door and went inside.

The room was very dark. Malcolm had duct taped a light tarp over the empty window frame. She flipped on the light. Blake's room was even neater than usual, since Athena had gone over it carefully as they cleared out the wreckage from the storm. It didn't look like a teenager's room, anyway. There were no posters of sports teams or rock bands. Instead, a framed architectural drawing of the Brooklyn Bridge hung over the bed and an engraved portrait of Beethoven frowned down upon Blake's desk on the opposite wall.

Cathy plugged in the vacuum cleaner and passed it randomly over the carpet as she looked around. The book bag wasn't on his desk or chair; it wasn't next to the night stand or in the bay window. She flipped up the edge of the comforter and looked under the bed as she vacuumed under it. Here, the machine caught a few tiny shards; she heard their sharp crackle as they made their way into the vacuum bag. *Fantastic.* Now she wasn't a total liar. There was nothing else under the bed, though.

Frustrated, she turned off the vacuum and wound up its cord. He probably kept his book bag in his closet. *What a freak.* She wasn't a very messy person, herself, but why couldn't Blake be normal and leave his stuff all over the place the way most teenagers did?

He's not most teenagers. He's something else entirely.

Cathy shivered. Did she dare taking a quick look in the closet, or should she play it safe and wait for another opportunity?

She decided to risk it. She turned the vacuum off and slid the closet door open. There was the bag, on top of neat rows of shoes— black canvas, with the logo of his old Manhattan prep school embroidered on the side. She bent over to grab it, but whirled in shock as the floor creaked behind her.

Blake stood between her and the door, sweating profusely and breathing hard. He wiped off his red face with the edge of his T-shirt and glared at her. How had she not heard him come in?

"What are you doing in here?" he asked.

Cathy gripped her cover story and held it up. "I . . . just wanted to make sure all the glass was up off the floor," she stammered. "I found some more under your bed," she added lamely.

"And now you're looking for some in the closet?" Suspicion poured off him in waves.

Cathy suddenly hated him. How dare he do drugs in their family's house? How dare he endanger them all with his reckless behavior? "That's right. You never know what you'll find," she said, raising her eyebrows and lifting her chin.

Blake stepped toward her and grabbed her arm. "What's that supposed to mean?" His fingers dug hard into the soft flesh above the inside of her elbow. Cathy kept herself from flinching through sheer force of will. Now she regretted taunting him; what had she been thinking? She had no proof he was doing anything wrong, and without it, any accusations she made would sound insane. He was much bigger and stronger than she was. She should retreat before she made him any angrier. Above all, she couldn't let him know that she knew who he really was.

"Nothing," she insisted. "I was just trying to help clean up." She twisted free of his grasp and tried to get around him.

Blake angled his body in front of her, blocking her escape. "You little sneak," he hissed into her face. His pupils were so dilated that his eyes looked black. "Stay away from me, and stay out of my business. Otherwise, you're going to get hurt."

Cathy laughed. "You sound like a bad movie. You're going to hurt *me?*" she asked, keeping herself from rubbing her throbbing arm.

Blake smiled, and fear made a sick pit in Cathy's stomach at the sight of his handsome, terrible face. He cocked his head toward the distant sound of video games and listened for a moment to the

sound of the little girls' chatter. "Yeah," he said simply. "I know how
to hurt you." Still smiling, he stepped out of her way.

Cathy walked past him and out of his room with her head held
high. In case he was watching, she took her time putting away the
vacuum and sauntered to her own bedroom. As she shut the door
with extra care, she wished it had a lock on it. Her bathroom did, but
she didn't exactly think of it as a safe haven. She wedged her desk
chair under her doorknob, then curled up on her bed and wrapped
her duvet tightly around her.

She was living with a monster. He hadn't actually said anything,
but she knew that Blake had been threatening her sisters just now.
She was going to have to find a way to get rid of him.

Her cell phone bleated from deep inside her pocket. She dug it
out and looked at its screen; Rich was calling.

Crap. Had he seen her come home? She hadn't talked to him in
four hours. He probably thought she'd blown him and their plans
off. What should she say to him? There was no way she could tell
him anything more about Bunny or Holly Place. Would Rich believe her story about Blake if she didn't tell him how she'd known
what to look for? She hated the thought of lying to her friend. It had
been bad enough lying to her mother. Maybe she should just avoid
Rich right now. She didn't want to hurt him, but it would probably
be safer for him and for their friendship if she did. She turned off her
phone and put it under her pillow.

It wasn't even nine o'clock yet, but exhaustion smothered her
fear and guilt. She didn't want to take that bath; she didn't even
feel like taking off her jeans or brushing her teeth. She reached up,
snapped off her light, and rocked herself until she fell into a wary
and fitful sleep.

CHAPTER TWELVE

CHOICELESS AS A BEACH

BUNNY WANDERS THROUGH the Harfords' dark house. Having been built so recently, it feels strange and slick to the weak senses of his spirit. Bunny has to keep moving in order to get any traction at all. Its walls exude no memories; its rooms hold no weight of past dreams and fears, no resonance of triumphs or fights or routines. It is still a shell, a void. It waits to be filled by the minutes and hours and days that will be lived by the family that has begun to inhabit it.

It is as unlike the old house in the woods as a house can be. That place is so thick with the residue of both memories and possibilities, it is almost like swimming through air when he is there. He feels grateful to have found that house. It is the only place he can find any peace; he certainly finds none in this place. After his father and his body moved to Kashkawan, Bunny wandered even more restlessly than ever. Ripped away from the city, the only home he'd ever known, he had even less purchase on the awareness of his former life and had been desperate to hold onto his flimsy sense of self.

He had been up on the big rock behind this house one night, unwilling to be any farther away from his body than that, when he had felt a sudden and unrelenting tug in the opposite direction, a pull even stronger and more compelling than the magnetic hold his body exerted. And it felt *good*, somehow.

Suddenly, he thought of something he hadn't remembered in years—a trip with his parents to Florida. He had forgotten that places like Florida even existed. The experience flooded his mind until he felt he was there again: standing in the warm waves holding his mother's hands and looking up into her smiling face; enjoying the gentle but insistent draw of the clear, blue water around his legs; feeling the grains of sand rush out from under his feet with the tide. Oh, his lovely mother, and that beautiful, warm place they had been together. But more than that, the recovery of the memory itself thrilled him; he hadn't felt this alive in more time than he could count.

Up on the rock, he had looked in on his body one more time, its face blue in the reflected light of the computer screen. Then he had turned back to the dark woods and followed the call of this new, ocean-like attraction. He had walked at first. Then, feeling stronger with every step, he had run.

The house loomed white in the darkness. It was the source of this pull; it engulfed him now that he was so close. He felt a rush of hope: could his mother be here? He ran up the steps and stopped in front of the door. Should he knock?

Come inside.

He had obeyed the invitation that had sounded in his mind, as clear as any words he'd ever heard spoken. He had found rest. Hope and strength filled him as little by little, day after day, he explored its rooms and all that they had to show him. He didn't learn everything; he didn't know how this girl Cathy was going to be able to help him. But he was certain that she was the key to his rescue.

And so he visits her night after night, here in the new home of his father and his enemy. The first time he tried to talk to her, he didn't know whether she would be able to see or hear him. He had tried to reach her through her bathroom mirror, and she had not reacted well. Later, the house in the woods had shown him how to appear to her—simply as himself. And miraculously, she responded with pity and friendship. He hopes he can repay her somewhat by trying to keep her safe in the unguarded moments of her sleep.

Out of habit, Bunny walks around pieces of furniture instead of through them, but walls and doors he tends to ignore. He moves through the kitchen and into the den. By the wan light of the moon, he can just make out shadowy forms in the photographs that sit on end tables and the tops of bookshelves. The chronicles of two families stand side by side. His father has looked the same for years. The girls smile out at him, posing in ballet costumes and school uniforms. In the past few weeks of nights that he has roamed the rooms of this place, he has come to recognize them through their various stages of growth. Their mother remains a beautiful constant despite subtle variations in hairstyle. He avoids any pictures of his body.

He goes up the back staircase and walks the hall that connects the house's five bedrooms. So much room; so much isolation. It makes him nervous. He looks in on the littlest girl, her blond hair sticking up everywhere and her cheeks flushed. Bunny smiles at the sight of her; even her sleep is fierce and exuberant. The stuffed animal she holds so tightly looks worn out from countless nights of similar intensity. Bunny puts out a hand and touches its fur, alert to the danger of accidentally brushing the girl's skin. This object is redolent of love. Stroking it, Bunny drinks in a little of the affection that has been lavished on it for years. He is overcome by a rush of longing and hurries out.

In the next room, the middle girl—the one who looks his own age—sprawls across her bed in a tangle of covers and legs and long nightgown. In sleep, she abandons the controlled demeanor she cultivates so carefully while she is awake. Her mouth is open, and her eyes move back and forth beneath their lids. She dreams—happily, Bunny hopes. He wonders who or what occupies the center stage of her mind at this moment. It is hard for him to remember the sweet bliss that is sleep and the carefree adventuring that is dreaming. He craves becoming reacquainted with both.

He continues with his ritual walk and continues to the room at the end of the hall. Here his father and his new wife sleep, spooned together as comfortably in Malcolm and Gail's old bed as if they had been together for years instead of mere weeks. Bunny stands at the head of the wrought-iron bedstead and peers at his father's face. As always when Bunny is near, Malcolm stirs restlessly. The faintest moan escapes his lips, and Bunny knows that his father dreams as well.

Does Malcolm remember Bunny's mother? Does he miss her as intensely as Bunny does, or has this new woman filled the hole that ached so long in his heart? Bunny is not jealous on his mother's behalf; he hopes his father has found comfort and balm for his long-cherished grief.

He gazes at Athena for long moments. She seems kind and calm. When Bunny has watched the family through the windows from the big rock in the back yard, he has seen that she moves with purpose and direction. Whether she is reading or preparing food or playing the piano, she seems to glow with a quiet satisfaction. He thinks he would be happy if she were his new mother. And despite the faceless newness of this house, he would be happy to call it home if he were restored to himself again.

Bunny goes back up the hall and visits Cathy next. How is it that she will be able to help him? When the old house first told him to seek her out, he assumed she would know what to do. He has since seen that she is even more bewildered than he is. He hopes the house will teach her the way to cast out Zared and restore Bunny—Blake—to himself. Why else would the house have appeared? It seems to have come into existence in response to his need; the universe would not be so cruel as to provide it unless it was a tool, an instrument to be used to help him.

Cathy is wrestling with sleep. Bunny hopes she will win her way past its rocky shallows and find quieter depths. Unconscious, without her bright eyes and smile to animate her countenance, she is merely pretty. But awake, walking, laughing, she possesses a beauty of which she seems to be unaware. Even without the prompting that she was to be his rescuer, he would have been drawn to her. Anybody would be, he thinks. Bunny watches her toss and struggle, and focuses all his will into sending her relief. A moment later, she relaxes and breathes more deeply. Bunny is surprised; has he helped her? Or is it just coincidence? Either way, he is relieved that she is calmer now. He has a sense that she will need her rest. He moves on.

He has reached the back stairs again. He pauses for a moment outside his body's door. Does he dare visit? No. Not tonight. Cathy has warned him to stay away. He should trust her. Zared may be awake and lying in wait for him. He stops himself from going in, as difficult as it is to resist the throbbing pull his body exerts. He goes back downstairs to the living room, where his mother's favorite chair sits next to a large window that faces east. In it, he curls himself up and waits for morning.

CHAPTER THIRTEEN

THROUGH A VEIL

CATHY TURNED HER PHONE on again after she changed out of her church clothes on Sunday afternoon. *Great.* Rich had left her two voicemails and texted her five times the night before. She forced herself to read his messages. He had kept his tone funny and light, masking his hurt pretty well—until the last one. This was her only friend in Kashkawan—her only real friend in the whole world anymore, actually.

She'd been a little surprised at how quickly her city friends seemed to have adjusted to life without her. She couldn't blame them, though, not even her best friend, Jessica. Manhattan high school classes were as rigorous as those at a lot of universities, and students spent their "free" time preparing for debate tournaments and theater productions, interning at the United Nations or Wall Street law firms, or volunteering at the city's countless homeless shelters and world-class hospitals. Cathy remembered how it was. She couldn't recall a single day last year when she hadn't been obsessing about how to enhance her resume so that she'd have the best edge possible in the cutthroat world of top college admissions, and she certainly hadn't been the only one. That was life in the city. She and her friends had talked endlessly and sent one another constant texts about their activities; they had had everything in common back then.

But the busy hive of Manhattan activity was myopic. She knew that it was as hard for her friends to imagine her new life here in sleepy upstate New York as if she had moved to the moon. And she couldn't relate to their life anymore, either. Rich was the only friend she had left—and he was a great friend—so funny and smart and kind. She didn't ever feel the need to compete with him. His comfort with who he was had infected her, and she had relaxed her usual frenetic pace and had been surprised at how much better she felt as a result. She needed him, and she couldn't afford to hurt him even unintentionally. She had to make amends.

It would have to wait until after dinner, though. The Wrights had always fixed roast beef, mashed potatoes, and salad for their post-church Sunday dinner, while the Harfords had always made pancakes and bacon. So far, the newly blended family was alternating traditions until Malcolm and Athena figured out what the new routine should be. Fortunately, today was a pancake day. Cathy had to admit that the Harfords' tradition was quicker both to make and to clean up. She'd escape to Rich's at her first opportunity.

An hour later, full of pancakes and lying opposite Rich in the giant hammock in his back yard, Cathy let the sun's heat bake her worries away. They swung gently back and forth together. Rich hadn't asked her yet about yesterday, and had accepted her simple "I'm sorry" with a smile and a shrug. She knew she eventually had to say something to explain, but she felt so comfortable right now. She could afford to procrastinate a little; she didn't want this moment to end. She gazed up at the flawless blue sky, then looked at Rich, who had his arms crossed across his chest and his eyes closed.

Her straight legs lay alongside his twisted ones in the taut fabric of the hammock. Cathy realized that if Rich hadn't been born with amyloplasia, he'd be much taller than she was. As it was, they were almost exactly the same height when Rich wasn't bearing weight on his crutches. This afternoon, Cathy had changed into a pair of shorts, but she'd never seen Rich wear anything but long pants. She wondered why he felt like he had to keep covered up all the time. Did he have scars from surgeries? She realized she didn't know much at all about his condition. It hadn't mattered to her, but maybe it was something he'd want to talk about at some point.

"Hey," she said, nudging his hip with her bare toe. "You asleep?"

Rich opened his eyes and grinned. Cathy's heart surprised her by flopping over in her chest. There was something almost exotic about the way his bright blue eyes turned up at the corners, and his smile was gorgeous. Another flop. With a jolt, Cathy realized that she was falling in love with her new best friend.

As she smiled back, she wondered what it would be like to kiss him. She felt her pulse accelerate as she thought about it, and breathed in through her nose in an effort to stay calm and cool. Did he ever think of her in that way? Had he ever kissed a girl? She imagined lightly brushing his lips with hers and having him put his arms around her, those tanned arms made strong by years of bearing his own weight. She could twine her fingers in the waves of golden hair at the base of his neck as the kiss got deeper and—

Gasp. She sat up with a start and hugged her knees to her chest, sending the hammock bobbing.

Rich sat up, too. "What's wrong?" he asked. "You're all red."

"I'm fine," Cathy lied. Maybe she was getting better at dishonesty, since she'd had so much practice lately.

Rich raised an eyebrow. "Seriously?"

Okay, maybe she was still a bad liar. "I think Blake is doing drugs," she said in a rush. Suddenly it seemed easier to talk about Blake than to confess what was really on her mind at this very moment.

Laughing, Rich said, "Blake? Come *on.* In the dictionary next to the term 'straight edge' is a picture of your stepbrother. I've never seen someone our age as buttoned down as he is."

"You don't know many city kids, do you?"

"Well, no. I've never really gotten that whole prep school scene. Look, I don't really know him, but he's about the last person I would suspect of partying."

"I think it's more than partying. I think he's snorting cocaine, or heroin, or something."

Rich's mouth dropped open. "That's pretty hardcore. How do you know? Have you seen him do it?"

"Yeah, sort of . . ." Terrific. Now she had talked herself into a corner. Why was she such an idiot?

"What, did you find his stash, or something?"

"Yes. No. I mean, I think I know where it is. I went looking for it yesterday in his room, but he caught me. I told him I was vacuuming up broken glass from the storm—and I really was—but he got suspicious. He didn't say anything, but he gave me the impression that he would try to hurt me if I kept snooping around. Or hurt Fawn or Mae, which would be worse. Way worse."

"Wow. That's psycho. But, wait a minute. Why did you suspect him in the first place?"

Cathy's throat went dry. She looked at Rich for a moment while she scrambled to come up with a safe answer. "Bunny. The boy who was spying on Blake. He was up on that big rock behind the house again, looking into Blake's room. Bunny told me all about the drugs yesterday afternoon."

"The weird homeschooler? His name is *Bunny*? Why would you believe him? You don't even know him."

"He gave me details about Blake that he wouldn't know unless he'd actually seen him."

"Wow," said Rich. "Now I can see why you didn't want to hang out last night. You must have been totally freaked out."

"You have no idea," Cathy muttered, resting her chin on her knees.

What was she going to do? She needed to get back to Holly Place to figure it all out, but when? And she had to find some way to keep track of time while she was there. She couldn't risk being late again, or her mother and Malcolm would be all over her. And how could she make sure Blake stayed away from her sisters while she was gone? She couldn't let him hurt them, couldn't give him a reason to take out his rage on them.

"Hey." Rich leaned closer to her and bumped her knees with his shoulder. "Look, it's pretty awful if that's really what's going on. But there has to be a way to find out for sure—without Blake knowing what you're doing. You just have to make a plan."

Cathy looked at him. His face was just inches away from hers. Those eyes of his—she'd never seen eyes that vividly blue before, fringed with dark gold lashes that would make any girl envious. He smiled again. Could he tell what she was thinking? Her heart thumping, she raised her hand and touched his cheek. Smooth and rough at the same time, so different from her own skin.

Rich's eyes widened and he covered her hand with his own. "Cathy?" he whispered. Closing his eyes, he bent forward and kissed her tentatively, running one hand along the side of her throat and into her hair. Oh, this felt even better than she had imagined.

After a moment, he pulled back and looked at her. "I've been wanting to do that for a long time," he confessed.

"Oh, yeah? Since when?"

"Since I fell on your lap in the mini mart."

Cathy laughed, giddy with relief that she hadn't messed up. "Really?"

"Pretty much. But I didn't ever think you would—" Rich pressed his lips together and stared off beyond her.

"What, want to kiss you? Why wouldn't I? You're gorgeous and you're an amazing friend."

"Friend." Rich echoed with a grimace and started to turn away, but Cathy reached out and turned his face toward her.

"I think I want to be more than friends," she whispered, feeling her face go hot again.

Rich smiled and kissed her again, more confidently this time. She melted into him and felt his arms go around her just the way she had hoped they would. Peace settled over her, and she realized that she felt safe for the first time since she'd left Holly Place the evening before.

"Being with you feels like coming home," she murmured into his ear as he trailed feathery kisses down her cheek toward the tender underside of her jaw. He smelled faintly spicy, like cedar and cloves and something else dark and smoky. Cathy inhaled sharply as Rich reached a tender spot behind her ear, giving the whole right side of her body goose bumps. She gazed out across the back yard and was just about to turn her own lips to Rich's earlobe when her unfocused eyes caught a flicker of movement among the dense trees along the edge of the lawn. She peered into the deep shadows, trying to see through the brush.

Bunny was looking straight at her and motioning her over. She stiffened, glaring, and shook her head very slightly. No way was she going anywhere with him right now. What was he doing here? Why did helping him have to mean ruining everything else? She sat like a statue in Rich's arms, willing Bunny to leave.

"I'm sorry," Rich said, pulling away. "I'm moving too fast, right? I'm really sorry."

"What?" asked Cathy, still staring at Bunny. "Oh, no." She looked at Rich and smiled. "No, not at all. I . . ." She let her eyes flick back to Bunny for the merest fraction of a second, but Rich caught her look and twisted around to see what she saw. Cathy held her breath. Bunny was climbing through the bushes and coming out from under the trees, moving as silently as ever, but very visibly.

Rich scanned the yard and the woods beyond and turned back to her. "Did you see a deer, or something?"

Rich couldn't see Bunny. Cathy fought down panic; somehow, that drove home the fact that what she was experiencing was not normal. It made sense, after all—Bunny was sort of a ghost, right? She had always been alone whenever she had seen him before—except for during the storm, with Blake. It didn't surprise her that the entity that had usurped Bunny's body would still be able to sense his lingering presence. She didn't have any other circumstances as proof yet, but she had to believe that other than Blake, it was she who was the exception rather than Rich. Bunny claimed he'd been following his own body around for years, and if just anyone could see him, surely Bunny would have mentioned it. Malcolm, for example. He was unaware of the entire situation—wasn't he?

Bunny now stood on the lawn just twenty feet or so from the hammock and continued to gesture to Cathy. "Oh, that must have been what it was," she said, trying to keep her tone light. "It was pretty big. I'm still getting used to all the wildlife around here." Another lame lie. But what else could she do? It was clear that Rich couldn't see what was so plain to her.

He knew there was something wrong, though. He was squinting at her just a bit, and a vertical furrow had developed between his eyebrows. *Think, Cathy; think. Find a way to distract him.*

"Hey," she said, giving Rich what she hoped was a flirty grin, but wincing inwardly at her lack of eloquence. She scooted around until she and Rich were both facing the same way, took his arm, draped it around her shoulders, and leaned back with him into the hammock. They lay, not speaking, staring up at the sky. She hoped that Bunny would get the message her turned back sent. "This is turning into a great day," she said aloud.

"Best day of my life," murmured Rich, kissing her lightly on the cheek. Cathy turned her face so that their lips could meet again, but there was Bunny, standing on Rich's side of the hammock and staring at her. She jumped, which made Rich jump, too.

"Okay, clearly this is making you uncomfortable," he said, sitting up and reaching over the side of the hammock to get his crutches. Bunny moved out of his way automatically.

"No, Rich, I'm fine!" she said. She sat up, glaring at the ghost boy.

Bunny spoke. "Cathy, I'm sorry. I know you're, um, busy. I just need to talk to you right now." Rich was inches away, but oblivious.

Cathy shook her head, so furious that tears started up in her eyes. *Ugh.* It was clear that Bunny wasn't going anywhere until he got what he wanted. She should just make a graceful exit rather than risk Rich seeing any more of what would look like insane behavior.

Rich got to his feet and swiveled around with the help of his crutches. "Is this . . . are we going to be all right after . . . this?" he asked.

Cathy could see hope and doubt warring in his eyes. Bunny would just have to wait for a minute. She vaulted out of the hammock and hugged Rich. Pulling back, she kissed him again, trying to put every ounce of tenderness she felt into it. "We are more than all right," she whispered. "But I, um, I should go. I've got some stuff to do. I'll text you later, okay?"

Rich smiled at her uncertainly. "Okay."

"No, really. I've never been happier than in the last few minutes. I'll be back."

"Okay," Rich repeated, nodding. "I trust you."

"Thank you. You have no idea what that means to me. I'm so sorry. Bye." Cathy ran to the gate, turning and waving as she let herself out of the yard. Rich nodded back at her, then swung himself across the lawn toward his house.

Bunny walked through the solid wood fence as she latched the gate. "I'm really sorry," he said again.

Cathy bent over and pretended to tie her shoe. "Somehow, I doubt it," she hissed. "I can't talk to you right here. Someone might notice me, and since Blake and I are the only ones who seem to be able to see you, I'll look like a lunatic. Meet me at Holly Place."

"Okay." He turned and ran, his big white T-shirt fluttering behind him.

Cathy watched him go, her frustration mounting. Why her? Why could she see and touch him and Rich couldn't? She glanced across the street at her house. No one was outside, and she couldn't see anyone at the windows. She started running down the street, her mind working furiously as she went.

She couldn't risk a time shift by going inside Holly Place—not until she could figure out how that worked. If she was going to help Bunny and keep her family safe, the first thing she had to do was keep herself out of trouble. Bunny would just have to tell her whatever he was going to tell her on the porch, and then she'd be back home again before anyone was the wiser.

CHAPTER FOURTEEN

A CROOKED MILE

HIGH, HIGH UP IN A sycamore tree between the absurd little boxes that pass for houses out here in the wretched wilderness, Zared watches the girl run after the eidolon. He seethes. He has seen her in the hammock with her deformed abomination of a friend. He has seen the eidolon's approach and successful badgering of the girl. That girl—that *Cathy*. Her very name leaves a bad taste in his mouth.

Zared should have found a way to keep Malcolm from marrying. He had thought that a romantic relationship and the care of other children would keep his "father" busy and distracted, but this has now gone too far. They have left Manhattan and its population that throbs and surges and caresses as relentlessly as the sea. Malcolm has brought them instead to a place nearly devoid of stimulation of any kind. And Athena and her three spoiled brats are turning out to be nothing but trouble. This one, especially. If Zared isn't careful, Cathy will ruin everything.

Though his wrath runs strong and bitter, he revels in it as it courses through his system. It dizzies him somewhat, and he climbs down the tree with care. He plans to get years' more use out of this body; now that it is nearly old enough to be autonomous, the freedom to do whatever he wants with it is tantalizingly close. He can't let that prize slip through his fingers after all this time. Before finding this body,

—left empty at such an early age! It was unheard of among the wekufe—

Zared had been bereft of temporal form for agonizing, soul-numbing decades. No drug-induced high or other physical response he has sought in the past eight years has compared with the sweet, shuddering release he'd gotten when he had first slipped inside this shell. Since then, the vivid tastes of water and food and air; the sting of sweat running into his eyes after getting this young, vigorous heart pumping during a long run; the response of his body to a beautiful woman—all these sensations that humans take for granted most of the time are a powerful drug to him, one he plans never to be without again.

But lately, ordinary sensation hasn't been enough. He craves more and stronger feeling, more exposure and surrender to the all-engulfing *now* of the physical body. He has found it in illicit substances and in a sea of intoxicating images downloaded from the internet. As he explores these new, more intense pleasures, he finds himself losing patience with the strictures he has abided for so long: following the rules, performing filial duties such as studying and achieving and performing. He is no longer sure he can wait for the unsupervised, free-wheeling haven that is modern college life. He yearns to be free to do whatever he wants, whenever he wants—*right now.*

He lopes after the girl. It's time to find out where she is going and what she is doing with the eidolon. That *garbage.*

Zared's throat fills with bile as he thinks of him. He has performed all the rituals known to his kind designed to distance oneself from an on-hanging spirit once its body has been appropriated, to no avail. Perhaps it is because of its youth, but the eidolon's tenacity has surprised and maddened Zared for years.

And why can the girl see the eidolon? What has the ghost boy said to her, and how has she made any sense out of what surely must be the inchoate ramblings of the long-dispossessed? Does she have some gift? If so, is it inborn, or is it generated by an amulet or other magical charm? He must find its source and wrest it from her.

Judging from her behavior last night, she suspects something; she knows something. He has tried charm and diversion and politesse with her; he has now moved to threats. But here she is, sneaking off again with his enemy. Clearly, she is not easily deterred. He must be rid of the eidolon. And if the girl keeps getting in his way, he'll have to find a way to get rid of her, as well.

Zared stays well back from his quarry, not wanting to chance her catching a glimpse of him. He sees her turn off the main thorough-fare. He follows her up the twisting, tree-choked dirt road. His heart pounds pleasantly; through the uncounted lifetimes he has stolen for himself through millennia, he has always loved a good chase. The increased circulation heightens all his senses and fires his imagina-tion. He begins to wonder how the girl's smooth skin would taste, how her body might respond to his touch, how he might find a way to dominate her completely and punish her for her disobedience and curiosity.

Perhaps another wekufe has the knowledge he needs—not that any of his kind would share such treasure willingly. They are solitary beings, forming alliances only when there is a possibility of overtak-ing a vulnerable body. Then, when the prize is freed from its eidolon, the wekufe turn on each other and rip one another to shreds until only the strongest remains to claim the prize. Zared has been such a winner many times. A cunning wekufe can absorb the magic a weaker one gives up when it dies and its intelligence dissolves into the ether. Zared has never had a need to hunt wekufe while embod-ied, but he acknowledges that now might be the time to search out one who might hold the key to getting rid of his problems—the eidolon and his "stepsister."

Now that there is little chance of their being seen, Zared accel-erates his pace, wanting to catch up to Cathy and confront her. Up the next rise and around a turn—

—and she is gone. Her footprints have faded to nothing and she has left no more broken twigs or bent grass leaves. No trace of her clean, young scent remains on the heavy afternoon air. All he can de-tect—other than riotous birdsong and the slight soughing of leaves in the breeze—is the sickly sweet smell of decay.

She has tricked him. She has sensed his pursuit and has escaped with the eidolon. But how? He runs all the way up where the road ends at a small lake, but she is not there. On the way back down the road, he follows a gravel driveway a few hundred yards until he comes to a chain link fence. A yellow sign mounted on it reads "Philipse Town Landfill" in large block letters, with the hours of operation and supervising personnel listed beneath. She is not beyond this fence; she can't be.

Roaring in frustration, Zared grasps the fence in his hands and shakes it until the rough metal cuts into his palms and blood runs down his forearms. The sight of it both soothes and frightens him. He licks the blood off his skin, savoring its coppery tang. He'll go home and tend to these cuts. Maybe he'll snuff a little more of the excellent heroin he has bought from a down-county dealer. And he'll wait.

CHAPTER FIFTEEN

UNDER THE SHADOW

CATHY RAN UP the wide stone steps of Holly Place. She looked down each end of the long, shadowy porch, her chest heaving. Bunny was nowhere to be seen. *Fantastic.* What now? She refused to go into the house—not without some way to keep track of how long she was inside.

"Bunny!" she called, scanning the dense underbrush beyond the lawn. "Bunny, you said you had to talk to me. I don't have time for games. Where are you?

"And thanks, by the way, for ruining possibly the best moment of my life," she added under her breath. She sank down on the top step and leaned against the baluster. Here she was again. She knew more about the house than she had the last time she'd sat on this porch, but she felt even more clueless. She hadn't asked to be anyone's savior. All she wanted was to go to school and enjoy being with her new boyfriend—the thought of Rich as her boyfriend gave her stomach a delicious twinge—and live her life. She'd rather read about magic houses than visit them in real life.

This *was* real life, right? She wasn't crazy? Because if this was somehow all in her head, she was going to work on having much more enjoyable delusions than this whole scenario.

Cathy raised her eyes and gazed up under the eaves. She could see bits of twig sticking out from above the intricately carved joists; small birds must have nested there. Were they affected by the house's ever-changing position in time? Did the house actually move through time at all, or was that just an illusion apparent to those who went inside the house? She listened hard, hoping to hear whether the birds' nests were inhabited.

No rustling or chirping met her ears, but she realized she could hear faint singing. Not birds—a person. She cocked her head. It didn't seem to be coming from within Holly Place. She closed her eyes and concentrated. A pure, clear voice sang something that had the chant-like rhythm of a nursery rhyme. Cathy got to her feet and started down the steps again, following the elusive sound. She walked under the massive holly trees that flanked the porch and turned the corner. Yes—the singing was definitely coming from behind the house.

Cathy followed the wide swath of lawn around the house. Holly Place and its grounds looked almost like an island, except that instead of being surrounded by sea, it was hemmed in by the thick and exuberant woods that covered any wild place in upstate New York. Who cut the grass and took care of the shrubbery that nestled against the buttery stone walls of the house? Cathy noticed rhododendrons and roses and the strap-like leaves of spring bulbs months past flowering.

Turning the corner again, she came to a wide stone terrace extending out from the back of the house. Near the center of it, a little girl jumped rope with her back to Cathy. She wore a pale pink taffeta party dress with big bell sleeves and a full skirt—exactly the kind of dress Cathy had always wanted when she was little. Her bare feet slapped the stone in perfect time with the gentle kiss of the rope. She sang softly but clearly as she jumped, never missing a beat or a note.

God guard me from those thoughts men think

In the mind alone;

He that sings a lasting song

Thinks in a marrow-bone.

That was an odd jump-rope rhyme—a little more abstract than "Bubblegum, Bubblegum." The halting, minor melody matched the words for strangeness. Cathy had never heard anything like it before.

Adding to her sense of disorientation was the sense that there was something very familiar about the girl. From the back at least, she looked almost like Mae. In fact, if Cathy had been a little farther away, she would have immediately assumed that this was her little sister. But this girl's hair was slightly darker and longer.

Cathy stepped onto the terrace. As she did so, the girl whirled around, her rope collapsing to the ground behind her. Cathy's mouth went dry. She was looking at herself as of about twelve years before. It was as if she had been twinned and frozen in time. It wasn't a mere similarity; this child was her clone. Except for her eyes—they were the same color and shape as Cathy's, but they possessed a wisdom and world-weariness that she'd never seen in a person so young.

"You're here," said the girl. Her voice was just like Cathy's had been as a child. The sound of it made Cathy dizzy somehow, as if her image in a mirror had started speaking to her. Which it had, not too long ago, she reminded herself.

She stretched her lips into what she hoped would pass for a polite smile. "Yes, I'm here. I was supposed to meet someone. You don't happen to know where he is, do you?"

"Bunny, you mean? He'll be here soon." The girl twisted the painted wooden handles of her jump rope, and Cathy could hear the ball bearings inside them swiveling.

"Great, thanks." Cathy paused. It wasn't rude to ask, was it? Hopefully it didn't matter. Kids that age usually preferred directness. "Who are you?"

"That depends," said the girl, and she began jumping rope again.

"On what?" asked Cathy.

"On what you need."

Cathy felt her face flush. This was ridiculous. Why all the talking in riddles? "What I need are some answers," she retorted.

Skip, *skip*. Skip, *skip*. The girl kept jumping, and Cathy's frustrations started to fade against her will with the regular rhythm of the rope.

"That's not what you need," said the girl finally. "That's what you *want.*"

"Same difference," Cathy snapped, her impatience flaring again.

The girl smiled, the same gap-toothed grin Cathy remembered from her own first grade school photo. "Not at all," she laughed, and began her strange rhyme all over again.

"Cathy!"

Finally. Bunny's voice reached her from the front of the house. Cathy looked away at the sound of it, then back to the little girl.

She was gone. She'd vanished in the split second that Cathy had taken her eyes off her. Cathy looked around the terrace wildly. There was nowhere to hide, not within several yards.

But on the flagstone where the girl had been jumping lay what looked like a necklace. Cathy picked it up and examined it. A white stone the size and shape of a small bird's egg hung from a long, braided gold chain. It looked as if it had been cut in two and then put back together. Was it a container of some kind? Cathy twisted the two halves until they split, and the scents of cloves and orange blossom and heliotrope poured forth. Inside was some sort of hard, waxy substance. Was it a kind of perfume? Cathy rubbed a bit of the wax on her pulse points and closed the stone again. Lifting her wrist to her nose, she inhaled. *Delicious.* The wax warmed to her body temperature and smelled even better than it had in the stone.

Why had the girl left such a precious thing behind? Had she really been there at all? Cathy didn't feel like she could just put the necklace back on the ground where she'd found it. Maybe she'd find a safe place to put it on the porch. She put the chain around her neck and slipped the stone down the front of her shirt so that it was well hidden. Hearing her name called once again, Cathy threw her head back and groaned, then circled back to the front of the house once more.

Bunny was sitting on the porch in nearly the same spot she had been just minutes before.

"Where have you been?" he asked.

"Behind the house, on the terrace," she said. "I heard someone singing."

"Really? Who was it?"

"I'm not sure. She looked like me—*exactly* like me—only from a long time ago. It was freaky. We talked for a minute, but she didn't tell me much. She seemed to know who *you* were, though."

Bunny frowned. "I've never been back there. I've never seen anyone else here—not *real* people. And I don't know any other girls, except for your sisters."

"Right. And it's not like you actually know them. And I'm not sure this girl *was* real."

Bunny gave her an odd glance, but said nothing. The silence between them stretched for a few long moments.

Finally, Cathy broke it. "Okay, I'm here now, and I'm not exactly happy about that. First you left me alone in the dreaming room yesterday. Today, you totally invade my privacy, mess up my afternoon, and beg me to come here so you can talk to me about something urgent. Then you're not even here when I show up. What do you need?"

Bunny hung his head. "I'm really sorry. I couldn't stay yesterday. What the house showed you scared me too much." He paused and peered at her from under his lowered eyebrows. "But I saw you at your house last night, while you were sleeping," he continued in a shy voice. "You seemed okay. I've just been wondering whether you have a plan yet."

"A plan," Cathy echoed.

"For helping me." Bunny sat up straight again. "For getting my body back." He smiled, and fresh hope shone out of his eyes.

Cathy felt like crying, but gritted her back teeth hard instead. "No," she admitted. "I have no idea how to help you. The dreaming room only showed me how bad the situation is. It didn't give me any sort of solutions." *And I'm not sure it can*, she thought to herself. How could it possibly?

"Okay, maybe it will today. Will you come in and see? Maybe we could go upstairs and—"

"Bunny, no," Cathy interrupted. "Slow down. I can't believe you brought me here just for this. I can't go in there, not today. Every time I do, I lose track of time, and yesterday I totally lucked out of getting into major trouble for that. I can't help you if I'm grounded, right?"

"I guess not." Bunny sounded dubious.

"Look. You go in the house and do whatever it is that you do when you're in there alone. See if the house will—I don't know—give you some sort of time-tracking device. Or whether it will agree to stay put while I'm inside. You've been out of your body for years, now. A few more days won't make a difference. Just try to be patient, okay? I'm really new to this rescuing business."

Bunny stood up. "Okay. I'll try. It's just that my mind is so much clearer lately, and I can't help wondering whether that's only temporary—and whether right now is the time to do something about Zared. Right now, before it's too late."

Cathy's heart thudded, and her face felt warm. What if Bunny was right? Maybe time *was* running out for him. Maybe this house wouldn't always be here for her to find whenever the mood struck her. She should go inside Holly Place right now and see what their next step should be. It would be worth the risk.

No, Cathy told herself fiercely. *I've got to be sensible and protect myself.* A chill washed over her, and her heart quieted. "Bunny, I can't. Not today."

The boy's face fell. "Okay," he whispered. He turned away and walked toward the front door. Cathy squashed the guilt and pity she felt rising up within her. "Come find me later, okay?" she called after him, but Bunny didn't turn or respond. She shrugged, ignored the sick feeling in her gut, and headed down the path toward home.

Cathy didn't have any real obligation to Bunny, did she? How had Bunny gotten himself into this mess? By looking for his mother, who was dead and gone. Try to fight that reality, and you get nothing but trouble.

Cathy wondered whether the idea to search for her father's departed spirit would ever have occurred to her. Her dad had died when she was twelve, not when she was four. Bunny hadn't gone looking for his mother until he was nine, but still. Cathy knew she was lucky. Fawn barely remembered their father, and Mae would never have the comfort that memories of their whole family together could have. Cathy loved reliving times with her dad, going back in time and doing her best to muster up his presence again.

Cathy stopped in her tracks. It hadn't occurred to her that she actually had a way to go back in time in her own life. Holly Place. It didn't work just for Bunny, did it? Cathy realized that she had been thinking of the house as an extension of Bunny, a lens for viewing the details of his particular challenges. But that traveling room—she could try to use it to go back in her own life, too. Maybe.

She turned around and ran back to the house and up the porch steps.

"Bunny!" she called as she shoved the heavy front door open. "Bunny, I'm here!"

No answer. Where could he be?

Cathy realized even as she scanned the balcony above that it was better this way—she could try out the traveling room on her own, without interference or embarrassment. Then maybe she'd have time to stay and help Bunny later. She squared her shoulders and walked to the traveling room's tall double doors.

How did this work? Cathy turned the ornate doorknob and pushed.

The room was empty. The first time she had been in it, it had looked like Blake's tiny, cluttered old bedroom in Manhattan. Now its grand architecture matched the rest of the house, but sat deserted and dusty. It looked cold and lonely, unlike the other rooms in the house that Cathy had seen. She shut the door.

What had Bunny done when he had brought her here the first time? Well, he'd known what he wanted to show her; maybe the room picked up on the user's intent somehow. Cathy realized that she had opened the door without any sort of expectation as to what she would see inside.

Keeping her hand on the doorknob, she closed her eyes and rested her forehead on the door's carved surface. She sorted through her memories. What did she want to see? Should she try for her favorite moment with her father, or go with the one she remembered most vividly?

She thought about the time that her family had rented a house in Mexico for a few weeks. Her mother had been pregnant with Mae. Cathy had been eleven, and Fawn had been two. The house had sat right on the beach, and its hand-carved wooden furniture had smelled like an exotic spice. Opening her eyes, Cathy opened the door again. Bright, warm air and vivid colors engulfed her.

Smiling at her success, she stepped onto glazed terra cotta tiles and looked around. The entry hall and living room were just as she remembered them. Vivid woven rugs hung on the white stucco walls. The huge windows allowed views of the back garden, the lap pool, and the beach beyond. The sun was setting over the jungle behind the house, and the ocean and the sky glowed with an otherworldly light. The whirring overhead fan stirred Cathy's hair as she walked through the living room to the sliding glass door that led to the patio. Hope made her heart thud as she looked outside.

Peter Wright lay sprawled in a deck chair next to the pool, a ragged fishing hat on his head and extra sun block on his nose. Tears welled in Cathy's eyes. He had been reading a paperback mystery, but now lay asleep with the book on his chest. His mouth was slightly open and Cathy guessed he was snoring a bit; he probably would have been embarrassed if anyone had decided to memorialize the moment with a photo.

Cathy heard yelling coming from the beach. A moment later, her own head appeared as she and Fawn charged up the rickety wooden stairs that linked the garden to the sand.

"Daddy, Dad!" she heard herself yell. "Daddy, come see the turtles!"

Her father lurched awake, his book falling to the concrete beside the deck chair. "Hey," he said breathlessly as his daughters launched themselves onto him.

"Dad, hurry!" young Cathy urged him. "Baby turtles are hatching out of the sand! Mom is filming them, but you have to come see!"

"Blue, Daddy!" added Fawn with her toddler lisp. "The teedles are blue! Like magic! Hurry!"

"Okay, okay," her father laughed. He scooped Fawn up and grabbed Cathy's hand, then heaved himself off the deck chair and ran for the beach.

Cathy watched them disappear down the hill and remembered what had happened next. They had gone back to the nest and watched dozens of tiny blue turtles come boiling up out of the ground. Each one would right itself, then push against the sand with all its might until it got to the ocean. They had squealed and cheered, clapping as each one made it to the water. Fawn had wanted to help one turtle that lay flailing on its back, but her father had stopped her from touching it. "It has to do it on its own," he cautioned. "That's how it builds up the strength it needs to swim and crawl. If you help it, you'll actually be hurting it."

Fawn had started to protest, but then nodded solemnly. She had bent over until her nose was inches from the struggling turtle. "You can do it, you can," she had urged it. Finally, the little animal had managed to flip itself over and start crawling to the water. Fawn, normally so reserved, had squealed and applauded until the turtle had swum out of sight. The last turtle had glided away, and her mother had put away the video recorder.

Soon, Cathy saw her family returning from their adventure on the beach in the fading light. She moved away from the sliding glass doors and backed up until she found herself in the front hall of the hacienda once more. She whirled when she felt someone's presence behind her. She felt her face go hot when she saw Bunny, who looked surprised to see her.

"What are you doing here? I thought you were too busy to come inside," he said quietly. He looked beyond her at her family, who were now coming inside the house. "Oh," he said.

Guilt flooded Cathy all over again. "I miss my dad. You, of all people, should understand that. I just got the idea that I could see him again, and I wanted to try it. That's all."

"Of course," Bunny replied. "I've done that lots. I get it. Take your time." After another wistful glance at Cathy's happy family, he turned and faded through the door.

Cathy bit her lip and returned her attention to the scene in the living room. Her parents bustled about, getting food out for dinner. Fawn sat on the tile floor playing with a stuffed animal. Her younger self stood at the window looking out at the sea. As interesting as it was to see herself as another person, Cathy found her gaze returning again and again to her father.

Turn around, she wanted to say to her younger self. *You won't have him around for much longer. In just a few months, he'll die. Turn around and talk to him. Don't waste even a moment that you have with him.*

Cathy watched him, bumping her mother's hip as he passed her in the kitchen, laughing and joking, chopping onions and grating soft queso blanco for their fish tacos. She realized that she had forgotten how tall he was and that his hair was going gray at the temples. She stared intently at him, wanting to emblazon every detail of him on her brain so that she wouldn't forget again.

Her mother, too, looked subtly different. Her eyes glowed and she smiled more here than she had in recent years. That was understandable; she had been grieving and enduring the challenging life of a single parent. Cathy realized that the cruelest part of death was how it stole away that glow, that light of a thriving love transmuted into pale memory.

Dinner was ready. Cathy's family sat and ate at the large wooden table near the windows. The twilight sky beyond them darkened into night. Fawn asked what turtles ate. Young Cathy asked when they'd be going to visit a Mayan temple she had read about before the trip.

The conversation was ordinary, yet Cathy found it more absorbing than the best movie she'd ever seen. Finally, when Fawn laid her head on the table and Athena got up to put her to bed, Cathy realized that a long time must have passed—both here and in the outside world.

Not again. She felt like an idiot. Cathy left the traveling room as quickly as she could. The windows in the front hall looked out on a rainy fall night, but Cathy knew she wouldn't know how long she had been gone this time until she was several hundred yards away from Holly Place and could check the clock on her phone.

"Bunny!" she called as she ran for the front door. "I'll see you later. I've got to go!"

CHAPTER SIXTEEN

THROUGH THE FIRE

IT WASN'T RAINING outside, and it wasn't fall, but it was definitely night. Cathy ran as fast as she could through the dark woods, which wasn't very fast. At least the path was well marked; she didn't worry at all about getting lost. Once she got to Route 403, she pulled out her phone.

3:07 a.m. Monday morning. As its clock updated itself, Cathy's phone buzzed with the notices of dozens of waiting texts and voice mail messages. The bottom dropped out of Cathy's stomach. She was so totally busted. Her parents must be sick with worry—and Rich would be panicked, too. *What have I done?* For a minute, she considered not going home at all. How could she possibly face Malcolm and Athena? She had no explanation for where she had been, none at all. Her parents would surely have checked with Rich; they had probably been out driving around and looking for her as well. Everyone knew she had no other real friends here in Kashkawan. What was she going to do?

And what about school? She hadn't eaten in hours, but she was too panicked to be hungry. Exhaustion was another story—she knew it was hiding right behind the extreme anxiety she was feeling. How could she possibly go to school in a few hours, assuming her mother and stepfather hadn't killed her?

Cathy turned right on Turley Lane and saw her house up the block. Sure enough, she could see the light on in her parents' bedroom. Blake's light was on, too. *Perfect.* How was she going to explain the fact that she had been gone for twelve hours? Shoving aside the strong temptation to go back to Holly Place and hide in a replay of some comfortable memory, she stood on the sidewalk and considered her options.

She could hear a train's plaintive whistle as it left Manitou Station, just two miles south of town. The Hudson Line trains ran along the river from Manhattan to Poughkeepsie 24 hours a day, though very infrequently at this time of night.

Yes. That was her alibi. She'd gone to Manhattan to see her old friend Jessica, who had been having boyfriend trouble and had been in crisis mode. When Cathy had gotten her text, she hadn't taken the time to go home from Rich's and ask for permission, because she had wanted to catch the train. She'd spent the evening sitting in an Upper West Side diner, talking Jessica out of her tree and calming her down. Once she'd seen her safely back to her apartment, she had taken the train from Grand Central to Manitou, and walked home.

It was a stupid, dangerous, totally uncharacteristic thing to have done, and she'd be grounded probably until college, but at least it was a somewhat plausible story. She pulled out her phone again and texted Jessica, just to cover her bases: Emergency: I was at your house last night. I'll explain later.

There was no use putting off the confrontation. *The longer I wait to go home, the worse it will be.*

Cathy took a deep breath, let it out, and walked slowly the rest of the way to the house.

On the front porch, she paused before opening the door. This was going to suck. But what else could she do? She had to face her family sometime. She opened the door and didn't take any extra care to try to shut it quietly; she didn't want her mother to think she was sneaking in. She went upstairs as fast as she could, wanting to make it to the master bedroom without encountering Blake. She reached the bedroom door just as it opened. Her mother stood there with tear-filled eyes and pale, lined face, and for the first time ever, Cathy thought that her mother looked her age.

"Well?" asked her mother quietly.

Cathy glanced behind her toward Blake's door. "May I come in?"

Athena opened the door wider without saying anything else and stepped back to let Cathy enter.

Malcolm sat in an easy chair by the bay window. He was usually so mild and quiet, but now he looked furious. Maybe there was a little more spice to him than Cathy had thought. Athena closed the door behind Cathy, then went to the chair next to Malcolm's and sat down. They both looked at her expectantly.

"I guess you're wondering where I've been," she ventured.

Athena let out half a laugh, and Malcolm said, "You could say that."

Cathy closed her eyes for a moment to gather herself. Then she opened them and launched into her alibi. Athena narrowed her eyes at her when she finished.

"Let me get this straight. You took the train to the city to see Jessica—without asking permission, or even telling anyone, including Richard, where you were going? Without calling or texting us on the train ride down? You have never done anything remotely this irresponsible. I don't believe it."

"It was an emergency," Cathy insisted. "I didn't stop to think—"

"That's certainly true," Malcolm cut in. "It seems as though you haven't been thinking for several hours. I'll admit that I haven't known you that long, Cathy, but this doesn't seem like you at all."

"I know. I'm really sorry. It was totally stupid. I am so sorry, Mom. I know you must have been worried."

"That's putting it mildly. I've been out of my mind. I assumed for hours that you were at Rich's, but when I called him, and he said you'd left very suddenly in the middle of the afternoon, I didn't know what to think. I started thinking maybe you'd been kidnapped or raped or hit by a car or shot by some crazy hunter in the woods. There are bears around here from time to time, Cathy. Do you have any idea how many different awful scenarios a mother can come up with in the space of six hours?"

Cathy stood and took her mother's words. She deserved it. She had been an imbecile to go follow a whim and go back into Holly Place again after all her resolutions to the contrary. Finally, Athena moved on from ranting.

"I'm glad that you wanted to help your friend, but there's no excuse for your inconsiderate and frankly stupid behavior. I know you're almost an adult, Cathy, but you live in my house. There have to be consequences for poor choices. Mercifully, you're safe. I'll be on my knees thanking God for that when we're done here. But before we try to salvage what's left of this night's sleep, tell me: what do you think is fair discipline for what you've done?"

Cathy hated it when her mother made her come up with her own punishment. Why couldn't she just dole out the consequences the way other parents did? She knew she had no choice but to answer, however.

"I abused your trust. I get that. So I have to try to earn it back. Which means I should probably stick around and be grounded for at least a couple of weeks."

Athena nodded, and Malcolm spoke. "Two weeks seems like the bare minimum to me. In addition, since it was the phone that got you into trouble, I think you should surrender it for the two weeks as well."

Cathy kept herself from protesting, even though she couldn't imagine what she'd do without her phone. She concentrated on the excellent and surprising fact that they seemed to have bought her story. She'd have to email Jessica from the school library tomorrow. She nodded and pulled her phone out of her pocket. She quickly cleared all her messages, powered it down, and handed it to Malcolm. As she was doing so, a soft knock came at the door.

"Come in," said Malcolm.

Blake poked his head in. "Hey, Cathy," he said with a big smile. "Whew! Man, I'm so glad you're safe. We were all pretty freaked out." He cocked an eyebrow at her mockingly.

Cathy seethed. If Malcolm and Athena had any idea what he'd been up to lately, he'd be way worse than grounded for two weeks. She maintained her composure; she didn't want to give him the satisfaction of seeing how upset she was. She raised her own eyebrow in return.

"Yep, I'm safe. Just got back from the City."

"Really." The single word dripped with sarcasm, as did his next. "Fascinating."

"You should get to bed, Blake," said Malcolm. "School starts in about four hours, whether we like it or not."

"Yeah, goodnight, Dad. Goodnight, Athena."

Cathy's mother smiled faintly at her stepson. "Thanks for all your help tonight, Blake."

"Sure thing." Blake grinned at Athena and gave Cathy another look. "G'night, Sis," he said, and closed the door.

Cathy wanted to kill him. She was burning to rat him out purely out of revenge, but knew that this was not the moment. She had no proof, and her mother and Malcolm would probably assume that she was just trying to deflect attention from herself. She folded her arms and turned back to Athena.

"I'm really sorry, Mom. I never meant to worry you. I hate the thought of giving you grief."

Athena rose and took Cathy in her arms. "I'm just so relieved that you're all right." She hugged Cathy fiercely and stroked her hair for a moment, then held her at arm's length. "Now, I'm betting you're a little bit hopped up, but try to get some rest. You'll be hating life even worse tomorrow during French class as it is."

Malcolm stood up as well. "I feel like maybe what you did tonight was in part a reaction to having me around. I know you certainly never pulled a stunt like this before I came on the scene. I hope this doesn't set a precedent. I want us all to be able to get along. I love your mother, and I can't stand to see her suffer."

"I understand," said Cathy, nodding and managing not to roll her eyes at her stepfather. A wave of distaste for Malcolm washed over her, and she wished bitterly for the millionth time that her father were still alive. Realistically, she knew that her dad would have come down just as hard or harder on her, but that would have been his right. She owed Malcolm respect for loving her mother and taking care of the family, but she didn't have to like him, did she? Right now, however, she just needed to get out of the room without anything worse happening. She smiled tightly, gave Malcolm a brief, one-armed hug, and left the room.

As she tiptoed down the hall to her room, she could see a line of light shining from under Blake's door. She didn't want to see him again tonight. But just as she got to her own door, she heard hinges creak behind her. *Ugh.*

She pasted on a smile and turned around. Blake leaned against his doorjamb and sighed.

"Wow," he said quietly. "You really blew it. I never thought I'd see the good girl brought down." He folded his arms.

"I was helping a friend," Cathy whispered. "It's none of your business."

"Yeah, I overheard that. I wonder what my dad and Athena will think when they find out your story about going to Manhattan is a total crock."

"I don't know what you're talking about." *Jerk.* If Blake blew her cover, she was toast. How did he know she had made the whole thing up?

"I saw you leave your crippled friend's house. You didn't go to the train station. You went into the woods, and you were in quite a hurry. Did you make it to your party on time?"

Cathy could feel her face turning red; fortunately the hall was pretty dark. How far had Blake been able to follow her? Had he seen Holly Place, or did he run into the dump the way Rich had? "What, are you stalking me now? What kind of freak are you?"

Blake dropped his casual demeanor and moved toward her. "The kind of freak who wants to protect this family."

Cathy stifled the harsh laugh that rose up in her throat. "Ha! That's rich," she snarled, still keeping her voice low. "The only thing you care about protecting is yourself. You are the most unbelievable

hypocrite I have ever met. I can't believe you are pointing fingers at
me about being dishonest. You. With what you've got going on."

Blake stepped even closer to her and now loomed over her. He
was a good eight inches taller than she was and outweighed her by at
least forty pounds. What was she doing? It was like taunting a bull,
except she couldn't see any way out of the ring.

"What *do* I have going on, Sis? What do you think you know?"
he whispered, reaching out and tucking her hair behind one of her
ears.

Cathy tried not to shy away from his touch. She didn't want him
to know how terrified she was and hoped he couldn't hear her heart
pounding. She realized she had to tell him what she knew, though, if
only as leverage to keep him from going to their parents and expos-
ing her lie.

"Don't call me 'Sis.' I'm not your sister. What do I *think* I know?
You're doing drugs, that's what." She raised her hand to cut off the
protest she saw coming. "Hard drugs. Cocaine or heroin—you're
snorting it. And porn. That's really nice stuff you're looking at on your
precious computer." She smiled a little at the fury she saw mounting
in her stepbrother's eyes. If she had doubted the visions she'd had in
Holly Place, she was sure now that they had been the truth.

"You filthy little sneak," he hissed. "If you breathe a word of this
to anyone, I'll kill you. I am not exaggerating. I will kill you, and I
know how to make it look like an accident. Do you understand me?"

Cathy was so scared that she thought she'd pass out, but she
couldn't back down now. Squaring her jaw, she raised her right forefinger and set the tip of it lightly on the center of Blake's ribcage.

"I know who you are, you psychopath," she whispered. "I know
what you stole eight years ago. And I'm going to get rid of you.
Forever." As she said the words, she knew they were true. She had
to keep her promise to Bunny—somehow. She thought she saw a
flicker of fear in Blake's eyes, but it was too dark to know for sure.

"Is that a fact?" he murmured. "I don't think you want to get
rid of me." He put his hand over hers and pressed it down until she
could feel his heart beating under the hard muscles of his chest. He

had a bandage on his palm; what had he been doing now? "Touch me again, and I'll assume it's an invitation, *Sis.*"

He squeezed her hand lightly and let it go. Cathy squelched the urge to wipe it on her jeans. Just looking at him sickened her, and physical contact was far worse. He was trying to intimidate her because he was scared; she could see that now. If he was afraid, that meant she had power over him. But she had to retreat. Her adrenaline was running out, and she felt wearier than she ever had before.

"I'm going to sleep now," she said. "You should, too. You're going to need your rest." She backed into her room and quietly shut the door in his face.

She held her breath, held perfectly still, and listened hard. After a moment, Blake walked back to his room and shut his own door. She sighed with relief and felt tears well up in her eyes. She felt nauseated, even though there was nothing in her stomach to throw up. Despite her bravado and her extreme fatigue, there was no way she would be able to fall asleep. She wished again that her door had a lock on it.

She flopped down on her bed and stared out her window at the setting moon. What was she going to do to get rid of Blake? *Not the real Blake—the fake Blake.* She chuckled despite herself.

"Blake is a fake, Blake is a fake," she chanted under her breath in imitation of Mae. Fake Blake. That was nearly gallows humor—it would be funny if it weren't so awful. She'd have to tell Bunny her new nickname for the usurper, since he was the only one who would get her joke.

Bunny. She hadn't been her best with him today, but she saw now that there was no putting off finding the way to restore him to his body. But how? Bunny seemed to think that Holly Place would provide the answer, but all it had done so far was show her things. It wasn't enough to see the truth; she needed the power to act.

She turned over onto her side, and as she did so, the golden chain holding the white stone slid out from under her shirt. She had completely forgotten about it. What was it, and who had that little twin of hers really been? Was she supposed to have this thing, or had it just been left behind by chance? She twisted the stone open and sniffed the wax within it again. It smelled heavenly, though subtly different from the way she remembered it smelling this afternoon. Earlier, she had thought of cloves and exotic flowers, but now it smelled like pine and the ocean. *Woods by the sea.* Romantic, but a little lonely and melancholy at the same time. She closed the stone, stuffed it back under her shirt, and got up to go to the bathroom.

She winced and squinted as she turned on the bank of lights over the mirror. After a few seconds, her eyes adjusted, and she stared at her image in the glass. She looked as haggard as she felt, but she realized that for the first time in weeks, being in her bathroom didn't freak her out. She had much bigger things to worry about now. Thinking back to that voice she'd heard in the mirror the day she'd met Rich—had it been some kind of signal, some kind of switch flipping on? Because that's when all this insanity had begun. Now it seemed like she was in the middle of it. There was no way out but through.

Cathy went to the bathroom, then washed her hands and splashed some water on her face. Her mouth felt fuzzy, so she brushed her teeth. Looking at the little clock she kept on the bathroom counter, she realized she might as well just shower now. She'd suck down Dr. Pepper at school all day if she had to. There was no point in trying to rest for the few minutes she had until it was time to get up and get going.

She twisted the shower spigot on and undressed as the water heated up. Ahhhh. Hot water was a gift, she thought as she let it pour over her. She scrubbed her hair and body vigorously, trying to scour away both her weariness and the memory of Blake being so close to her.

Blake. How could she possibly find a way to fight him as long as she was grounded? There must be a way to defeat the usurper. Otherwise, why would Holly Place even exist? Without access to the house, however, she felt cut off from her only source of wisdom on the matter. Her stomach twisted as she imagined the kind of trouble Blake could cause her in the next two weeks while her wings were clipped.

One day at a time, she told herself. One step at a time. I'll find a way or make a way. Isn't that what Dad used to say?

CHAPTER SEVENTEEN

THE LIGHT OF TRUTH

RICH SAT IN FRENCH class trying not to crawl out of his skin. His teacher, Miss Baldwin, had been alternately boring and entertaining him and his fellow students with various tics and eccentricities since seventh grade, but right now he was half convinced that she was actually a sadistic alien from deep space. How could he be expected to concentrate on the obscure intricacies of compound verb tenses when his whole world was falling apart?

It was driving him nuts that Cathy wouldn't talk to him—wouldn't even look at him. She had sat next to him on the bus that morning, but she had been a million miles away. Rich had tried to ask her about the night before. Where had she gone, and why? What was up with her mother? He hadn't known what to say when Mrs. Harford had called his house the night before wondering where her daughter was. She had been cheerful and polite, but Rich had sensed great strain beneath her careful questions.

Rich had a ton of questions of his own. Had he blown it by kissing Cathy yesterday afternoon? She had seemed so happy at first, and relief and joy and hope had flooded him. He had not been able to believe his incredible luck. Never in a million years had he dared hope that he might have a girlfriend, let alone one who was so close to perfect. But then Cathy had left in such a hurry—something had obviously upset her, and Rich couldn't help but think that it was his fault. She hadn't answered a single text or phone call for the rest of the day and night.

Miss Baldwin turned away from the class as she wrote out the pluperfect subjunctive conjugations of *retourner* on the chalkboard.

Rich looked over at Cathy, who sat two rows over and one seat up. She looked terrible—wilted somehow. Normally, Cathy took copious notes in class, but now her binder wasn't even open. She sat hunched over with her chin on her hand as if she were barely able to stay conscious. Her usually creamy skin looked almost a ghostly gray. What was wrong with her? And when could Rich get some answers?

Class stretched on even longer than the usual eternity, but at last, the bell rang. Rich scrambled to shove his papers and books into his backpack so that he could catch up with Cathy, who was already slipping out the door. He called out her name, but she didn't seem to hear him. Rich threw on his pack, hoisted himself up onto his crutches, and hurried after her.

"Cathy!" he called again. She was halfway down the hall. A few other heads turned, but she kept moving. Was she ignoring him, or was she so out of it that she really didn't hear him? He swung himself along as fast as he could through the crowd of students, praying that Cathy would have to stop at her locker.

The heavens heard him. As he negotiated his way through the crowded hall, he saw her stop and struggle with her locker's perpetually jammed door. It came open with a crash just as Rich reached Cathy's side.

"Hey," he said more sharply than he had intended. She barely seemed to notice.

"Hey," she mumbled, not looking at him. She pulled her gym bag out of her locker and tried to close the faulty door; Rich leaned against it to hold it open. He ducked his head down, trying to get her to look at him.

"Cathy? Hey, remember me? What's going on? Why won't you talk to me? What happened last night?"

Cathy glanced up at him and looked away again, her eyes hard and her jaw set. "I can't talk right now. I've got to get to gym."

"*Screw* gym. This is more important. You don't look like you could manage a single jumping jack, anyway. Cut class and come with me to the library instead. No one's there this time of day."

Cathy pulled on her locker door again. Rich felt its sharp metal edge digging into his shoulder. "I can't cut gym," she said. "I'm already grounded. If Mrs. Kilpack calls home, I'll be even farther up the creek."

"Grounded? Why? What happened?" Rich waited for an answer, but apparently one wasn't forthcoming. "Cathy, come on. Yesterday, you told me I was a great friend." Rich looked down at his feet and swallowed hard. He went on, trying to keep his voice even. "You said you wanted us to be something more, and you seemed pretty happy about that, at least for a few minutes. And now you'll barely look at me. Don't I deserve an explanation?" He looked up, hoping to meet her eyes.

She gazed steadily back at him for a few seconds. The hall was nearly empty now. The bell rang a moment later. Cathy rolled her eyes at the sound. "I'll tell you a secret," she said. "I was this close to asking my mom if I could just take the GED and skip senior year, you know that? I'm so sick of being shoved around by bells and schedules and what other people want from me." She sighed and pinched the bridge of her nose.

"Yeah, fine," she said finally. "I'll go to the nurse and tell her I feel like crap. *That* won't be a lie. I'll ask her to write me a study hall pass, and I'll meet you in the library in a few minutes. Okay?"

"Okay." Rich moved aside so that Cathy could shut her locker. He gave her a tentative smile. "Thanks. I'll see you there."

The school library felt like a sauna. Streams of dust motes danced in the bright sunshine that poured through the tall windows. Rich sat at a double carrel in a corner near the foreign language shelves and fidgeted with a hinge on the brace of one of his crutches. Time felt like it was grinding to a halt, but after a few minutes, Cathy came in. The shadows under her eyes looked even deeper in the strong afternoon light. She saw him, came over, and flopped down next to him.

"Okay, spill it," he ordered in a low voice.

"Right. When I left your house yesterday, I got a text from my friend Jessica in the city. Her boyfriend broke up with her, and she was super upset. I took the train down to Manhattan so that I could hang out with her and help her calm down. I lost track of time and took a really late train home. My mom and Malcolm were waiting up for me. It wasn't pretty. I'm grounded for two weeks, and they took my phone away."

"You went to the city," Rich said slowly. *Not bloody likely.* Her whole explanation sounded rehearsed, but also hollow, as if she didn't even believe it herself.

"Yep," Cathy replied, looking straight into his eyes as if she dared him to argue with her. She was treating him like a stranger. Rich's frustration made him want to take her by the shoulders and shake her until this ridiculous wall she had put up came tumbling down. He tried for logic instead.

"Cathy, that makes no sense. Maybe your parents believed you, but I don't. Why would you go there straight from my house without telling anyone what you were doing? Why would you sit on the train for an hour each way without answering a text or a phone call? Why wouldn't you go home to get a book, or at least a windbreaker? You haven't seen Jessica in months, right? Isn't she the one who went to band camp for the whole summer right after your mom got married? How come you're the one she would call, when you two haven't even been that close since you moved up here?"

Cathy stared at him, her wall still firmly in place. He could tell that she had shifted from defiant to scared, though. Rich just had to be patient and bank on the hope that she'd eventually get around to what had really happened. Finally, she relented.

"I know, I know," she whispered, lowering her eyes. "It's a lame story. I came up with it right before I got home. I can't believe they bought it. I know Blake didn't."

"You saw Blake last night?"

"Yeah, you could say that. I was hoping to avoid him, but he couldn't keep himself from mocking me after I got grounded. He got me so mad that I blew it. I told him I knew he was using drugs, and then he went all *Godfather* on me. He threatened to kill me, and I don't think he was bluffing, either. I was so freaked out that I couldn't sleep. Not that two hours of sleep would have done much for me, anyway."

"Two hours?" Rich repeated, a little louder than library protocol. Cathy had left him at around three o'clock yesterday afternoon. Where had she been for over twelve hours?

"Cathy, please," he said. "Trust me with the truth. How bad can it be?"

She nodded, chewing on her lips. What was so awful that she couldn't confide in him? Suspense was making Rich sick to his stomach, but he held his tongue. Finally, she spoke.

"The truth's pretty bad, actually. I was at Holly Place."

"The house in the woods. The one that burnt down. The one that used to be where the dump is now."

"You asked for the truth. That's the truth."

Right. "Okay," he said aloud. He'd take her at her word and show trust so that he could get the real story. "What were you doing there for so long? What's so great about it that you would blow your curfew to hell to be there? Why did you have to rush there all of a sudden?" *Were you late for a date with the Mad Hatter?* Cathy, the girl that he loved, who was so smart and funny and kind and gorgeous— Cathy had to be delusional. This was so sick and wrong. Rich tried to shove aside both his grief at her mental state and his skepticism at her insane story for the moment. Maybe there was something he could do to help her. He took her hand in his and squeezed it. She looked at him again.

"Remember last week, when I first found the house and I wanted you to come see it, too?" she asked. "You said that you thought I was perceptive, and that you would try to trust me. Is that still true?" Her eyes were huge and haunted in her haggard face; even though she looked terrible, she was still the most beautiful thing Rich had ever seen. Just looking at her made his heart hurt. He tried to arrange his features into an expression that would pass for acceptance.

"Yeah, of course. Just tell me what happened."

Gripping his hand like it was a lifeline, Cathy took a deep breath and started talking.

His girlfriend was crazy, and Rich had no idea what to do about it. It figured that anyone attracted to him would turn out to be insane. He sat on the couch in his dark living room and stared unseeingly at the blathering television, going over in his mind what Cathy had told him earlier that day. When she had started talking to him about the magic house and the ghost who was actually her real stepbrother, it had been clear that she was telling what she thought was the truth. Rich had asked Cathy to bare her soul, and she had trusted him enough to do so, spinning a tale that was so outrageous, it sounded like *she*—not the evil entity that was pretending to be a part of her family—was the one using drugs. He regretted not just accepting her initial cover story the way her parents had.

"You asked for it, Mallory," he muttered. He flipped from channel to channel, hoping to find some distraction. Aliens. Idols. Game show hosts. Desperate housewives. They all seemed so sure of themselves and their purpose in life. They all saw themselves as the heroes in their own personal dramas. Rich figured that it was that way in real life, too. People who did bad things worked hard to rationalize their behavior. Abusers were really victims. Killers only wanted justice. Crazy people were actually just defending themselves by building a new reality when the old one became too painful.

For some reason, Cathy felt like she needed to be a hero. Was she that mad at Malcolm for trying to take her father's place and for bringing his son into the family mix as well? But Blake getting high all the time—if he really was getting high all the time—seemed like enough of a crisis for her to try to solve. Why did her subconscious need to manufacture all this other nonsense?

However disorienting it must be to try to live in a newly blended family, that didn't seem like enough trauma to justify Cathy's delusions. Maybe the whole situation had just been a trigger, bringing to light some psychosis that had been growing within her all her life. Whatever had happened was beyond Rich to try to figure out. Cathy needed professional help. She didn't seem about to ask for it on her own. Should he stick his nose in her business and go to her mother?

If he did that, Rich could count on the fact that Cathy would hate him for the rest of her life. Yesterday, life had seemed too good to be true; today had proved the accuracy of that bit of intuition. So what was he supposed to do now? He couldn't just pretend that everything was normal—smile, kiss Cathy, and wish her well on her quest to exorcize a demon and give new life to a ghost. As much as he wanted to, he couldn't go back to yesterday, either. The only way out of this nightmare was through it—Cathy had said that herself. He had to do something to help her get better, even if it meant giving up their budding relationship. A hopeless quest involving sacrifice, pain, and misunderstanding—Cathy and he actually weren't all that different. Rich twisted his lips at the bitter irony; maybe he needed to be a hero, too.

CHAPTER EIGHTEEN

WITHOUT ABSOLUTION

BEING GROUNDED SUCKED. Cathy knew her bad attitude was a ridiculous teenage stereotype, but there it was.

Evening deepened into night all around her. She threw a tennis ball against the garage door and moved to catch it as it bounced back to her, over and over and over again. Eventually, her mother would come out of the house and ask her to stop, come inside, and get to bed. But for now, the mindless rhythm and repetition served to numb her. Her dancing, bobbing shadow tripled in the light of the halogen spotlights that illuminated the grass-littered driveway. Blake had mown the lawn rather sloppily earlier in the afternoon, and its fresh, green smell rose up lazily like smoke in the humid evening air. The ceaseless hum of cicadas accompanied Cathy's improvised handball game. She wondered how far into fall they continued their song. Would they all be dead by her birthday?

She was weeks away from turning eighteen—nearly old enough to be out of her mother's house and on her own. She could enlist in the army if she wanted to, or get her own apartment, or hitchhike across the country. Instead, she was under house arrest by her own consent. She had broken family rules and lost her mother's trust; there had to be consequences. She got that. It was fair, but that didn't make it any easier to bear the fact that she was less than twenty-four hours into her punishment, and the next thirteen days stretched before her like an endless desert.

Under normal circumstances, she could cope with the occasional grounding. She'd read and bake and hang out with her sisters, biding her time and distracting herself as much as possible. But things weren't normal, not by a long shot. She was living with a depraved, lawless addict who had all the confidence and resources she lacked. She had to protect her family from him, no matter what. And what about Bunny? Even though she had no idea how to keep the promise she had made him, she certainly couldn't do it under the confines of her punishment.

I hate this. I hate this. Cathy's mind made up words for the regular beat of the tennis ball. Slapping at the sudden sting of a mosquito on the back of her neck, she felt the chain of the white stone against her sweaty skin. She batted the tennis ball away and watched it roll until it came to rest under the box hedge that lined the driveway. She fished the little egg out from under her shirt. She had slipped its chain on again after her shower early this morning and had not noticed it since. As she held it up to the bright light of the spotlights, the stone seemed to glow from within, shimmering and shifting as if it were alive somehow. What was it for?

She opened it and breathed in its powerful aroma once more. It had changed again; now it smelled sharp, haunting, and clean. *Wind over the moor,* she thought, even though she had never been to Scotland and had no idea what heather smelled like. She dabbed a little of the wax on the pulse points of her wrists again and closed the little container. Lifting her wrist to her nose, she inhaled again. The scent seemed almost to be speaking to her. What was it trying to say?

She felt a subtle shift in the air behind her. Turning, she saw Bunny standing deep in the shadows on top of his rock. He looked so young and frail. Sometimes when he was talking to her, his sadness and desperation made him seem much older than he was. But he was really just a kid. He raised his hand in greeting; she nodded back.

She wondered why it was that Bunny's spirit had not aged once it had been separated from his body. Was that what happened when you died? And what would happen if they were actually able to get him back where he belonged? How would someone who had been frozen in time at age nine be able to handle the very different physiology of a seventeen-year-old body? Would he even fit anymore

after all these years, or would his body refuse to recognize him and
end up rejecting him in the way that transplant patients had trouble
with donated organs?

There was a lot she didn't know about this whole situation, but
staring at Bunny, a curtain suddenly parted in her mind. Insight
chased away her confusion and depression. She had to take action
now; she had to go. She had to follow Bunny back to Holly Place
again, go inside, and find the way to restore him to his body once and
for all. It didn't matter how much time it took, or what happened to
her afterward. Helping him would help her family; it would solve all
her problems. She saw that clearly now.

She looked back behind her at the house looming up against the
night sky, its windows illuminated with the flow of normal life going on within. She couldn't go back inside and pretend to go along
with that flow, not when everything so desperately needed fixing.
She was never going to solve this mess by keeping one foot in reality and one in . . . whatever dimension Holly Place represented. No
matter the consequences to which she had agreed the night before
in her confrontation with Malcolm and her mother. That would all
sort itself out later. Sometimes you had to break promises in order to
keep more important ones.

She had to keep her promise to Rich, too, the promise they had
made to one another with that kiss yesterday afternoon. Those lovely
moments seemed much farther in the past than just a day ago, and
a huge distance stretched between the two of them right now. She
had seen the painful disbelief on Rich's face this afternoon in the
library as she had told him every bizarre detail of the past several
days. He had tried to hide it, hugging her and telling her that they
would figure it all out, but Cathy knew full well that Rich thought
she was out of her mind. That misperception hurt, and she wanted
with all her heart to be able to prove to Rich that it wasn't true. If
she could get rid of Fake Blake once and for all, then she and Rich
could have a shot at a real, normal relationship. First things first, as
her father used to say.

Through the windows over the garage, Cathy could see her family going through their normal weeknight routine. Fawn and Mae

worked together on kitchen duty, no doubt half-heartedly bickering as they loaded the dishwasher and wiped the counters. The faintest sound of dramatic chords struck on the piano reached Cathy's ears. Blake was playing Chopin, or maybe Liszt. Malcolm sat in an armchair grading a stack of essays, his brow furrowed and his glasses on the top of his head. Athena was curled up with her knitting on the couch, her beautiful face serene as she counted stitches.

Cathy thought about all the worry she had already caused her mother, and almost lost her resolve. She clenched her jaw against the fear and doubt she felt welling up inside her. No. Athena would be fine; she was a strong, resourceful woman. And Malcolm would watch over her and the little girls. Cathy had to have faith that if she went forward with this seemingly impossible task, her family would be taken care of in return. She turned back to Bunny, who still stood high up on the rock where she had first met him. She nodded again, and his face lit up in understanding. He whirled and disappeared into the darkness.

Cathy watched him go. It was time. She had to leave now, before her mother came out onto the porch and called for her. She didn't know how long she'd be gone, or how she'd eat or sleep or do anything while she was figuring out the exact nature of the task before her. Since she had no idea what she was doing or what she would need, she didn't see the point of going back in the house and trying to pack anything. There was no way to explain her quest, so writing a note wouldn't make her disappearance any less painful for her family. There was nothing left to do but take the first step. Cathy sighed. Putting the stone egg back under her shirt, she walked quickly across the back lawn, up the side of the massive rock, and into the night woods.

CHAPTER NINETEEN

FOUND OBJECTS

FOR ONCE, REALITY INSIDE Holly Place seemed to be in sync with what she had just left behind. The front hall was lit only by the radiance of the harvest moon rising above the dark, thickly leaved trees. As always, the house stood silent.

"Bunny! I'm here. Where are you?" She looked inside the dreaming room and the traveling room. Bunny was nowhere to be seen. Now what? Standing directly under the unlit crystal chandelier, Cathy considered her options. She knew what lay behind the doors to either side of her. Could Bunny have gone upstairs into a room where he couldn't hear her? Why would he show up on the rock outside her house and then disappear once she let him know she was coming?

Cathy decided not to worry about it. As crazy as it seemed, she felt sure that she was doing the right thing. There was a curious freedom in leaving her entire life behind and stepping alone into the unknown. Whatever happened, happened. She would get on with the job that she'd been given. Why not climb the stairs and see what there was to see?

She walked forward and put her hand on the intricately carved newel post. Immediately, she felt the slow, steady thrum of what she had come to think of as the house's heartbeat. It startled her at first, but she calmed herself and focused on it to steady her nerves. She took a step up with each beat.

When she reached the top step, she looked around. It was almost too dark to see, but she could tell that the landing ended in a window at either end, and to her left, she could just make out the break in the balcony's railing where the other staircase descended. A wide hall opened up and ran to the back of the house perpendicular to the landing, but it was entirely in shadows. Was there any way to find a light, or should she just find somewhere to try to rest until the sun came up again? No, she wouldn't sleep—not yet. There must be a reason why she had felt like she should come here right now, instead of waiting until morning to run away. She had to find a way forward.

The Voorhees family had built Holly Place long before the invention of electric lights. The sconces on the walls had been made to hold candles, but they were all empty as far as Cathy could see. She moved toward the window at one end of the landing. The first stars were appearing in the sky outside. She looked downward to where the narrow lawn that ran around the side of the house should be, but saw only darkness.

That wasn't exactly true, she realized. There was a dim light below her eye level, but it wasn't coming from outside. Instead, a faint glow reflected on the surface of the window—a glow that must be coming from her. Looking down at herself, she gasped. A light shone from underneath her shirt. The stone. She pulled it out and looked at it lying in her hand. Pale and milky, it shone just enough to light her way.

Holding it out like a flashlight, she turned and went back down the landing until she came to the wide, unexplored central hallway. She still couldn't see more than a foot or two in front of her, but it was enough.

An elaborate Persian carpet lay under her feet and completely silenced her footsteps. Dark wainscoting lined the walls on either side of her, punctuated by oil paintings whose subjects were too much in shadow to identify. Cathy passed doors that mirrored one another across the hallway. She decided that she would walk the length of the hall before trying to go into any rooms. It was longer than she thought it would be; the house must be deeper than it looked from the outside. After passing more doors on either side, she finally could go no farther. Heavy curtains hung from the ceiling and pooled on the floor before her. There must be windows behind them—that was why this hall was so much darker than the other areas of the house. Why were these curtains drawn when all the others in the rest of the house were not?

Reaching out to the curtain, she rubbed the nap of it between her fingers. Velvet, soft and thick. Holding up the egg for light, she drew the substantial fabric aside. It concealed a deep seat enclosed by a tall bay window. What looked like a thousand mullioned panes glimmered in leaded frames. Lavish, inviting cushions in deep jewel tones filled the seat—and lying nestled in them was Cathy's little twin, fast asleep. One hand clutched a finely woven blanket to her chest, and her other arm was flung out across the cushions. She still wore the same taffeta party dress, and her hair was tousled as if she had not gone to sleep easily.

The light pouring out of the stone brightened, and Cathy drew back, not wanting to awaken the girl. But it was too late; her twin opened her big, brown eyes and squinted a little in the egg's alabaster glow.

"Cathy," she whispered with a smile, then yawned and stretched like a cat. She sat up and brushed her hair out of her eyes. "I was wondering when you would be back. You found my necklace."

"Oh—yes. I didn't know what to do with it. I was planning on giving it back to you if I saw you again." Cathy held out her hand. "Here. Thanks. It came in handy just now."

The girl drew back just a little and shook her head. "No, I left it for you. I'm glad you took it. I'll make another one if I need to."

"Okay, um, thanks. It's really beautiful." Cathy felt obscurely uncomfortable, as if she had just failed a small but important test. "I'm not sure what to do now," she added.

"I can tell," answered her twin, eyes sparkling with suppressed amusement. Was she making fun of Cathy? She seemed to have a talent for pushing Cathy's buttons. Had Cathy herself been this annoying when she was younger?

"Who are you? No, wait—I know what you're going to say. I suppose it depends on what I need, right?" Cathy could remember her first conversation with the girl almost perfectly.

"You're a fast learner. Do you want to sit down?"The girl scooted to the side of the window seat and patted the cushions beside her.

"Sure," Cathy said with a sigh. "I don't have anywhere else to be at the moment." She let the stone fall to her chest, clambered onto the deep, soft bench, and settled in. The weight of her decision to run away now weighed like a millstone around her neck, and exhaustion settled upon her like a cloak.

"It's comfy, right?" The girl bounced up and down a bit, and Cathy felt a pang of strong homesickness for Mae.

"It's super comfy." Cathy looked at her twin, who seemed to alternate between mysterious sage and mischievous child with dizzying speed. Maybe the girl wouldn't give a question a direct answer, but Cathy had the sense that she held the key to what to do about Bunny. She decided she'd lay it all out and see what information she could glean from any responses she got.

"I'm trying to help my stepbrother," she said. "Blake. He calls himself Bunny; I guess that was his mother's nickname for him. It seemed like you knew him—or at least who he was—the last time we met, but he claimed he didn't know who you are. He's . . . a bit lost, and I need to help him get home. That's why I'm here."

"A lost stepbrother! I read a fairy tale like that once," said the girl. "I think I have it here somewhere." She reached down into the cushions and dug around a bit. She pulled out her jump rope and set it on her lap. A bedraggled china head doll and a threadbare stuffed dog followed out of the depths. Finally in her fishing around she came up with an old, leather-bound book. "It's in here," she said, handing the book to Cathy.

Cathy opened the book, which was heavier than it looked. The pages were brittle and nearly brown with age. Dense, ornate handwriting filled nearly every bit of their surfaces. The tongue of a ribbon bookmark stuck out about a third of the way through the volume. Cathy turned to the place it marked. The writing ended there; only blank pages followed. Even when she held the egg close to the page, she couldn't make out any of what the writing said. But then, when she turned a page back, a word jumped out at her. *Hulsthuys.*

Holly Place. Scanning the rest of the writing, she now understood why she hadn't been able to read it; it appeared to be written entirely in Dutch.

Had this book belonged to someone who had lived here? It must have. "Where did you get this?" she asked the girl, who shrugged.

"It's always been here," she replied.

Cathy handed the book back to the girl. "Sorry, but I can't read Dutch. I guess you can, though. What happens in the story?"

"A little boy gets kidnapped by an awful monster, and his stepsister is the only one who can find him and save him. She has to solve riddles and find her way through a maze and kill the monster. It's a really good story."

Cathy nodded politely. "It sounds good. My stepbrother wasn't kidnapped, though. His body was, uh, stolen from him. He needs to get it back."

"That makes your job much harder than the stepsister's in the story. It's easier to kill monsters than it is to evict them."

"Is that what I have to do? Do you know how I'm supposed to go about 'evicting' this thing? Because it—he—has threatened to hurt my sisters. I believe he will, if he can. He's pretty deranged, and he doesn't seem eager to return what he stole."

"No. I know what he is. He is very tenacious. He'd rather kill Bunny's body than give it up. If he can't have it, he'll make sure Bunny can't have it, either. His kind is particularly vicious in that way."

Cathy thought about that for a moment. What had Bunny said the spirit's name was? Zoram? No, Zared—that was it. Zared would stop at nothing to win this fight, and he would have the advantage of desperation. What had her father said so often—possession was nine tenths of the law? What possible leverage would Cathy have against the thing that possessed her stepbrother's body?

"You stand on the side of right," said the girl, apparently reading her thoughts. "That is more powerful than you would believe."

Cathy gazed into the girl's eyes and again had the uncanny feeling of looking at herself in some sort of time-traveling mirror. "I don't feel powerful. I don't know why I'm the one to help Bunny, but he seems to think that I am. I've decided that I'm ready to do whatever it takes to make that happen. I don't know what I'm supposed to do next, or how long it will take, or how I'll survive until it does.

"I know what I need now," she finished, realizing it was true as she said it. "I need help."

Her twin grinned with what looked like relief. "My name is Januarye."

CHAPTER TWENTY

THOSE WHO WANDER

IN THE ATTIC of the old house, shadows whisper and shift as if alive. This does not frighten Bunny. This house has had a rich life. Faint memories rise up from its floors and chase one another like dancing motes of dust—these keep him company and help him pass the long, long hours. Tonight, he perches on top of an old steamer trunk, hugging his knees to his chest and rocking slightly back and forth. Cathy has followed him here, but he will not go to her. The house has told him that she must find her own way. For now, he needs to wait.

But this makes him impatient. Will he have no active part in his own salvation? He realizes the massive advantage that the embodied have over the dispossessed. He has almost no power to rise up out of this enforced passivity, this exile into which he was thrown so long ago. For many long years, Zared has successfully kept him away, and time has slipped by in an inexorable stream. But now, surely he can do something. He has felt so strong and alive of late, and he has great confidence in Cathy's abilities.

He longs to go visit his body, but the risk is too great. Although it is the quietest part of the night, Cathy is not home, and Bunny doubts that Malcolm and Athena are able to sleep. Worry and fear and frustration surely have put them into a state of emergency—and if they are awake, Bunny is sure that Zared is also awake. Instead, perhaps he will go to the dreaming room and see what it shows him. That should help pass the time until he next meets Cathy. He can spy on his body from here without worry. He has always been safe within the walls of this house.

Bunny floats down from his high perch and glides down the narrow, steep stairway. This part of the house must have been the servants' quarters at one time. On the second floor landing, he passes linen closets and clothes presses before going down another set of stairs to the dark, cavernous kitchen. A huge, black stove looms, flanked by ranks of cupboards and shelves. No one has cooked here in decades, but the kitchen still feels inhabited. Bunny lands, lighter than air, on the rough, stone floor. He goes to the large double doors that lead to the dreaming room and walks through them, closed.

He supposes he could have just floated down through the ceilings of the upper floors. Even the densest physical barriers are mostly empty space—space between the atoms that make them up, and more vast expanses within the atoms themselves— making it easy for the finer matter of his spirit body to penetrate. He finds, though, that he likes to keep the appearance of normality most of the time. His system of moving about is inconsistent, but it feels right, somehow. He hopes to be back in his body soon, and when he is, the ability to pass through walls and doors will be a luxury he will gladly leave behind.

A lovely fire burns in the fireplace of what was once the house's dining room, casting a warm glow on the walls and ceiling. Who lights and tends it? Bunny has never seen anyone else in this place, but it never has the feel of an abandoned building. Or is the fire just an illusion? If so, it is perfect in every detail. Bunny can't feel the heat of the fire except as the faintest breath, but the warm air rises up and away from it in shimmering waves. Its flickering light seems to set the figured wallpaper in motion, and Bunny allows himself to be drawn into its hypnotic dance. His intuition is accurate. He sees into what should be *his* bedroom in the house on Turley Lane. Zared is awake—

Blake, wearing a T-shirt and pajama bottoms, is slumped over his computer. Its screen is filled with awful images that dissolve into one another like a slideshow. His face is slick with sweat. The circles under his eyes look like bruises in the monitor's pale light. After a moment, however, he jerks straight up and looks around. He goes to his bedroom door and ensures that it is locked. Turning back to his desk, he glances around again, as if expecting to find someone in the room with him. His eyes brush right over Bunny's vantage point, Bunny shivers a little and then relaxes. He remembers that he is invisible, peering into his usurper's lair as if through some sort of metaphysical camera. He does not know how the dreaming room works, but it has never betrayed him before.

Blake sits down again, but now can't seem to get comfortable. It is as if he knows he is being watched. His eyes dart from the computer to the newly repaired window. He jumps up, rushes to the window, and slides it open. Pressing his forehead to the screen, he cups his hands around his eyes and peers out into the night. Bunny realizes that Blake is looking out at the rock that Bunny has visited so often. A few seconds later, Blake straightens up, closes the window, and draws the shade. As he steps back toward his desk, he scans his dark bedroom once more. His gaze sweeps past Bunny and beyond, and then—

Zared's eyes lock onto Bunny, recognition and hatred filling his face. He raises his left hand and mutters something unintelligible. How has Zared seen him? Bunny tries to rear back from the vision and withdraw into the safety of the dreaming room, but he finds to his shock that he is no longer in Holly Place. He looks behind him in panic. Zared has brought him forward somehow out of the dream and into Blake's actual room.

Zared smirks in triumph. He quickly twists his left hand clockwise, makes a fist, and thrusts his arm backward and down, all the while whispering in a language Bunny does not recognize. Bunny must get away, must sink through the floor and out the wall of this place and retreat to safety once more. He tries to force himself down through the carpet, but the floor has become as solid as if Bunny were embodied. He flings himself backward against the wall, but meets another impenetrable barrier.

Bunny lets out a wail of desperation, though he knows no one in this house will hear him. Stamping his feet against the floor, he realizes that Zared has trapped him in an ingenious snare. He has somehow filled the empty spaces between atoms with the immeasurably fine material that makes up spirits. Bunny tries to rush at Blake, furious and more frightened than he has been in years. He hopes to get past his body to try exiting through another part of the room. Instead he slams into another wall, invisible, but unmistakable. Zared has boxed him in. He can find not even the tiniest crack in his prison, not even when he shoots up to the ceiling to try going out that way.

When did Zared learn to do this? Only recently, Bunny guesses, because he surely would have trapped Bunny like this long ago, had he been able. Bunny pounds his fists on the air in front of him and screams again. Zared raises his eyebrows and hands. *What?* He mouths and points to his ears. *I can't hear you. Sorry.* He shrugs and mocks a big-eyed pout at Bunny. Then he laughs and pumps his fists in the air. Waving to Bunny, he leaves the bedroom and shuts the door carefully behind him.

Bunny sinks to the floor of his prison in horror and replays what has just happened in his mind. Where did he go wrong? What has he done? And how can Cathy help him now?

At Holly Place, the fire blazes on in the hearth of the dreaming room, but only the constantly shifting patterns of the wallpaper are there to notice.

CHAPTER TWENTY-ONE

CLOUDS OF ERROR

"Januar-I?" Cathy echoed. "Like the month, except with an 'eye' at the end?"

The girl nodded, still grinning. "My mother named me after a poem she liked."

"Then . . . you're not me? Some form of my past self, or something like that?"

Januarye broke into laughter and shook her head. Once again, Cathy felt like an idiot. Had it been that bad a guess? She and the girl looked exactly alike, and anything seemed possible in this place. Finally, Januarye got her mirth under control, with only the occasional giggle escaping. She looked at Cathy and put her hands to her mouth.

"I'm sorry," she said, her eyes bright. "I am many things, but I am not you. I could see why you would think that, though. It was a reasonable deduction, under the circumstances. You haven't had much to go on, have you?"

"No, I haven't," Cathy said shortly.

Januarye opened her mouth to reply, but then her eyes bulged and her hands flew to her throat as if she were choking. Her face flushed crimson at first and then paled to a sickly gray. As Cathy leaned forward and grabbed her to try to help her, Januarye drew in a huge gulp of air and started coughing. Cathy pounded her on the back between her shoulder blades until the spasm subsided. Januarye leaned back into the cushions and closed her eyes. Tears streamed down her face.

"Are you all right? Januarye? What happened?" Cathy asked, bending over the girl. She shifted some of the cushions to try to make the girl more comfortable. The stone swung back and forth on its chain as it dangled from Cathy's neck, casting its light about wildly as it moved.

Looking down, Cathy noticed bright red seeping through the bodice of Januarye's pale pink party dress. Cathy wadded up the beautiful blanket that had covered Januarye while she was sleeping and pressed against her side. She frantically tried to remember the first aid she had learned at Girl Scout camp years ago. She should keep the girl's head up and stop the bleeding . . . at least, that's what she thought was the right thing to do. What next? Cathy couldn't exactly call an ambulance. Should she try to carry her out of the house and find her way to help?

Januarye was breathing in shallow little gasps, and the pulse in her neck fluttered like a desperate bird. Her eyes flew open and she stared into space.

"Januarye?" Cathy tried to get her attention. "Can you hear me? I don't know how to help you. Do you know what's going on?"

The girl made no response. Cathy wondered if Bunny were somewhere nearby. "Bunny!" she yelled. With her free hand, she parted the curtains that hid the window seat and presumably muffled all sound pretty efficiently.

"Bunny!" she called out into the dark hallway at the top of her lungs. "Bunny, come here right now!"

"He's not here," came a weak whisper from behind her. She turned back to Januarye, who stared right through her. "He's been ripped away from here. He was downstairs, but now he's gone."

"What does that mean—ripped away? Someone came in here and took him?

Januarye nodded, her breath coming in pants. "Yes, just now. The one who has his body. I'm sorry," she whispered.

A huge flash of light burst out of the egg, so bright that Cathy reared back and squeezed her eyes shut. Splotches of neon green throbbed behind her eyelids for several seconds. When the after-images faded, Cathy opened her eyes. Januarye was gone. By the now-faint light of the stone, Cathy could see that the bedraggled toys, the old book, and the bloodstained blanket remained; if that had not been there, Cathy might have thought she had hallucinated the entire episode.

Something disastrous had happened. Had it killed Januarye, or had she gone wherever she had gone the last time she disappeared, hopefully to get some help? And how could Bunny have been taken away? Cathy had assumed that Holly Place was a safe haven. Apparently not. Now she was here alone, and suddenly that didn't seem so wonderful anymore. She shivered, wishing that the blanket weren't ruined. She pulled the long end of one of the curtains up onto her lap from where it pooled on the carpet and wrapped herself in its heavy folds. Rocking back and forth slightly, she chewed on her lip and tried to figure out what to do next.

Where was Bunny, and how did Januarye know what had happened to him? Cathy realized she was asking the wrong questions. A girl who could appear and disappear at will and create glowing stones filled with aromatic wax probably had lots of other unearthly powers. What was the point of wondering about them, when she knew so little? She tried to focus on what she did know.

Januarye had said that Bunny was downstairs when he was . . . ripped away. He hadn't been in there when Cathy had arrived, so he could have gone into either the dreaming room or the traveling room while she was on her way to the window seat. Though, Cathy realized, there must be a lot more to the ground floor than what she had seen so far. She had only explored perhaps half of what should be down there. This deep hallway and all the rooms it adjoined was proof of that—assuming that Holly Place followed the normal rules of architecture. But maybe that was a big assumption, for all Cathy knew.

It was all so overwhelming. Cathy fought back the relentless tide of fatigue and despair. She hadn't slept at all the night before, and that lack was catching up to her now. She wished she could go home and forget all about this whole quest, if that's what it was, and just sleep. How nice it would be to wake up and have all these problems solved. But she couldn't go home. She'd left again with no word, and she had to get rid of Fake Blake permanently before she dared face her mother—and the consequences of her actions—again.

She knew she had to find out what had happened to Bunny—and what had hurt Januarye so badly—but she couldn't make herself go downstairs and investigate, not in the dark. What if whatever had taken Bunny was still down there and was waiting for her? For that matter, what was stopping it from coming up here and finding her? Suddenly she felt very exposed. She let the curtain fall and burrowed deep into the window seat's cushions for warmth instead. She hid the stone under her shirt again to muffle its light. Hugging her knees to her chest, she let her head sink to the side. Exhaustion ate away at her panic and confusion, dissolving everything into a grainy haze. Cathy let her head sink back into silk-covered down and slipped under a wave of sleep.

She woke up with a crick in her neck, a nasty taste in her mouth, and huge hollow feeling in her stomach. Wind lashed the branches of the oaks and maples outside, and the rain pelting the mullioned windows made her realize that she urgently needed to find a bathroom. What time was it? Did that question mean anything at all within these walls? Cathy sat up and stretched. She felt like an idiot for having left home without a toothbrush, and what was she going to do for food?

First things first. Did this house even have a toilet? Cathy didn't think so, not if it had burnt down when Rich had said—and hadn't been modernized when it came into being in this dimension, or whatever. Did that mean finding a privy somewhere outside? Cathy wrinkled her nose, but knew she couldn't afford to be choosy. She climbed out of the window seat and shoved her way past the curtains, which she could see now were a deep, dark green. They had looked black the night before.

Cathy walked fast down the hall and paused at the top of the stairs. Was it safe to go down? The front hall stood empty and bright in the light of late morning. Her bladder cramped, and she decided she would risk it.

As she descended the stairs, inspiration hit her. She could use the traveling room. If she could choose any destination, that should include the bathroom of her choice. She ran to the double doors and paused with her hand on the knob. Where to go? Not into any strong memory; she didn't have time to get sucked into the pain and joy of seeing her family again. Someplace neutral. Her stomach rumbled. Bathroom first, food second. Could she take care of both with one destination? She smiled to herself. The Upper Crust Cafe in the city would do nicely. She and Jessica had often gone there on their way home from school. Fixing the memory of its familiar French doors and wrought iron tables firmly in her mind, she opened the door and walked in.

It was crowded, as always. A long line formed along the pastry case, and harried workers shouted to be heard over the bustle of chatting customers. Cathy saw herself and Jessica at the corner table they liked best, drinking hot chocolate and sharing a huge, pecan-covered pastry. She felt a pang of homesickness for her old friend and their familiar routine. Sidling past school children and nannies with high-tech strollers, she made her way to the lavatories in the back of the restaurant. It was odd, being able to touch things, but at the same time invisible (and hopefully intangible) to the press of people all around her. She could see herself in the mirror of the bathroom, but no one else paid her the slightest attention, not even when she flushed the toilet and exited the bathroom stall.

After she washed her hands, she drank directly from the cold water faucet. New York City tap water was the best in the world, and it was free. Wiping her mouth with the back of her hand, she grimaced in the mirror as she realized something. Water might be free, but food at the cafe was not, and she had no money with her. She was invisible, but she could definitely interact with her environment, and she didn't want to abuse the privilege. Stealing was stealing, whether you were inside an inter-dimensional magic house or not.

She could go home through the traveling room and raid her fridge, though—carefully choosing a time when she wouldn't have to see anyone in her family. She'd go back to the Kashkawan house, not their old apartment. Athena had a bigger budget for snacks now that she and Malcolm were married.

Cathy left the cafe bathroom and shouldered her way back the way she came. Easing herself past a team of loud-mouthed utility workers on a break, she caught sight of someone familiar out of the corner of her eye. The bottom dropped out of her stomach and she flinched. It was Blake, wearing his old prep school blazer and tie, a lacrosse stick and backpack slung over his shoulder. He and two friends laughed and jostled one another as they headed toward the front door, which was exactly where Cathy needed to go.

"He can't see me, he can't see me," she whispered to herself. She tiptoed anyway and let a harried-looking woman with a double stroller follow directly behind the boys. She could see Blake in profile as he teased one of his friends. As he reached the door, he stiffened and looked back into the cafe as if he had heard his name called. He scanned the crowd, and Cathy couldn't help ducking once more. She peeked over the shoulder of the mother with the stroller. After a moment, Blake turned back to his friends and left the cafe. Cathy watched him saunter down the sidewalk through the glass door. After a few seconds, she followed.

Back in Holly Place's hall, Cathy leaned against the double doors and took a few deep breaths. How had she managed to go to the Upper Crust at the exact moment Blake had been there? Cathy didn't remember having ever seen her stepbrother at the café before, but there was no reason they couldn't have been there at the same time before they had ever met, since they had lived mere blocks apart nearly all their lives. But it seemed like an odd coincidence, and Cathy didn't like it, especially since he appeared to have been looking for someone just before he left. Was it risky to go back to Turley Lane through the traveling room, even if Cathy used a memory of a solitary midnight snack? Had Zared somehow gained the power to manipulate what happened here in Holly Place?

Cathy's stomach gurgled. Okay. She could beat this. She cast her mind back to a time in Manhattan before Malcolm and Athena had met. New Year's Eve two years ago—Cathy's mom had gone out with friends and left Cathy in charge of the younger girls. Post-Christmas snacks abounded. Perfect. Back she went through the doors.

She walked through the entryway of her old apartment and into the tiny galley kitchen. School flyers, and Christmas cards, and photos of all three girls covered the surface of the refrigerator. Pots hung from a rack above the gas stove; Athena had maximized every bit of space in their small apartment. Cathy could hear strains of familiar music—a sweeping, orchestral score—coming from the living room. Of course—she had watched *The Scarlet Pimpernel* that night after Fawn and Mae had fallen asleep in order to keep herself awake until midnight.

A plate of peanut cakes sat on the radiator cover under the kitchen window. Cathy got a paper towel and grabbed four of the delicious little pastries that Athena only made once or twice a year. Then she got into the fridge and got an apple and a couple of cheese sticks; that would do for now. Her mouth watering, she bit into one of the peanut cakes and started chewing. Heaven. Swallowing, she decided that she'd better take a couple more.

As she reached toward the platter, a shrill tone made her jump and almost drop her loot on the floor. The phone on the wall rang, its volume set loud enough to be heard in the back bedrooms. After she got over her scare, Cathy frowned. She didn't remember anyone having called their apartment that night. In fact, Athena had apologized for *not* phoning when she had gotten home shortly after midnight. Cathy waited for her other self to pick up the handset in the other room. She didn't, and the obnoxious ring kept bleating. It was time to go; Cathy was getting a little freaked out. As she passed the phone, she noticed its silver plastic surface was covered with something white and grainy that steamed slightly in the warm kitchen air. Frost?

Cathy hurried toward the front door of the apartment. As she approached, the intercom to the lobby below buzzed. Now Cathy *knew* something was wrong. The doorman had never called upstairs on New Year's Eve two years ago. She looked at the little screen with its row of black buttons and glanced back toward the living room.

No one was coming from there to answer the door, and that would only be because Cathy and her sisters *didn't hear the buzzer.*

They weren't meant to hear it. Someone was trying to break into her memory—trying to reach *her,* the present-day Cathy who had traveled back in time hoping to score some breakfast. She shuddered. It had to be Zared. Condensation dripped down the intercom's screen and formed tiny icicles that dripped onto the parquet wood floor. She had to get out of here. Juggling her food, she leaned as far away from the intercom as she could get, flung open the apartment door, and stepped back into Holly Place's hall.

Letting her back slide down the carved wood of the traveling room doors, Cathy sat on the stone floor and set her food at her side. Holly Place was feeling less safe to her by the minute. She knew that fear made some people lose their appetites, but she was still starving. In fact, she was feeling a little shaky and lightheaded. She ate a couple more of the peanut cakes, then unwrapped a cheese stick and downed it as well. Okay. That was better. She wrapped up the rest of the food in her paper towel and set it on the bottom step of the nearest staircase. She should try to figure out what had happened to Bunny.

She went through the doors to the dreaming room. The room looked exactly as it had the first time she had visited it, except for two things. No fire burned in the grate. And just to the right of the massive marble fireplace, a huge, irregular stain darkened the wallpaper and paneling. Everywhere else in the room, the dizzying patterns kept up their eternal shifting, but in that place the wall looked diseased and stagnant somehow. Cathy walked nearer to it so that she could examine it more closely.

The stain was the color of dead leaves and looked wet, as if it were some sort of seepage. Fine green mold had begun growing along its edges. Cathy bent to examine it more closely, but a strong smell of soggy cigarette butts and rotting vegetables rose up from the stain, making her gorge rise. She drew away from the wall, breathing shallowly through her mouth. This was more than some sort of mundane leak from the outside. She couldn't help feeling that this had something to do with Bunny's disappearance and whatever it was that had happened to Januarye. Had Bunny stood right here, looking at something through the wallpaper when he was taken? What if it happened again?

Cathy had to get out of this room. The back of her neck itched as she walked quickly back to the front hall. She was now sure that Holly Place's defenses had been compromised in some way. But how? Had Zared mounted some sort of attack? How did he even know about this place? There had to be some way to find out.

Even though she had closed the doors of the dreaming room, she felt like the rancid smell of the moldy wallpaper was still clinging to her. She needed fresh air to clear her mind. She strode to the front door and flung it open, expecting to find the green-smelling, humid air of an Indian summer morning. Instead, she encountered thick, dark fog that swirled so densely that she could barely see the porch steps, let alone the trees in the front yard. She ducked her head back into the house. The windows showed a sunny, clear day outside. Which view was the correct one?

As she stood in the doorway trying to see anything at all beyond the pillars of the front porch, the fog sent a wave of chilly, damp air toward her. She shivered and slammed the door. A little of the mist curled under the bottom crack of the door like seeking fingers before dissipating. What next? Both parts of the house that she knew best felt unsafe to her now. And was it her imagination, or was the smell of the wallpaper stain growing stronger? It was time to go back upstairs.

Back at the window seat, she stowed her extra food on its stone sill. She picked up the old book that Januarye had found for her. She opened it and scanned its pages again. Did it really contain a story that was similar to her dilemma? The script looked so tantalizingly familiar, as if she should be able to read it. She stared hard at the spidery words, but their meaning seemed to be just out of reach. She closed the book carefully and put it back down on the cushion.

With a pang, Cathy thought of Rich and wished desperately that he were with her. Once he got over the shock of having his logical, rational world turned upside down, his orderly mind and good humor would be definite assets to the situation. When would she see him again? It looked like that wouldn't happen until she did whatever it took to get rid of Zared. Assuming she was successful, that is.

"I can do this," she whispered to herself. She couldn't let loneliness, fear, and despair overtake her. She thought of her mother and sisters. She had to make sure they were going to be all right. She looked back down the hallway, which was still dim despite the hour. With a shove, she opened the curtains that hid the window seat to let more light in. Dust motes whirled in endless, pointless dances as she considered the double row of doors she faced. It was time to see what lay behind them.

CHAPTER TWENTY-TWO

CHASE THE GLOWING HOURS

THE DOORS ALL looked identical. Where should she start? After hesitating, she decided to be methodical about it. She strode to the first door on her left and tried to open it, but it was locked—as were the second and third doors. The fourth hid a large linen closet, with shelves and shelves of snowy, embroidered sheets and towels and tablecloths. The fifth opened onto what looked like a bedroom crowded with draped furniture.

Going back down the other side of the hallway, Cathy tried four more locked doors before coming to the one nearest the window seat. She paused for a minute, considering. She had circled back almost to where she had begun just a few minutes before. This investigation felt a little anticlimactic to Cathy after having discovered the wonders of the downstairs rooms on her previous visits. If this door was locked, she figured she would search the linen closet in greater detail. Or look under all the drop cloths in the bedroom. Or try to find a way to the back of the house downstairs. She realized that she still had options, even if she couldn't get into this last room. But when she tried the doorknob, she found that it moved freely. She opened the door and stepped inside.

She stood in a library. Rows of mahogany shelving ran around its perimeter and all the way up to the high ceiling. Books of all shapes and sizes filled each one, with no apparent order or organization. Brightly colored paperbacks stood next to ancient-looking tomes with peeling leather spines: Stephen King and Edmund Spenser, A.S. Byatt and St. Augustine, Mark Helprin and Julian of Norwich all seemed to cohabitate happily in this place. It surprised Cathy to see modern books within the walls of this house; she realized she had assumed that Holly Place was like some sort of relic from the past preserved in amber, with no real connection to the present day. But that, along with her assumptions about Januarye's identity, were proving to be totally wrong.

Cathy closed the door behind her. This room looked like heaven. A few thick rugs punctuated the expanse of gleaming wood floor. Plump leather chairs sat before the room's two tall windows, and a crimson silk-upholstered couch faced a marble fireplace similar to the one in the dreaming room downstairs. A huge painting hung over the fireplace, providing the room's only decoration other than the books themselves.

What was its subject? Cathy couldn't tell. It portrayed some sort of dark landscape in unrelieved browns and grays. Its somber sky blended into a deserted plain with not a figure, or even a rock or tree, in sight. "Not what I'd hang in *my* library," she murmured. She turned toward the walls of books again. Climbing one of the wooden ladders that ran on little wheels along brass rails around the room, she trailed her fingers along the backs of books that were her favorites, books she hoped to read someday, and many, many more that she didn't know at all.

Cathy could picture herself becoming utterly distracted in this room, sinking into that comfortable-looking couch and reading book after book in glorious escape. She deliberately pushed that fantasy from her mind and descended the ladder. A movement caught the corner of her eye, and she turned with a jolt of adrenaline.

There was no one else in the room, as she had thought for a wild second. But looking up, she noticed that the painting had changed. Now it showed a busy Manhattan street from the perspective of someone sitting in the branches of a tree. By the look of the tree's just-budding branches, Cathy guessed that it was very early spring. Among the people walking under it and along the rows of brownstone townhouses that lined the sidewalk was a young girl in a pink party dress. She was barefoot and held a helium-filled balloon; it was Januarye. As Cathy gazed at her, the girl cocked her head and smiled straight into her eyes. Looking up at the emerald green balloon, she deliberately let go of its tether and watched it float up through the branches of the tree and out of view. Then Januarye smiled at Cathy again and beckoned to her.

What did she mean? Was Cathy supposed to get closer to the painting? She pushed the library ladder around the curved corner and as far down the rail as it would go, right up to the brass finial that capped it at the fireplace's edge. Then she climbed up again and leaned over sideways until she was eye level with Januarye. At this range, the painting should have dissolved into an indiscernible mess of colors and brush strokes, but it actually seemed even clearer now that she was up very close.

Januarye nodded and stepped into the well in the sidewalk that held the tree and clambered up its trunk. She wore purple spandex shorts under her dress, and Cathy experienced a chill of recognition. She had worn shorts under her dresses just like that when she was little, terrified that someone would get a glimpse of her underwear otherwise. Again she wondered whether the girl was somehow a reflection of herself despite everything she had said.

Januarye stood up on a near branch and held her arms out for balance. Bracing one hand against the tree's narrow trunk, she held her hand out to Cathy. She reached closer and closer until her hand emerged from the painting itself, sticking out like a coat hook from the center of the canvas. She wiggled her fingers, and Cathy guessed that she was supposed to take Januarye's hand. She stretched as far as she could, but she was still a good foot away from meeting the girl's grasp. She eyed the mantel and wondered whether it would hold her weight. It should; it looked like solid stone built right into the wall. She climbed another rung on the ladder and slid one knee onto the marble surface of the mantel. Could she possibly keep her balance on it until she reached the center of the painting? And what then?

Forcing herself to look at it logically, she saw that the mantel had to be at least six inches deep. Cathy knew the balance beams in gym class were only four inches wide. She should be able to do this if she leaned against the painting as she moved toward its center. She shifted her weight from the ladder and, pressing her cheek and upper body against the canvas, she inched her way along the cool marble until she could touch Januarye's outstretched hand. The girl immediately caught hold of her and pulled back slowly and gently.

Cathy's own hand moved into the painting, and her arm and head followed. Incredibly, now she could hear the sounds of the city all around her. Januarye let go of her hand and stepped back on her branch, and Cathy reached up, grabbed a branch for leverage, and pulled the rest of her body through the surface of the canvas. She hugged the tree trunk tightly, fighting off a wave of momentary vertigo. She looked behind her, hoping to see some sort of window into the room she had just left, but all trace of Holly Place had disappeared.

She turned back to Januarye, who looked perfectly healthy and had no blood staining the bodice of her dress. "You're all right, then? I'm so glad. I was afraid maybe you had died last night."

The girl shook her head. "I'm tougher than I might appear, though I'm still quite badly hurt. I'll be all right, don't worry. Healing just takes time. But right now I can't get back into *Hulsthuys* in the usual ways, so I had to bring you here."

"Where are we, exactly?"

"West 73rd Street, between Central Park West and Columbus. But you probably weren't asking quite so literally. You are looking for a way to help Bunny. I need to show you what you're fighting so that you can figure out how to do that. Come on." She bent down and used the branch beneath her like a monkey bar, swinging down and hanging, then dropping into the impatiens plants at the tree's base. She stepped over the low fence back onto the sidewalk and looked up expectantly. Cathy sighed and copied her young friend awkwardly; it was harder than Januarye had made it appear.

Safely on the sidewalk, Cathy asked, "What next?"

Januarye took her hand and headed toward Central Park. The sun shone brightly, but the air carried enough of a chill that Cathy shivered a bit in her jeans and T-shirt. Januarye seemed impervious to the cold, her bare feet slapping lightly on the concrete as they walked.

"All around us, there are three worlds superimposed upon one another. Most mortals live exclusively in the seen world, never realizing that they walk through two others at the same time. Long ago, young Blake went looking for one of the unseen realms, but accidentally stumbled into the other. When he did so, he had no idea what he was doing."

"He went looking for his dead mother."

"Yes, but there was never any chance that he would find her—not in that way. Those who die go to Aaru, or Paradise. From there, they can observe the mortal realm and the other unseen world—that of the wekufe. They can influence those mortals with whom they shared a strong connection in life, and can even visit the other realms temporarily. But eidolons—mortals temporarily loosed from their bodies—cannot get into Aaru, not until they are called to die. They are tied to this realm—or that of the wekufe—for better or for worse.

"Bunny had no way of knowing this. He was just a small boy, as you know. He had no training and didn't realize the risks of what he had taught himself to do. He left his body without safeguarding it first, which is how Zared stole it from him." Januarye looked up at Cathy. "Do you understand?"

"I think so. Bunny showed me what happened to him. I just don't know how to put things back the way they were."

"It won't be easy. But you can do it," Januarye promised.

"You've said that before, and I guess I believe you. But I still have a question. I have a lot of them, actually. But the one I keep coming back to is—why me?"

Januarye stopped in her tracks and turned to Cathy, looking up at her for several long seconds. "Why *not* you?" she whispered finally, tears glistening in her dark brown eyes and her bottom lip trembling.

Shame washed over Cathy, and she nodded. She didn't understand the reasons why, but she had promised to do this thing, and she had to honor that. Perhaps understanding would come later.

"Okay. Never mind. I guess that doesn't really matter."

Januarye dashed the tears from her face and beamed. "Come on."

They walked until they got to one of the many playgrounds that dotted Central Park. Dozens of children played on the climbing toys, and more lined up for their turns on the swings. Though it was early spring, the fountain in the center of the playground gushed water, and a few intrepid toddlers splashed their hands happily in its spray. Januarye led Cathy through the gate, then stopped and surveyed the dark green wooden benches that ran along the boundary fence.

"Look," she said, pointing to the far corner of the playground and moving toward it.

Cathy followed and obeyed. A young Jamaican woman lay curled up on a bench, her hungry eyes fastened on another woman who played with a young child in the sandbox. She realized that the woman in the sandbox and the first woman looked like they could be sisters, though the first woman looked much younger. Mother and daughter, perhaps?

No. In a flash, Cathy saw it: the first woman was a spirit and the second was her usurped body. Just then, the sandbox woman cast a furtive look of hatred at the woman on the bench. Cathy took a quick step backward, shocked by the intensity of her hostility, even though it wasn't directed at her. She grabbed Januarye's arm for support, though she didn't know whether she could count on the girl for actual protection. Whatever lurked in that woman's body was as evil—or worse—than Zared.

The thought of it horrified her. This woman must be employed as a nanny; the child next to her in the sandbox was obviously not hers. The thought of someone like Zared being entrusted with the care of a baby made Cathy sick. How common was it for people to have their bodies stolen from them?

"It's actually quite rare," Januarye murmured. "But keep watching."

After a few minutes, the woman in the sandbox asked another nanny to keep an eye on the child for a moment. She went to a stroller parked nearby, brushing off her long, multi-colored gauze skirts as she went. She pushed the stroller over to where the spirit lay huddled on the bench and hissed something at her while pretending to look through a diaper bag. The spirit cowered at first, then jumped up and fled through the fence and into the thick undergrowth beyond. A smile of satisfaction spread over the nanny's face as she sauntered back to her spot in the sandbox and serenely resumed entertaining her young charge.

"The wekufe—the usurper—has more weapons at its disposal than intimidation," Januarye observed. "Those in bodies always are stronger than eidolons, and most thieves of this kind have powerful magic besides. Some can even move between the realms, as we are doing, though only the strongest and oldest have mastered those skills. You'll see that the wekufe and his or her stolen body can never elude the eidolon for long, though. Every banishment is only temporary, and is painful for both. And, in a way, the wekufe depends on the eidolon. If its time comes to move to Aaru, the body dies, and the wekufe becomes homeless once more."

"I just don't see how I can fight something so powerful."

Januarye nodded. "These creatures are formidable. But you must understand that Zared has no right to the body he has stolen. It was not created for him, so it does not fit him perfectly, no matter how long he inhabits it. That is a weakness, a chink in his armor, so to speak. He also has been abusing the body lately, which will weaken his hold on it more than he realizes. There will be a way."

Cathy watched the spirit of the young woman creep back through the bushes toward the iron fence. She looked through the bars for a few seconds, then passed through them and resumed her huddled position on the bench once more. Cathy felt terrible for her.

"I wish I could help," she whispered.

Januarye put her arm around her waist and hugged her. "Watch."

Cathy now noticed that she and Januarye were not the only observers of the wekufe. A man with hollow, haunted eyes wearing a long, black trench coat stood by a drinking fountain. Two haggard women perched on the edge of one of the jungle gyms. All three watched the embodied wekufe with voracious intensity. Unlike the eidolon, who looked defeated and desperate, these three looked strong and hungry. Children and their caregivers passed by them as if they were not there.

Cathy clutched Januarye's hand. "Other wekufe," she whispered.

Januarye nodded. "They are ruthless and vicious, far worse than animals. Sometimes they tear each other apart just because they can. These plan to attack the embodied one and take the body for their own. Their alliance will last only that long."

"Which will take it?"

"Whichever is the strongest."

"But what about the eidolon? Does she have a chance against all of them?"

Januarye opened her mouth to answer—

Bang. Something slammed into the fence right behind where they stood. Cathy whirled around. A group of teenagers with lacrosse sticks ran around the adjacent lawn. They laughed and shouted as one of the boys ran over and rooted through the dense ivy near the fence. Finally, he held up a small, orange ball and waved it happily at his friends. As he ran back to the group, Cathy grew cold. They were far away, but one of the other boys looked very familiar.

As if he felt her gaze, the boy turned and looked at her. Cathy tore her eyes off him and turned toward her young guide. "That's Blake over there. Zared, I mean." She glanced back over her shoulder. The boy was now jogging lazily over to the playground.

"Cathy! Hey, Cathy," called Blake as he reached the gate. "Come here for a second. I want to talk to you." Cathy could see that his smile did not reach his eyes.

Januarye's eyes widened. "He should not be able to be here. Hurry. We need to leave." She grabbed Cathy's hand and ran toward the playground's fountain.

"Take a deep breath and hold it," Januarye cried. With a leap, they cleared the cement lip of the fountain and jumped into the water.

It should only have come up to their ankles, but Cathy and Januarye plunged into a pool that was much deeper and darker than any New York City fountain. Januarye released Cathy's hand and started swimming. Her face and limbs glowed faintly, but as she moved away, it got harder to see her through the murky water. Cathy wondered briefly whether at some point she would get used to being constantly surprised. She kicked her legs strongly and followed after Januarye as fast as she could.

CHAPTER TWENTY-THREE

A SHADOW CAST

ZARED STANDS AT the edge of the playground's fountain, frustrated for the moment. He can now sense when Cathy ventures into the unseen realms and can track her with increasing accuracy. For all her otherworldly talents, she is as predictable as any young human. The factor that keeps throwing him off is that guide of hers. What is her connection to Cathy, and whence does she derive her significant power? She looks like a child, but Zared senses that there is far more to her than her appearance would indicate.

He glances around the playground, noticing the other wekufe, their target in the sandbox, and the pathetic eidolon cringing on the bench. All of them look at him with curiosity, their own struggle forgotten for the moment. He knows none of the wekufe by sight, but after sizing them up, he can tell that he is more powerful than any of them. He scowls and fakes a lunge in their direction, spreading his arms wide, then laughs as the woman flinches and the wekufe and the eidolon scatter like crows.

He breathes deeply and assesses his situation. Cathy has eluded him for the moment, but she has not gone far. He is closer to finding his way into that mysterious house, his eidolon's former haven—closer to destroying this constant threat to his security. Casting his senses out farther, he can't quite get a fix on Cathy's exact location, which seems to fluctuate between the realms. It is clear, however, that the girl and her little helper are worried. He cannot follow Cathy and her guide into the fountain, but he can complicate their escape route. Passing his left hand in a circle above the surface of the water, he mutters a spell of darkness and obstruction. There. That should keep Cathy busy and distracted until he can find his way past her defenses.

He'll continue to go over every inch of the boundaries of their hiding place until he finds another way in. And when he does, he'll dispose of Cathy as securely as he has caged his eidolon. Her having run away from home yesterday gives him the perfect alibi; Malcolm and Athena need never know what has happened to their daughter.

With a blink and a mutter, Zared is back in his bedroom and in his own time stream. He glances at the prison he has created in the corner. His eidolon remains secure and unseen to all but Zared.

What a stroke of good fortune it had been for him to have come upon a solitary wekufe in town just the day before. No, it had to be fate, the universe moving in Zared's favor after centuries of unjust treatment. The lone wekufe was old and wise, but had been rendered weak from untold decades of bodilessness. Capturing it had taken Zared only a matter of moments. He had tortured the thing for fun until it expired, but before it did so, it gave up many invaluable and intriguing secrets. Zared had sucked up its vast intelligence and experience like soda through a straw.

He spent the rest of the day sorting through his newly assimilated knowledge, trying out spells and experimenting with the increase in the force of his will. By combining these new capacities with the element of surprise, he seized the moment when he discovered his eidolon spying on him and promptly and simply removed the nagging burden of its constant proximity. The eidolon is now unable to harass Zared, but that is not the only benefit of this new confinement. This body's true owner is also safe and unable to move to Aaru, whether voluntarily or forcibly. Because of this, Zared now revels in a freedom he has never before enjoyed. He glories in the fact that, after centuries of waiting, the day of his full power has come. Every earthly pleasure can be his now, as long as he is very, very careful.

Even though it is the middle of the night, Zared finds that hunting for Cathy has made him ravenous. He steals downstairs and wolfs down cold casserole with a fork straight from the refrigerator. He barely tastes it; he is after an ever-elusive feeling of satiety and does not stop eating until his belly is bloated and tight. Wiping his mouth on his sleeve, he finds that he is still restless. Lately, he's been numbing that feeling with a quick snort or two, but tonight, he instead wants to hone and sharpen it to a finer peak. He considers the porn site he has hacked his way into, but the thought of it bores him.

Images are losing their potency to stimulate him. He feels that only the touch of real skin will satisfy him tonight. Unfortunately, his problem is access. He has made friends with girls at school, but he doesn't know where any of them live, or how he would find them at this time of night. He will have to content himself with the waning pleasures of the internet.

Or will he? Maybe he doesn't have to leave the house for the close contact he craves after all. Leaving the dark kitchen, he climbs the stairs and stops in the hallway. He has tried to manipulate Cathy before with threats against her sisters. Perhaps it is time now to prove that he does not bluff. He weighs his options. Fawn is lithe; with her long, tan legs, she looks older than she is. But she is too smart for her own good, and too careful as well. The younger girl is less appealing, barely out of plump babyhood. But she would be easier to intimidate and shut up if necessary. And would anyone believe the misguided imaginings of a kindergartner, anyway?

He listens outside Mae's door, then eases the door open and peers inside. The five-year-old is snoring slightly, sprawled across her bed in a tangle of blankets and stuffed animals. He slinks to the side of her bed and gazes down on her. She is luminous despite her graceless, penguin-covered pajamas. She sweats with the effort of deep sleep, and her fine, blond hair sticks to her temples in damp waves. He trails his fingers across her forehead and down the side of her cheek. So soft, the down on them feels silky under his sensitive fingertips. He moves his hand to the pulse at her throat, as rapid as a bird's. His heart beats faster in response, and he feels delicious heat rise up within him. Mae is a heavy sleeper; the whole family knows this. He traces her tender collarbones and slowly circles the hollow between them. How much can he touch without awakening her? Is it worth the risk?

A sound out in the hall startles him, and Zared snatches his hand away from the girl. Someone else is awake. Panic extinguishes desire. He moves quietly to the doorway and peers out into the hall. Malcolm is shuffling down the stairs. Why? Hunger? Another of his interminable bad dreams? Zared guesses the latter. Idiot. He has gone from tolerating and placating the man to hating him actively, but he knows he must be more cautious. He could ruin years of careful compliance by chasing one impulse. Hearing Malcolm's bare feet on the kitchen's tile floor, Zared knows he should get to safety. He glances back at Mae once more, then slips across the hall to his own bedroom and closes the door quietly.

Now that he has escaped detection, his fear turns to exhilaration. He brushes his fingertips across his palms, remembering the velvety feel of Mae's cheek and shoulders. He gets into bed and rides his rush down, then turns his thoughts toward his next assault on Cathy.

CHAPTER TWENTY-FOUR

INVISIBLE IN DAYTIME

THE WATER GOT DARKER and darker. After a few strokes, Januarye had disappeared. Cathy's lungs begged for air, but in the black depths, she had no idea which way was up. And if she made it to the surface, would she be back in the Central Park fountain, confronting the monster pretending to be her stepbrother with no idea how to defend herself?

Cathy had been holding her breath for so long that bright green stars began to burst and stream before her eyes. The urge to inhale overtook her mind until it was all she could do to fight it. Her fingers brushed against something—cold, rough stone, furred with algae. She ran her hands along its flat surface. Was it a floor, or a wall? There was no way to tell. Finally, she chose to believe that she had reached the bottom of whatever body of water this was; she wasn't going to find a way out by sitting here and dithering. She bent and angled her body so that her sneakers were flat on the stone and pushed off with all her might. Her lungs burned with the effort of holding in dead air, so she exhaled through her nose and battled the desire to breathe in again.

Finally, her head broke the surface. She gulped huge, sweet breaths and treaded water until she had had a chance to settle into a rhythm. Her racing heart calmed. She strained to see anything at all, but the darkness was absolute. The cold water lapped quietly, and the dank smell of moss and wet earth nearly overwhelmed her. Where was she?

"Januarye?" she called. By the shortness of her voice's echo, she could tell she was in a large chamber of some kind—a cave? She swam slowly forward, reaching out with both hands and feet for any purchase at all. Her arms soon grew tired, and just as she wondered whether she should float on her back and rest for a while, she encountered a stone wall. She reached up as high as she could and found that it had a lip. She grabbed its edge with both hands and shoved the toes of her sneakers into cracks between the rough blocks of the wall, trying to lift herself out of the freezing water. But her hands slipped and she tumbled back, scraping her chin on the wall as she fell back into the pool.

Warmth trickled down Cathy's neck. She wondered how badly she was bleeding. She had to get out of this water and into some light. She reached up and felt along the wall, searching for better purchase. Inching herself along, she came to what felt like a large metal ring embedded in the stone. She gripped it with both hands and pulled herself up again. This time, she got her leg up and over the edge, then levered the rest of her body out of the water. At first she lay on the stone to rest, but before long, she sat up. The cold seeped into her bones, and her wet hair and clothes did not help. She was afraid to move, though. What if she fell back in the water, or into something worse?

She had a potential source of light, she remembered. She fished the stone out from under her shirt and held it in her hand. She hadn't made it glow before—at least not consciously. It had seemed to sense and respond to her distress before, only changing its intensity when Januarye had been wounded. How could she get it to work now that she needed it again?

Cathy rubbed the egg between her palms. She breathed on it and whispered to it. Nothing. Stumped, she unscrewed it and held it to her nose. Did the scent change every time she opened it? Now it smelled spicy and warm, like her grandmother's cedar closet. She inhaled deeply, hoping somehow that its warmth would find its way inside her. She shivered, then dabbed a bit of the scent behind her ears and closed the stone again. She let it drop to her chest and put her hands on the floor behind her. The fingertips of her right hand slipped into a crevice in the rock. Running her fingers along the crack, she realized that the floor was made up of cut and fitted tiles.

Turning around, she traced the shape of one of them. It seemed to be a trapezoid about eighteen inches wide. She ran her hands around the next tile and found it was the same shape and facing the same way. Odd. Trapezoids going in the same direction didn't tessellate, at least not on a square or rectangular surface.

Aha. But they would tessellate around a circle—and maybe the pool out of which she had climbed was circular. Was it a well of some kind? Scooting forward on her knees, she felt her way across the stones. Yes—the edges of the tiles curved inward. Therefore, if she crawled away from the edge of the pool, keeping herself oriented perpendicular to the trapezoidal stones, she should at some point find the wall of this chamber without danger of falling back into the water. And if she found the wall, she could move along it until she found a door. Would there be a door? There was only one way to find out.

She knelt, facing away from the pool, with her ankles hanging over the edge. Groping along the tiles' edges one at a time, she inched forward through the black, chilly air. After a few minutes of shuffling along on her knees, she stubbed her fingers against an obstacle. She rubbed her palm up its cold, smooth surface. She had reached the wall. "Okay," she breathed, ignoring how creepy the echoes of her voice were as they whispered through the darkness. She stood up, determined to trace her way around the room and find a way out.

But what if there were another potential hazard awaiting her in the dark? She couldn't assume that the room was empty except for the well. She had no idea where she was or why she was here. She shivered in her sodden clothes and listened to her stomach growl. It felt like hours since she had gone back in time and raided her mother's kitchen. When would all of this be over?

"You can do this," she whispered to herself, gritting her teeth to keep her welling tears at bay. As her final 's' hissed around the dank walls of the room, she thought she saw a light bobbing ahead of her. She flinched and covered her eyes—it threatened to blind her after so long in total darkness. Gradually, she lifted her fingers away from her face and unclenched her eyelids.

"Hello?" she called, her echoes chorusing after her.

"Cathy? Is that you?"

Her heart leapt. It was Rich's voice. How had he found her? The light seemed to be coming from a corridor just ahead of her. Squinting around in the gloom, Cathy saw that she was in a high-domed room with a large, circular opening in the center of the floor. She was pleased that her theory had been correct, but froze when she saw what lay ahead of her along the sloped wall. Every few feet, a large opening appeared in the floor. One lay just inches before her feet. Looking down into it in the dim light, she could see no bottom. If she had gone forward with her plan to walk the perimeter of the chamber, she would have fallen. Her stomach dropped at the thought. She had been very lucky.

The dancing light grew stronger, and then Rich appeared around the corner.

"Hey!" he said, his gorgeous grin warming Cathy's heart. Holding a camping lantern, he skirted the edge of the pit between them and came to her side. Cathy threw her arms around him and bit back a sob.

"I can't believe you're here," she said. "I've missed you so much. How did you know I would be here?"

Rich wrapped his free arm around her and rubbed her damp back. "I couldn't sleep. I thought about everything you told me the other day, and I've been frantic about you and your crazy disappearing act. Your parents are, too, by the way. I'm pretty sure life is going to suck for you when you get home.

"Anyway, I went out to the hammock in my back yard to hang out and hope for sleep to come, and there was a little girl sitting in it. She looked just like you—at first I thought she was Mae. She told me where you were and that you needed my help. I never would have believed her if you hadn't filled me in on what's been going on with you. So I grabbed a light and came to find you.

"Here," he said, stepping away and slipping a heavy jacket off of his shoulders. "I heard you might need this. What happened to your chin? It looks painful."

Cathy took the jacket and put it on, zipping it up and hugging herself. It hung on her; it probably belonged to Rich's father. It didn't matter, though; she already felt much warmer. She smiled gratefully at Rich. "Thank you so much. I scraped my face trying to get out of that." She pointed, and Rich turned around to look at the pool. Cathy hugged herself and reveled in the bit of warmth the jacket was holding in. "I can't believe how cold I am. What is this place, do you know?"

"This is one of the Cat Rock caves. They used to be part of the Voorhees estate, and the family used them for storage. This one is obviously an auxiliary well, but it was also used as part of the Underground Railroad for slaves escaping north to Canada. Kashkawan fourth-graders tour it as a field trip every year when they study the Civil War, so when that little girl described it, I knew exactly where you would be. Who is she, and how do you know her?"

"Her name is Januarye. She's . . . part of Holly Place somehow. I'm not sure whether she's actually a person, as bizarre as that sounds. She's helping me find a way to get Bunny back into his body. At least, she was. I keep losing her."

"She thinks she can help you do that? How?"

Cathy looked into Rich's eyes as she considered his questions. There was something different about him, but she couldn't put her finger on exactly what it was. A rush of dizziness hit her, and she bent over and put her hands on her knees and waited for it to pass.

"Cathy, what's wrong?" Rich set the lantern down on the floor. "What can I do to help you?"

"Nothing," Cathy panted. "I think it's just because I'm so hungry all of a sudden. I remember the last time I ate; I just don't know how long ago it was. I know that doesn't make any sense." She slowly straightened up and smiled. "I don't suppose Januarye told you to bring any food with you."

"As a matter of fact," Rich said, slipping his hand into the breast pocket of his plaid flannel shirt. "I happen to have an emergency Snickers bar right here." He produced it with a flourish and a half-bow. "Your feast, my lady," he said, holding it out.

Cathy accepted it, her mouth already watering as she tore the wrapper open. Bringing the chocolate to her mouth, she looked at Rich again and paused. There it was again—a flicker of something not quite right. What was it about him that had changed? She had just seen him the other day, and she thought about him all the time. What was wrong?

"Eat," he urged her. "Then we'll walk home and you can tell me about this Januarye person."

"I can't go home—not yet. I'll be in lockdown when I do that, and I have to help Bunny first."

"Okay, well, I don't think staying here is an option. I can walk you back to the dump, I guess. Maybe we'll get lucky, and I'll be able to follow you to Holly Place this time. But eat first. We've got a good couple of miles to cover, no matter where we end up. You'll need a little energy."

Cathy took a couple of steps backward and furrowed her brow. Rich followed her fluidly, eager eyes locked on hers, and it hit her.

This wasn't Rich. The wavy, yellow hair and sky-blue eyes were the same. The captivating grin and slightly crooked chin were just right.

But this Rich had no crutches and stood a good four inches taller than she did. He frowned at her and took another step toward her.

"Cathy, eat. You look all gray. I don't want you fainting on the way home," he said, reaching out to touch her cheek.

Cathy shied away from him. "Don't touch me," she whispered.

Rich cocked an eyebrow. "Hey," he said with a short laugh. "I thought I was your rescuer. Where's the gratitude? Is that any way to treat your knight in shining armor?" He moved closer until he had backed her up against the wall.

"You're not here to rescue me. I don't know how you're doing whatever it is you're doing, but I know who you are, Zared."

They stood in the shadows a few steps from the lantern, but Cathy could see the change that came over his face as she said his true name. All trace of Richard Mallory disappeared, and the body of her stepbrother now stood way too close to her. His grin turned to a snarl as he closed the distance between them and covered her mouth with his own. Cathy screamed and struggled against him, but even on a day when she wasn't hungry and exhausted, he had the advantage of strength.

After kissing her hard, he muttered, "I've wanted to do this for a long time, little sister." He laughed as he bit her lips and throat. His teeth grazed the raw patch on her chin, causing it to bleed again. He pinned her arms against the unyielding rock with one hand and un-zipped the jacket he had given her moments before with the other. Thrusting his hand inside, he fumbled with her shirt.

"No!" Cathy shrieked, and kicked him in the shin as hard as she could manage.

"Oh, yes," he grunted into her ear. He trapped her hips against the wall with his and gathered her shirt in his hand as if to rip it off. Then his whole body jerked as if he'd been shocked. He let go of Cathy and grabbed his right hand, howling in pain. Cathy smelled frying meat and looked on in horror. Blake's hand was *sizzling*. What had happened?

She looked down at herself. Lying on her half naked chest, the stone egg glowed with a fierce, sharp light.

"You little whore," he hissed, and lunged at her again. This time, Cathy charged him, down and low, hitting him squarely in the gut. He stumbled back, roaring in frustration—

—And fell into the pit at their feet.

His voice was swallowed up as if it had never sounded, and Cathy was alone. She sank to her knees and wept with horror and relief and fatigue. Zared had transformed himself and completely fooled her at first. Why? She thought back over their conversation. He had want-ed information—about Januarye. He had somehow learned enough about Cathy's situation to trick her, but he didn't know everything, or he wouldn't have come to her with this elaborate ruse. Had it all been lies, or had he twisted the truth to suit his sick purposes? She gagged a little as she remembered his mouth on hers, and scrubbed her lips furiously to try to wipe the taste of him away.

She looked down at the stone glowing gently on her chest and buttoned her shirt with shaking fingers. It had burnt him some-how—why? Had he reacted to the stone, or to the substance inside? For the thousandth time, she wished that Januarye were with her to answer her unending questions. For now, she would assume that it was her only weapon against Zared. She had no illusions that she had gotten rid of him forever—nor did she want to, not until he was out of Blake's body permanently.

She glanced at the Snickers bar he had given her, which she had dropped when he attacked her. She was hungry enough to eat it despite the fact that it had fallen on the damp floor. But Zared had been awfully eager for her to eat it. Was it poisoned somehow? If he had given it to her, it couldn't be good. She kicked the candy bar into the pit. Then she reluctantly took off the jacket he'd given her and threw it in as well. As cold and as hungry as she was, she couldn't risk keeping his gifts.

Which meant the lantern had to go, too. Cathy hated the thought of that, but the egg glowed steadily once more, and she trusted its pale radiance would lead her out of this place. She picked up the lantern and held it over the edge of the pit. Its light only pen-etrated a few feet, leaving the hole's depths in inky blackness. Taking a deep breath, she let go of the lantern and watched it plunge down until its light winked out. She never heard it hit bottom.

Should she leave the way Zared had come in? Looking around the chamber, she saw another opening in the wall directly across from the corridor he had used. She wanted to stay as far away from him as she could. He might come back this way and be better pre-pared to force himself on her; she felt this in her gut. As adrenaline drained from her, she shivered once more. She had to get moving and use the light as long as she had it. Quickly walking around the well, she went to the far corridor. With one last glance around the chamber, she left.

CHAPTER TWENTY-FIVE

KICK THE BEAM

TRAPPED IN A CAGE he can't even see, Bunny feels himself start to fade away again. He is cut off from all stimuli other than the occasional appearance of his body in his bedroom. His usurper has changed somehow—gotten stronger and much more clever than ever before. Clever in some ways, at least. Bunny has no way of knowing how much time is passing, but over and over again he watches his body doing drugs of some kind—sniffing a yellowish white powder up his nose, then sitting back on his bed in a glassy-eyed stupor. This infuriates Bunny; that is *his* body that is being abused, and who knows what the consequences of such heavy drug use will be? Will Bunny even want to be back in his body, assuming that Cathy can still help him?

But he learns quickly not to show signs of anger. Zared laps his fury up like a kitten drinking milk. Bunny refuses to give him that satisfaction, when Zared has taken so many others from him over the long years.

Bunny wonders where Cathy is. Has Zared trapped her, too? He thrusts that fear from his mind. He holds on to ragged shreds of faith as fiercely as he clings to his slowly eroding memories. He was this way before finding Holly Place—listless, unsure of who he was anymore—and he had hoped never to lose his sense of self again.

He sits hugging his knees on the transparent, inflexible floor of his prison. Rocking slightly back and forth, he sings the song the house had sung to him the last time he was there.

God guard me from those thoughts men think

In the mind alone;

He that sings a lasting song

Thinks in a marrow-bone

It's an odd melody with even odder words, and it has a way of sticking in his head. What does it mean? Bunny barely has the energy to wonder. But it comforts him, somehow, and makes him feel as if Cathy is all right. She has not come home. Bunny is sure she is still at Holly Place. Perhaps if he keeps running those strange words through his mind, it will act as a beacon for her, a way for her to find him, despite the security of this place that is not a place in which Zared has imprisoned him.

The bedroom door opens. Bunny keeps his head on his knees, unwilling to acknowledge the presence of his enemy.

"Who are you?"

It is not his body speaking. Bunny looks up in shock into the eyes of a young girl. Cathy's smaller sister stands right next to him and looks right at him.

"I'm Bunny," he answers. "How did you know I was here?"

"I heard you singing. That's a weird song, but I like it. Why are you in Blake's room?"

Bunny scrambles to reassess his situation. He had assumed his prison was soundproof, but that doesn't seem to be the case. He doesn't know how to answer this girl, either. He doesn't want to scare her, though she seems unflappable so far.

"I'm stuck," he says finally. "I don't know how to get out of here."

The girl measures his cage with her eyes, as if she can actually see the barriers that he can only feel. Then she puts out her hand—

—And it goes through the barrier that has been as hard as stone for him. As if there is nothing, in fact, there.

"I see why you're stuck, but I can't touch it." She giggles. "It's just like in my video game, when I need to catch a rainbow star to get through the magic window. Otherwise, I can't get through. Are you real, or are you like a video game?"

"I'm real," Bunny assures her. The girl squints at him, then reaches through his cage again and touches his thumb. He feels the light pressure of her finger for a second, before she snatches her hand away and puts her finger in her mouth. Tears well up in her dark brown eyes.

"You shocked me," she whispers. "That hurt."

"I'm really sorry," he says. "I didn't mean to. I'm so sorry."

She sucks on her finger for a few seconds, then takes it out of her mouth and inspects it. "It's okay. It's better now. Wow, I've never gotten a big shock like that before. Is that your superpower?"

Bunny laughs. He cannot remember the last time he has laughed. It feels wonderful. "I don't think I have any superpowers."

"Well, you're sitting on air. Or inside a magic invisible box that I can't touch. That seems like a power to me."

Bunny considers the girl. "I think you're the one with the superpower. I can't get out of my box, see?" He bangs his palms against the wall in front of him. The girl imitates him, but her hands pass right through the barrier again.

"You really can't get out?"

Bunny shakes his head. "I really want to, though. I've been in here a long time, and I don't like it."

"Did Blake put you in there? Is it like time out?"

Bunny laughs again. "Yes, he did put me in time out. And, um, I guess he forgot about me."

"I can go get him, if you want," offers the girl. "He's downstairs playing the piano, can't you hear him?" She starts to run for the door, and Bunny calls out to stop her.

"No! Please—what's your name? I forgot."

"I'm Mae," she says, her hand on the doorknob.

"Mae. I think . . . Blake . . . would be really mad if he knew that you came into his room. You shouldn't tell him that you saw me in here."

Mae hops on one foot and looks at the ceiling while considering this. "I think you're prolly right," she finally admits. "He likes his stuff private."

I'll bet he does, Bunny thinks. "It's okay," he says aloud. "I'm glad you came in here. It's nice to talk to someone. I've been really lonely. In fact," Bunny feels a surge of clarity, and thinks for a moment. "Mae, do you have any gloves?"

"No, gloves bother me. I can't make the fingers work right. But I have mittens," she says. "They're in my bottom drawer of my princess dresser, I think. I haven't used them since we lived in the city. Are you cold?"

"No." Bunny smiles. "But I thought maybe if you put them on, you could touch me without getting shocked. And maybe you could pull me out of the box, if you think you're as strong as a superhero."

Mae stuck her chest out. "I am very strong," she declares. "I'll be right back."

"Just make sure that Blake is still playing the piano."

"I can still hear him. Can't you?"

"I can't hear anything but my voice and yours," he says.

"That's a bad box," Mae observes. "I'll go get my mittens."

A minute later, she returns with pink wool mittens on her hands. "I hope these give me hit points against your superpower," she says. Gingerly, she extends her hand through the invisible box and touches the very tips of her fingers to Bunny's outstretched hand. She grins with relief.

"They work! Wait until I tell my mom that she made me magic mittens." She clasps Bunny's hand and then takes his other hand as well. She pulls back, and Bunny tumbles out of the box as if it were not even there. He rights himself and makes sure to stand on the floor. He doesn't want Mae to see any more of his "powers."

"You did it, Mae. You freed me." He smiles down at her. Now he can hear the piano, but he can't risk staying here any longer. "I'm going to hide now, so that Blake doesn't put me back in time out. Don't tell anyone you saw me, okay? You're old enough to keep a secret, right?"

Mae rolls her eyes. "Of course. Will you come back and see me some time, though? I like you."

Blake squeezes her hands. "I will. Very soon, I promise. Now, you leave first and go put your mittens away, and I'll sneak out after you. Okay?"

"You got it, Bunny. That's such a funny name. I never met a boy named 'Bunny' before." Mae giggles again and runs out of the room. Bunny watches her go before fleeing out the side wall of the house and to his rock. What will Zared do when he discovers that he has escaped? Bunny has a feeling he won't have to wait long to find out.

CHAPTER TWENTY-SIX

CASTAWAY

THE DARK CORRIDOR seemed to go on forever. How long had Cathy been walking? She had no idea, except for the fact that her chin had crusted over and her clothes and hair had dried somewhat. The humidity had lessened; her feet kicked up small clouds of dust as they scuffed along, step after step. Her stomach felt hollow and light, and her mouth was parched. She had not passed a single door or window since entering this hallway. The walls looked the same, her mysterious egg glowed the same. She had the nagging feeling that she was actually walking on a treadmill, making no progress at all.

Where had Januarye been trying to lead her when they had jumped into the fountain, and how could Cathy find her again? Should she turn around and go back to the chamber with the well? Was Zared skulking somewhere nearby, preparing another disguise to try to trick her again? How had he done that, anyway? And why did she seem no closer to finding a way to get him out of her family's life forever? Questions chased each other like rats around her tired mind. Before she could find answers to any of them, she had to find some food and water and a safe place to rest for a while.

She stumbled over a crevice in the floor, saving herself from falling by throwing out her arms and bracing her hands against the walls of the narrow corridor. After she caught her breath, she examined the crack in the floor. It formed a square about eighteen inches on each side, the crevice making a border of about a finger's width. In the center of the square was a small oval hole. After looking at it for a second, Cathy stepped over the stone and continued up the corridor. But after a few feet, she came to a blank wall blocking any further progress. What? Had she come all this way, only to reach a dead end? If so, what was the purpose of this corridor?

Stumped, tired, and ravenous, she turned around and walked back to the spot where she had tripped. This square was the only thing on her entire journey that stood out from the featureless tunnel. She touched the little oval with her finger. Could that be a keyhole of some kind? Maybe this was a trap door that led out of this place. If only she had the key. A moment later, she realized she had something that would fit perfectly in that hole: her stone egg. She took its chain from around her neck and inserted it into the oval. It fit as snugly as a puzzle piece, going in nearly all the way and glowing much more intensely as a result. Cathy heard a deep rumble, and the square moved slowly down and away.

She hurried to remove the egg from the hole as the door slid under the rock floor on which she stood. There was no way she wanted to risk losing her only source of light—and what seemed to be her only potent weapon against Zared. The rumbling stopped. The opening yawned, as black and lightless as the pit in the well chamber had been. She knelt and, after wrapping the chain around her wrist several times for safety, lowered the egg inside the hole so that she could see what was down there. Its now bright light revealed a large room filled with wooden boxes and barrels. There seemed to be a door in the wall farthest from her, but she wasn't sure.

Cathy gauged the distance to the floor. It didn't look that far down—maybe seven or eight feet. If she let herself over the edge and then hung by her hands, she would have a drop of no more than a yard. Should she go down? It didn't seem like she had any other option. She put the egg around her neck and moved it on its chain so that it hung down her back. She lowered herself onto her stomach, then let her legs down into the hole and slid backward until all of her weight hung from her shoulders. She gripped the edge of the opening tightly and lowered herself until she dangled a few feet above the floor. Closing her eyes, she let go and dropped to a crouch. She rolled an ankle as she landed, but it seemed okay after she massaged it for a minute.

She brought her makeshift flashlight around to the front of her shirt once more. Looking around, she sniffed. That was a good smell—fresh fruit? Cathy opened the crate nearest her and nearly cried out in surprise. It was full of ripe, red apples. Without hesitation, she picked one up and took a bite. It was the sweetest thing she had ever tasted, and she gobbled the rest of it down, carefully wiping its juice off her sore chin with the back of her hand. She took another apple and started looking in some of the other boxes to see if she could find anything else to eat. The first held walnuts still in their shells and the second contained dry beans. The third held gold—a large round of pale yellow cheese nestled in straw. Her mouth watered, and she looked around for some way to cut it.

After a few minutes of rooting through barrels, she came upon a felt-swaddled rosewood box that held a set of pearl-handled knives. Perfect. She no longer had any compunction about taking food that didn't belong to her. This room and its contents seemed heaven-sent at the moment, and she needed all the help she could get. She drove the knife into the cheese and brought out a fat slice. It looked better than cake, and it tasted delicious—smooth, creamy, and tangy. Cathy finished it quickly and chased it with the second apple. She felt infinitely better. It amazed her what a little food could do.

She cleaned off the knife with some of the cloth that had wrapped the rosewood case. She lifted the box's lid to put it away, but hesitated. Should she keep the knife as protection? She mulled it over and decided against it. She had the stone, which seemed to have some sort of protective power, and she didn't like the idea of stabbing anyone.

With her stomach full, Cathy realized that she had no option but to rest. When had she last slept? On the window seat on the second floor of Holly Place? That felt like it had been weeks ago. She looked around the low-ceilinged room. It looked like some sort of basement or cellar, but of what? Was she under the Voorhees family's Cat Rock mansion, as Zared had told her, or had that been a lie? She was almost too tired to care. She couldn't find her way out of this place and help Bunny (wherever he was) if she couldn't think straight.

In the corner behind several wooden casks lay something large and rolled up. A carpet, maybe? That would certainly make a softer bed than the stone floor. Cathy went to it and lifted up its corner. It was heavy, woven fabric—definitely some sort of rug or wall-hanging. She looked back over at the barrel with the knives in it and had a flash of inspiration. She went to it and unwrapped several boxes that were inside and then rolled up the felt wrappings into a sort of cushion as she walked back to the carpet. She lifted up the loose edge again and climbed on top of the roll, pulled the flap of fabric back over herself, and laid her head on her felt pillow. It wasn't the most comfortable bed, but she was warm and had at least the illusion of security. Anyone coming into the room wouldn't be able to see her without some diligent searching. Snuggling back against the wall, she drifted toward sleep. Her last conscious thought was a hope that the egg's light would not go out before she awakened again.

She opened her eyes and found herself in a place of strange textures. She stood in a golden field of grain that waved and rippled in a stiff breeze. The sun beat down on her, and she closed her eyes and smiled up at it. She had been in the darkness for so long. After basking for a minute, she opened her eyes and looked around. The field stretched as far as she could see in every direction, rolling over slight hills until it met the cloudless, blue sky at the horizon. It was beautiful, but it all looked subtly unreal, as if she were in the middle of an Impressionist painting. The far edges of the field stood out in perfect clarity, but the stalks of grain nearest to her had a blotchy quality to them. She couldn't figure out what was so odd about it.

Only one thing stood above the field's undulating surface—a tree near the horizon to her right. What was she doing here? The grain rustled and whispered all around her, but communicated no clue as to her next move. With no real idea why other than to break the monotony of her situation, she walked toward the tree. It was both bigger and farther away than she had assumed at first. She traveled for a long time and didn't seem to find herself appreciably closer to her goal. She got sweaty and thirsty after awhile; the field provided no relief from the constant sun.

And constant it certainly was. Cathy could now look behind her and discern her path clearly through the grain. It stretched back nearly as far as she could see in that direction. She had to have been walking for at least two hours, but the sun had not moved at all from its position directly overhead. Despite her fatigue, she picked up her pace. She wanted to get to the dense shade she could now see under the spreading branches of the giant tree. The golden light that had caressed her when she had first arrived now felt like a punishment.

Finally, she reached the tree. It towered over her, but some of its enormous branches arched back down toward the ground, nearly touching it in some instances. It looked like an oak to Cathy, but she couldn't really tell, because up close, its surfaces broke up and refracted the way the grain had. If she leaned back and looked at its highest boughs, she could see individual leaves. The branch hanging a few feet from her looked out of focus, almost as if she were wearing someone else's glasses.

What was this place? Looking up again, Cathy noticed something she had not seen before. Little scrolls of paper hung from every branch like strange and plentiful fruit. The array of the scrolls was somewhat regular, but not completely symmetrical. She looked at the branch closest to her. A few of the papers hung along its length. Cathy walked to the nearest one and unrolled it, squinting to bring it into focus. In large, jagged, cursive letters, it read "Michael Crane." Other scrolls on that branch contained other names, all with the Crane surname, except for one: Karen Torelli.

Odd. Was it a memorial of some kind? It reminded her of a Christmas tree she had seen once that had been decorated with origami animals, each bearing the name of someone who had died in a big tsunami that year. She felt compelled to go to the next branch over and read its scrolls. These were all Martins—Robert, Christina, and Melissa—except for a Camilla Crandall. A very small scroll had no name at all on it.

She moved on. After examining the scrolls on several branches, a pattern emerged. These were families. Each branch had one female with a different surname. That must be the mother of each branch, listed by her maiden name, Cathy realized. Looking around, she saw that she had traveled around the tree and had almost reached the place where she had started. Only one more branch was low enough for her to examine. Her heart beat faster, as if it knew something that she did not. Unrolling the first scroll she reached, she saw her own name. With shaking hands, she looked at the rest of the scrolls on the branch. The names of each member of her family were spelled out on them. Her parents and her sisters. Malcolm, his first wife Gail, and Blake. "A family tree," she breathed, and felt obtuse for not realizing it before. She looked up. Suddenly, she had to know what the names were on the next branch up.

Hooking one leg over the branch, she pulled herself upward and balanced on her family's branch. She reached up; she could just grasp a scroll and open it. It held the name of her uncle Stephen, who had died when her mother was a teenager. She couldn't reach any more scrolls from this position, but she counted the ones on the same branch, and the number corresponded to the number of people in her mother's family. She climbed up and up, unrolling and reading scrolls as she went, no longer recognizing the names once she passed those of her grandmother and her great-grandmother.

A few more branches up, she got a jolt of surprise. The mother's name on this branch was Catalyntje Voorhees. She knew Voorhees was a Dutch name, so Catalyntje—that must be a Dutch variant of Caitlin or Kathleen. She peered down through the leaves at her feet and counted the number of branches she'd climbed since finding her own name. There were ten. Did she have Dutch blood? Could this woman with the name she half recognized be her ancestor? She had to assume that that was true. Her grandmother's and great-grandmother's branches had been just above her mother's, and she had climbed in a straight line ever since. She moved up to the next branch. These were all Voorheeses, except for the mother, Annetje Van Doren. The next higher branch broke the pattern; this was also a Voorhees branch, it appeared, as was the one after that. So this must be a tree representing the Voorhees family, then. Cathy wondered why she hadn't seen any Voorheeses when she had gone around the tree at first. It must be that the male lines had all died out through the generations, with no one to carry the name forward.

Were these the same Voorheeses that had built and lived in
Holly Place? If so, and if they were Cathy's ancestors, perhaps that
explained her ability to get to the magical house when Rich could
not. Maybe it was her birthright, somehow. Cathy remembered how
drawn her mother had felt to Kashkawan when she and Malcolm
had been searching for a house. Was it because of some familial pull?
Did her mother realize that they might have this connection to the
area? Cathy smiled as she thought of giving Rich the news. He loved
local history, and she had just discovered that she might be an actual
piece of the puzzle that was Philipse County's heritage.

As she neared the top of the tree, she realized that the sunlight
did not shine with the bright, merciless glare that it had when she
had first gotten here. She looked out across the field and saw that
the sky was now full of heavy rain clouds. The wind rushed over
the grain and bent the huge tree's branches as easily as if they were
blades of grass. Lightning cracked the sky open. The accompany-
ing thunder made Cathy's ears ring and throb. Seconds later, rain
beat down. Cathy knelt under the storm's onslaught and clung to
the branch that supported her, which waved in the wind like the
car of a wild carnival ride. The driving rain had made its surface
perilously slippery. Flinching as the next stroke of lightning hit the
top of the tree with a shower of sparks, Cathy lost her grip on the
branch and fell. She screwed her eyes shut as the ground rushed
up to meet her.

She woke up with her own screams still echoing around the cellar. Panicked, she threw aside her makeshift bedding and sat up. The
stone still glowed, fortunately. How long had she slept? She wasn't
sure whether it was adrenaline released in reaction to her dream, but
she felt wide awake and somewhat refreshed. And hungry again—
that must mean that she'd gotten a decent amount of sleep, she realized as she calmed down. Helping herself to more cheese and apples,
she plopped back down on her bed and ate. She gazed around absently as she munched, but she stopped chewing when her eyes fell
on the roll of fabric on which she sat.

It was a tapestry. She stood and pushed against the giant cylin-
der of fabric so that she could unroll it a bit more. She lifted up the

loose end and held it up so that she could examine it in the light. Its subject appeared to be a large tree on a gold and blue background. The tree bore countless names embroidered onto little scrolls woven into its design. She recognized some of them. The Voorhees family tree. How had it infused itself into her dream? She had to see the whole thing.

She spent several minutes pushing the boxes and barrels against the far wall, stacking them wherever she could so that the floor could be as clear as possible. Then she knelt and unrolled the tapestry across the cold floor. When it lay completely spread out, she crawled across it, searching until she found her family's names. She traced the branches up until she found Catalyntje's name again, then turned and went back to the base of the tree's trunk. A large scroll spread across the bottom, with the words "Familie Voorhees" woven into it.

Unbelievable. It was real. Who had made this? It looked like an antique, but the information on it was very recent. Athena and Malcolm had only been married a few months, but Malcolm's name—and Blake's, and his mother's—appeared right there where Cathy's branch divided in two. She shivered. If she got married someday and had children of her own, would they appear on this tapestry as well? She brushed its woven surface and realized why everything had seemed so blotchy in her dream. She had actually been *in* the tapestry somehow. But where had the storm come from, and why?

She wished she had the luxury to sit and contemplate the tapestry at greater length, but she realized she should get moving again. She rolled the tapestry back up. She looked around at the boxes and barrels she had moved and decided to leave them where they were. They hadn't appeared to be in any sort of order before.

Where to now? As she looked around the shadowy room, she saw no outlet other than the trap door she had used. But maybe she had missed something. Hadn't she seen a doorway when she had been up above? She held the egg out and examined the walls carefully. In the far wall, she found another oval carved into a brick. Looking up and around, she could see the outline of a large, arched door.

Where did it lead? "There's only one way to know," Cathy whispered, and she placed the egg in the oval. Just as before, its light increased. Just as before, the stone began moving aside, revealing only darkness beyond.

CHAPTER TWENTY-SEVEN

AN EASY GAME

RICH JERKED AWAKE and nearly fell out of his hammock. He hung on to its sides as it settled and looked around. What was he doing outside? Darkness had just begun to lift at the eastern edge of the sky. Had he really been out here all night long? He knuckled his eyes free of grit and grimaced at the foul taste in his dry mouth. His legs ached even more than they usually did in the morning. He should get inside and take a hot shower, for starters.

His crutches lay wet with dew in the grass below him. He leaned over and picked them up, fitting their cuffs onto his forearms. They felt slick and cold; the last bit of Rich's sleepiness vanished at their clammy touch. He swung himself out of the hammock and across the damp grass toward the back door of his house. As he went to open the screen door, he paused. Red and blue lights flashed, reflected in the glass of his house's windows. He turned and looked over the fence that separated the back yard from the front. A police car and an ambulance sat outside the Harfords' house. *Cathy.* Had they found her?

In a panic, Rich went to the gate, let himself through it, and hurried down the front lawn to the sidewalk. It looked like every light in the house had been turned on. As he watched, unable to decide whether he should cross the street and try to find out what was happening, the front door opened. Two emergency technicians wheeled a gurney onto the porch and carried it down the steps and toward the ambulance. In the gray light of dawn, Rich could barely make out the pale form that lay strapped down and covered with blankets.

It was Blake, not Cathy. Rich's relief was so strong that he felt sick to his stomach for a minute. Two police officers left the house next, followed by Mr. and Mrs. Harford. Blake's father hugged Cathy's mother tightly, then ran down the steps and got into the ambulance after the gurney was loaded in. One tech closed the back doors and the other quickly drove out of the subdivision. The police followed. Mrs. Harford stood on the porch and watched them go, her arms wrapped around her body. She looked slim and elegant in her long, red bathrobe, but her shoulders sagged with stress and fatigue. As she turned to go back into the house, she caught sight of Rich. She stopped and waved sadly.

Rich knew it probably wasn't the politest thing to do, but he had to know what was going on. He crossed the street and swung up the sidewalk as fast as he could.

"Mrs. Harford, hey," he panted. "Is everything okay? I mean— the answer is obviously no. What happened?"

The tall woman closed her eyes for a moment, seeming to gather herself. "We're not sure. Blake appears to have overdosed on some sort of drug. A huge thud woke us up, and when we went to check on him, we found him unconscious and barely breathing on his bedroom floor. I don't know what he's done, but the emtechs couldn't revive him. The police confiscated the drugs they found. They'll test them and call the hospital and compare their results with his blood work."

She buried her face in her hands. "First Cathy disappears, and now this. It feels related, somehow. I don't know what's happening to this family. We've barely begun to *be* a family." She took a deep breath, then lowered her hands and gave Rich a tired smile. "I'm sorry, Richard. That was probably more than you wanted to know. I should go in and try to get some rest before the regular day begins. You should do the same. I apologize for having awakened you. I hope the rest of the neighborhood hasn't been too bothered by all this."

"It's okay. I was already out and about. Sorry to be nosy; when I saw the police and the ambulance, I thought maybe they'd found Cathy."

The grief on Mrs. Harford's face was so deep that Rich didn't know how she was even standing up. "I wish that were the case, but we haven't heard from her. If we do, I'll let you know right away. Thank you for being such a good friend to our family, Richard. I'll see you later." She turned, went into the house, and shut the door softly behind her.

Rich made his way back down the sidewalk. He stopped when he heard the Harfords' front door open again. Little feet pounded down the porch steps and lightly struck the concrete behind him. He turned around again. Mae, wearing long john pajamas with pink and blue kittens all over them, hopped from one foot to the other. Her eyes were huge with agitation. Right behind her was her older sister Fawn, looking very sleepy and rumpled in her Sleeping Beauty nightgown.

"It's my fault," Mae blurted. "It's all my fault, but Mama won't listen to me. I told Fawn everything, but she's not old enough to do anything. You are, though. You'll help me, won't you?"

"Yeah, Mae, of course. What's up?"

Fawn interjected, "Let's go sit on the steps and talk. I don't want to be too far away from Mama."

"Good idea." Rich followed the girls and sat down with them on the bottom porch step.

"It's my fault," repeated Mae. "Last night, I heard someone singing in Blake's room, and I knew it wasn't Blake, because he was playing the piano downstairs. I thought for a minute that it was Cathy, and I got all happy, but then I went into Blake's room and found this little boy there instead. Well, he was bigger than I am, but still little. Like Fawn. Blake had put him in time out because he was angry. I guess Blake was babysitting him, or something, but he said Blake had forgotten about him, so I helped him get out."

"You helped him get out? Why couldn't he get out himself?"

"He was in a magic invisible box. He said I had a superpower, because I could get through it, but he couldn't."

Rich stopped himself from sighing out loud. Six-year-olds certainly had imagination.

Fawn seemed to sense his disbelief. Gritting her teeth, she said, "Mae is little, but she doesn't lie. Ever. When she says something, it's true. When she told me she had met a magic boy named Bunny, I believed her, even though that's a weird name for a boy."

The bottom dropped out of Rich's stomach. "Bunny?" he whispered. He remembered all of Cathy's insane-sounding ramblings the other day. Maybe she hadn't been crazy after all.

"Yeah," said Mae. "Why? Do you know him?"

"No, but your sister Cathy does. I can't believe it. Where is Bunny now?"

"He left after I let him go. I don't know where he is now. See, that's why Blake's accident is my fault. When he got done playing the piano, I heard him go into his bedroom, and he freaked out and threw stuff around for a while. Mama and Malcolm didn't hear him, because they were watching a movie downstairs in the den, but we did."

Fawn nodded in agreement. "We were in Mae's room, and we peeked out her door and spied on him. He came out of his room and went into Cathy's. Maybe he thought Bunny had gone to hide in there. Then he came out again. His face looked crazy, like a monster. We were scared. But then he went in his room again and didn't come out, not even for dinner."

"Yeah, and Mama made chicken marsala, Blake's favorite," put in Mae. "But he told Malcolm that he was sick, and he stayed in his room all night. After dinner, we went to bed, just like usual."

"Then I heard a big noise a while ago," Fawn continued. "Mae didn't. She sleeps through everything. She didn't wake up until the police and the ambulance guys came upstairs. I guess Blake fainted and knocked some stuff over when he fell. But Malcolm couldn't wake him up."

"I think Blake got so mad when he found out that Bunny was gone that he had a hot attack," Mae cried, her eyes shiny with unshed tears. "I shouldn't have let him go." She put her head down on her knees and started sobbing.

Rich put a hand on her back, trying not to smile. The poor thing. "A heart attack, you mean? I don't think Blake had a heart attack. Besides, Mae, I think you did the right thing. And this is not your fault. Blake wasn't supposed to put Bunny in time out. Blake knows that Bunny and Cathy are friends, and he's super jealous. I think he put Bunny in the box to keep him away from Cathy. That was a mean thing to do."

"Do you know where Cathy is?" Fawn asked, her face tight with worry.

"I think so. And I'm pretty sure Bunny is with her. Look, you guys, I think it's going to be okay. I'm going to go look for Cathy a little later, because I think she can help Blake."

Fawn raised her eyebrows. "Cathy's just a teenager. She's not a doctor."

"I know. But trust me. If you can believe in magic invisible boxes, believe that Cathy is working hard to make it so that your step-brother doesn't have any more 'heart attacks.'"

Mae lifted up her head and wiped her nose with the back of her hand. "Really? Are you sure?"

"Yeah." Rich smiled down at her. "I'm sure. You guys should go inside before your mom figures out you're not in your beds. I'll hope-fully go find Cathy, and we'll have a big party when everybody is back together again."

Mae's eyes lit up. "Let's have pancakes at our party. No, wait— waffles! With berries and chocolate chips and whipped cream."

"Sounds great. I'll see you later. And Mae—" Rich reached out to her as she jumped up from the step. "Thanks for telling me all this. You've really helped me a lot." The little girl grinned at him and ran up the stairs, followed by her sister. Fawn gave a little wave as she went inside and shut the door as carefully as her mother had.

Rich sat and thought. Dawn spread rosy pink across the sky and then faded as the sun rose. His girlfriend had disappeared, her step-brother had just overdosed, and he felt absurdly happy. Clearly, he was an awful person. But he couldn't get over the relief he felt that the world had proved itself to be nothing like he thought it was.

Ghosts and demons and inter-dimensional travel—he suddenly decided that he preferred this reality to the rational one, in which the person he loved best in all the world was crazy. He had to find Cathy and tell her that he believed in her, and then he had to try to help her fix this situation. Would Blake come out of his coma if Bunny were able to get back into his body?

Rich had no idea, but he was getting ahead of himself. The first thing to do—after he got some food, showered, and brushed his furry-feeling teeth—was figure out how to get to Holly Place. She had to be there, he felt sure. Should he head for the dump and hope he got lucky? That didn't feel right. Where, then?

He'd go to the library instead. That didn't seem logical, but he felt like he should trust his gut for once instead of trying to plan things out according to a mental flow chart. He planted his crutches, lifted himself up off the Harfords' porch step, and went home.

Once he had eaten and washed up and felt human again, he realized he could catch the school bus into town and walk to the library from there. That would save time and energy. He didn't know how far he'd have to go to find Cathy. He was strong, but he felt like he should conserve his stamina for whatever lay ahead.

At the library, Mrs. Greenlese greeted him with surprise. "No classes today, Mr. Mallory?"

"Independent study project," he answered. "I'll be in the Reference Room, if that's all right."

The ancient librarian eyed him knowingly over her glasses, but said nothing as she handed him the key.

The silence of the Reference Room settled upon him like a comforting quilt. He looked around. He was still running on pure instinct and didn't have any idea what to do now that he was here. After hanging the key on its hook near the door, he went between the tall shelves holding encyclopedias of all kinds and toward his favorite seat by the window. As he came around the corner of the last of the stacks, he stopped and gaped.

A girl about Fawn's age perched on a glass case that held some of Kashkawan's oldest historical relics. Except for her lank blond hair and the dark purple circles under her tired eyes, she looked just like a younger version of Cathy. She had bare feet and wore a filthy, fancy dress that might once have been white or pink, and she clutched a brown-stained blanket around her shoulders.

"I'm so glad you're here, Richard," she said, her smile belying her wretched state.

Rich tried to recover himself. "Does Mrs. Greenlese know you're in here?" he finally asked. As the words came out of his mouth, he mentally slapped his forehead at his idiocy.

The waif laughed. "I wouldn't put anything past her. She's much older than she looks."

"Who are you?"

"That depends," she answered. "And it doesn't really matter right now. You're here to look for Cathy, yes?"

Rich nodded.

"Thanks for coming here." She stood up on the glass, and as slight as the girl looked, Richard doubted the display case could hold her weight for long. "I hoped you would pay attention," she continued. "I'm glad you did. I need your help, and we have to hurry." She extended her hand to him.

"What are you doing up there? That glass is going to shatter."

"Come and see," she said, and pointed down at the display between her muddy feet.

Despite his confusion, Rich obeyed. Looking down into the case, he saw that an engraving of Holly Place lay inside, alongside a fancy metal key, a crystal bird, and what looked like a spoon made out of tortoiseshell or horn. Rich had never seen that engraving before, but he knew that Mrs. Greenlese rotated the contents of the case frequently.

"I'm hurt," the girl said. "I can't stray far from the house, but its image here helps me. That's why I'm here instead of in your backyard. Give me your hands."

Rich looked up. The girl looked like she was eight or nine, but her eyes seemed far older. "I can't," he said. "I'll fall if I let go of my crutches."

"Trust me," she answered, and reached down to him. When he hesitated, she said, "What else are you going to do?"

Rich smiled tightly and nodded. Bracing himself on one crutch, he held up his right hand to her. She grasped it, then grinned and wiggled the fingers of her other hand. Rich exhaled and put aside the fear that he was going to fall to the floor and drag this girl down on top of him. As fast as he could, he dropped his crutch and lunged up to reach her. As he took her hand, heat surged down his arms, through his torso, and along each twisted leg. He looked down in awe as his twisted legs straightened before his eyes. He lifted one foot, then set it down and lifted the other. He had never borne all his weight on his own two legs before. He looked back up at the girl, unashamed of the tears streaming down his cheeks.

"I'm very sorry, but it's only temporary," she said.

Rich swallowed a lump of disappointment. "That's okay," he muttered. "This is miracle enough, even if it's only for five minutes."

"Now, climb up here with me," she directed. "You don't need to worry. The case will bear your weight."

"If you can fix my legs, I'll believe anything you say," Rich said. Still holding the girl's hands, he clambered up on top of the case.

"Don't let go," she ordered. "And you might want to close your eyes."

Rich obeyed, and for the second time that morning, he felt his stomach lurch as if he were falling a great distance.

"All right," the girl said quietly. "We're here."

"What?" Rich opened his eyes, fully expecting to find them still balanced atop the Reference Room's display case. Instead, they stood inside the vast front hall of a mansion. Rain pelted its many windows, with wind and water coming in through several broken panes and soaking the faded curtains. Lightning flashed repeatedly, with the loudest thunder Rich had ever heard crashing right behind it.

Dead leaves scudded across the dusty floor, coming to rest against the base of twin staircases that looked too rickety to use. Moss furred the tiles of the floor nearest the windows and the sagging front door.

"It's real," he breathed. "This is Holly Place? But how can it be pouring here when it was perfectly clear in town? And what happened? Cathy told me the house didn't look abandoned. This place . . . has seen better days."

"You are right; it has. Zared—the being who stole the body of Cathy's stepbrother—has been mounting attacks of increasing power and efficiency on us. Now he has made a mistake, and by so doing he has been forced to leave the body he stole years ago. This makes him both stronger and more vulnerable. And though he has left the body, he has not released it—nor will he, unless forced. Cathy needs to break the bond that Zared has created with Bunny's body. When that happens, and Bunny is restored to himself, the house will heal."

The girl let go of Rich's hands. He wobbled and threw out his arms for balance.

"I don't know how to walk," he said.

"I shouldn't think so. But you'll learn quickly. Follow me."

She moved to the wainscoting on the wall between the two flights of stairs. She pressed one of the carved wood panels and turned another panel forty-five degrees at the same time. A door that had previously been invisible opened outward, revealing another staircase much more modest—but sturdier-looking—than the two that flanked this great hall. She turned and beckoned to him.

Rich lifted one foot and half stepped, half fell forward. He found his balance and tried again. He gained confidence with each step; by the time he got to the girl's side, he was feeling pretty steady.

"Well done. Now—we go up. We'll have to take the back stairs to the very top of the house."

"Is that where Cathy is?"

"No. She has been in the deepest cellar for quite a while, as time is measured in your realm. But the only way to reach her there is to go up." A huge peal of thunder shook the house at her words, shattering nearly all of the windows behind them. Glass crashed to the stone floor in a shower, and the wind howled in with greater fury.

"Hurry," the girl urged. While she turned a lever that closed the door behind them, Rich grasped the banister and obeyed.

CHAPTER TWENTY-EIGHT

THE SHARP EDGE

NARROW, CRUMBLING STAIRS led downward from the cellar's arched doorway. Cathy held out the stone egg, but couldn't see beyond a few feet. No railing provided support for the perilous descent. When Cathy reached out to the wall instead, she snatched her hand away again immediately. Cathy looked more closely at the wall's slimy, cold surface. Water ran down it in rivulets—all the way down to the steps, she could see now. She wiped her palm on her jeans and looked down again. She didn't have any choice but to go down; she'd just have to watch her step very carefully.

Down, down, she went. After at least a couple hundred steps, her thighs ached with the monotonous effort. After many, many more, she reached the bottom. Water pooled on the floor and trickled away into the darkness. The walls looked much rougher here; this seemed to be a true cavern as opposed to something man-made. Cathy shivered as the cold seeped into her bones. If she kept moving, the exercise would help keep her warm. She had to crouch as the tunnel narrowed and the ceiling got lower and lower. Finally she had to get down on her hands and knees in order to keep moving forward. Would it keep getting smaller until she got trapped? She tried not to wonder how many tons of rock and earth lay above her head. She couldn't panic now, no matter how dark and cold and wet it got down here.

Condensation dripping from the tunnel's ceiling had completely soaked her, and black slime covered her arms and legs. The sound of her breathing seemed amplified as it bounced off the wet rock that surrounded her. Finally, when her hands got so cold and numb that she couldn't feel how badly the rough floor had scraped her palms, the tunnel opened out again into a much bigger cave. She sat back on her ankles and held up the egg. She could see nothing in any direction.

But she could hear. A faint muttering and whispering came to her through the cold gloom. Was someone down here with her? Cathy's heart thudded faster. She had nowhere to hide and no real way to protect herself, and she couldn't sit here in this dim, cold place forever.

"Hello?" she called out. Her echoing voice sounded as frightened as she felt. *Get a grip*, she told herself, and forced confidence she did not feel into her next words. "Is there anybody out there?"

The muttering stopped. Then came a voice Cathy would know anywhere, even though it sounded rough with disuse, and even though she hadn't heard it in five years. "Cathy?"

Tears sprang into her eyes, and a wave of emotion threatened to close her throat. "Dad?" she choked. "Dad, is that you?" She jumped to her feet and started looking for her dead father.

She found him slumped in a corner of the cave behind a large stalactite that had grown until it fused to the floor. He clasped his knees to his chest and swayed back and forth. He seemed younger than she remembered him, but paler and thinner, too. He wore his oldest, most comfortable sweatpants and a faded Columbia T-shirt—the clothes he'd always worn on Saturday mornings when he'd gone out to get the newspaper and fresh bagels. Despite his haggard face, he had never looked better to Cathy, and her heart felt like it would burst with too much joy and pain. She fell to her knees and reached for him, but he shrank away and threw his arms up to ward her off.

"You can't touch me," he said. "I haven't ascended yet. Besides, your hands will go right through me." Letting his arms drop, he looked at her and gave her a crooked smile. "It's good to see you, though."

"Yeah, likewise," she managed, knuckling the tears out of her eyes. "Daddy, what are you doing here? I thought you'd be in—"

"Heaven?" he finished when she hesitated. He gazed beyond her for a moment. "Heaven and Hell are all around us all the time. But I've stayed here in this world because of you."

"What do you mean? How did you know I was here?"

"Cathy, my darling. You burn so bright and fierce, I'd know where you were no matter what. I haven't been far from you all along. I've watched your struggles against the wekufe. But it's your need that allows you to see me now."

Cathy nearly started crying again at her father's tender tone. To hide her emotion, she looked around at the little bit of the cave she could see in the dim light. "But I don't know what I'm doing, or even know where I am," she admitted. "I was in this house in the woods, and then a little girl took me to Central Park—even though I don't think I really left the house when we went there—and now? I don't know what day it is or what I'm doing here. I'm sick of wandering around in the dark. I just want to get out of here and find some answers."

"You have all the answers you need."

Cathy hung her head in frustration. "You sound like Januarye," she said. "And I have seen how strong the wekufe are. What could I possibly do to defeat Zared?"

Her father stood and indicated for her to do so as well. "The wekufe has made a grave error. He gained power and got careless as a result. He has harmed Blake's body to the extent that he has been forced out of it. It will only heal properly if it is restored to its rightful owner, but Zared will do everything he can to keep that from happening."

Cathy looked up at her father's kind, handsome face and hugged herself to keep from reaching out to him. "Forced out of it? Did this just happen? Then Bunny doesn't need me anymore. He can just get back in his body now, right?"

"Yes, if he can get past Zared and the wards that he has put around the body. But Zared would rather kill the body then give it up, and even disembodied, he is more powerful than Bunny is. But he is not more powerful than you." Her father bent down until his shadowed, brown eyes were level with her own. "You have that," he nodded at the egg. "And you have your heritage, which is potent, indeed—especially in this place, where your mother's ancestors lived for so long. You are a worthy opponent of even this wekufe." His gaze held hers and seemed to infuse her with strength and warmth. Then he straightened. "I must go now," he said.

"No!" cried Cathy. "Not yet. I've missed you so much! And I have so many questions. Please don't leave me alone here."

Her father grimaced as if with great pain and put out his hands as if to cup her face between them. "I wish with my whole heart that I could stay right here beside you," he said. "But I will not be far away, I promise. When you need me, you will know that I am watching you. I love you, Cathy." And then he vanished, as if he had never been there at all. Alone once more, Cathy sank back down to her knees and sobbed.

She flinched when she felt a gentle hand on her shoulder. She looked up to see Rich standing over her—without crutches—and screamed.

CHAPTER TWENTY-NINE

A LONELY HUNTER

HOLDING THE LIMP HAND of his comatose son, Malcolm lays his head on the edge of the hospital bed's mattress. Sadly, his body remembers this position well. He spent many nights at Gail's side during the last few weeks of her losing battle with cancer. He has slept little recently. Efforts to find his oldest stepdaughter and Athena's panic at their failure have kept him from getting much rest. And now his only child has done something unthinkable to himself.

After many tests, the doctors have confirmed that Blake's heroin overdose has damaged his brain. The medical team in charge of his care has not yet reached consensus, but it seems likely that Blake will never wake up again. Fear and anger and disbelief war within Malcolm. How has he not noticed that his own son has been abusing drugs? In his mind, he runs over all the stereotypical signs—withdrawal from family life, flouting of rules, slipping grades, radical changes in appearance and friends and musical tastes—Blake has not exhibited a single one of them. But perhaps Malcolm has not looked closely enough. Has he been so busy and happy with Athena and their new life together that he has overlooked symptoms that he should have seen?

Despite this turmoil of worry, his physical discomfort, and the beeping and whirring of the machines keeping Blake's body alive, Malcolm slides into an uneasy sleep.

A gentle touch on his shoulder rouses him. Lifting his head, he sees Gail standing beside him. Wonder and relief course through him. He stands and takes her into his arms, his head fitting over the top of hers just as it always did. He hugs her tightly and wishes that he could lose himself in her embrace. After a moment, she leans up and whispers into his ear. Her words are so faint that he does not catch them.

"I'm sorry," he says, "What did you say?" He draws away from her and looks into her beautiful eyes. Tears gleam at their edges, threatening to fall at any moment.

"This is not our son," she repeats.

"What are you talking about?" His uneasy storm of emotions has returned, along with something new that he never imagined he would feel toward his long-dead wife: suspicion.

She squeezes his arms gently and runs one hand up his shoulder to caress his face and hold the corner of his jaw in her hand. "You know what I'm talking about," she says. "Our son has been gone for years. You know this. What is here," she gestures to the bed, "Is just his shell. You must let him go."

Malcolm shies away from her touch. "What do you mean?" he asks, but he can no longer meet her gaze. He knows.

The knot in his stomach, the one that has been there for nearly as long as he can remember, confirms the truth of her words. He does not know how or why, but Blake has not been truly himself since he was about nine years old. He remembers his oft-recurring dream about Gail and Blake and suddenly sees its meaning and import for the first time. Guilt chokes him. In his grief over Gail's death, he deceived himself, unwilling to acknowledge that his son left him as surely as his wife did.

"You have lived a lie," Gail says, her eyes and voice turning to ice. Her words cut him to the core; never when she was living did she speak so harshly to him. "An impostor took over our son's life, and you allowed it to happen. You turned a blind eye to his suffering night after night. I never would have believed that you had such selfishness within you. But you can end this now."

Malcolm shakes his head. "What could I have done? I know I have handled things badly, and I'm sorrier than you can know about that. But what can I do now? You are suggesting that I . . . end his life. I can't do that; I can't kill my son. He could come back, couldn't he? How can it be too late? Is there no other way to fix what went wrong?"

"There is no other way. This is your responsibility, Malcolm. No one else can do this."

Malcolm tears his eyes away from Gail. He never would have guessed that she would be capable of such calm cruelty. Looking down at his son's pale face, he acknowledges within himself the wrong that he has done by omission. The lively, intelligent person who has been his closest companion for years—that was not his true child. But will releasing Blake's body atone for Malcolm's wrong, or will it compound his sin infinitely?

"Where is he?" he whispers, tears sliding down his cheeks. "Where is Blake, really?"

Gail moves to his side and clasps his hand, her tone gentle once more. "He is in a kind of hell." Regret tinges her words. "He came looking for me and was taken advantage of. He has been out of his body for so long that he cannot even remember who he is. He is powerless to move on while his physical shell lives. You must release him so that he can come with me."

Fear nauseates him, but Malcolm sees that Gail is right. The right thing, the unselfish thing would be for him to relinquish Blake. He gulps back a sob and nods his head. "Tomorrow I will tell the doctors that I want to let him go," he says. Sinking back into his chair, he takes Blake's hand again and lets his grief drip onto the starched white sheets. His dead wife bends over him and lays her cheek on the top of his head.

"That is right," she whispers. Malcolm feels her move away, but does not watch her go. In the morning, he will follow her counsel and give the order to terminate Blake's life support. For the rest of this night, though, he will keep vigil and pray for forgiveness.

CHAPTER THIRTY

NIGH UNTO AN ANGEL

"GET AWAY FROM ME!" Cathy shrieked, shoving Rich with all her strength. He stumbled backward and fell, and she jumped to her feet. She backed up and held out the egg as if it were a knife. "I don't know how you found me, but I will hurt you again. Stay on the floor where I can see you."

Rich stared up at her with a wounded look in his eyes. "Cathy, what are you talking about? I came here to help you."

Cathy laughed wildly. "Very funny. We've had this conversation before, you freak. Don't you remember, before I pushed you into that pit?"

A skeletal, nearly bald child dressed in rags limped into the egg's pale circle of light. She looked at Cathy with hollow, bruised eyes, and Cathy suffered a shock of recognition. "Januarye? Is that you? What did he do to you?" she cried.

Januarye shook her head slowly. "This really is Richard," she rasped. "He hasn't done anything to me. Zared's attacks on *Hulst-huys* keep weakening me. He is very close to destroying me entirely."

"But how can that be Rich?" Cathy firmly squelched the desperate hope that rose within her and tried her best for sarcasm. "Did you heal his legs somehow?"

Rich spoke up. "She did, but it won't last. She gave me some of the last of her strength, and it will only keep me walking as long as I stay within Holly Place's walls. Or under them," he finished, looking around. "We went through a door in the attic. I thought we'd end up on the roof, but instead—" He cocked an eyebrow and grinned.

This actually was Rich, Cathy realized. She rushed to him and held out her hands. He grasped them and levered himself upright, then caught her up in a tight hug. "You were right," he murmured. "You were right all along about all this crazy stuff. I'm sorry for doubting you."

"Don't worry about it, Mr. Logic. And I'm sorry I pushed you just now," she said.

"Yeah, what was that?" Rich drew back and looked down into Cathy's face.

"I thought you were Zared. It's a long story. I'll tell you about it later." Cathy glanced at Januarye, who stood shivering and wheezing beside them. "What now?" she asked the girl.

"I need Rich to stay with me. Zared shouldn't be able to find his way down here, not for a while at least. If he manages to do so, he will destroy me. You need to walk between the worlds and stop him, or I won't be of use to you any longer—and your chances of helping Bunny will shrink to nearly nothing. Rich will watch over me here so that I can help you as long as possible."

"Help me? How?"

Januarye pointed to the egg. "That stone contains a good portion of my essence. Normally it can be replenished, but there isn't time and I am not strong enough."

"You mean—if I use it, I'm slowly killing you?"

"It's for a good cause," Januarye flashed a tired smile. "And it's not killing me, not exactly. Your using the stone is the least of my worries. But go now. Get to the hospital. Both Zared and Bunny should be nearby the body. Malcolm will be there, too."

Cathy rolled her eyes. "Stupid Malcolm," she said through gritted teeth. "He's always in the way."

"Put aside your personal feelings for him and remember what it feels like to blame yourself for the death of the one you love most."

Her father. How did Januarye know that? Hanging her head, Cathy sighed. "I'll do my best."

"I know," Januarye said simply. "Remember what you saw in the park. And use the stone. You'll know the right thing to do at the right time ..." Januarye's voice faded and she collapsed.

Rich knelt and picked her up, cradling her gently in his arms. He leaned over her for a moment, listening intently. "She's still breathing," he said after a moment. "And I think she can hold on a little longer. You heard her; go. I'll do what I can to keep her safe." He moved to the sheltered, dry spot where Cathy had found her father and lowered himself to the ground. He inclined his head toward the part of the cavern that Cathy had not yet explored. "There's a door that way. That's how we got here. I don't know how you're supposed to 'walk between the worlds,' but I'm guessing that going that way is the first step."

Cathy crouched next to him and felt Januarye's forehead. The girl burned with fever, and her breathing was fast and shallow. "I hope she'll be all right," she whispered. Then she leaned over and kissed Rich, savoring the feel of her lips on his. "I hate to leave you here in the dark."

"We'll be okay. You should go, though."

"Yeah. Let me just go slay that dragon, and we'll be back together doing our French homework before you know it." She grinned, and added, "Be safe. I'll come back as soon as I can." She stood up and walked in the direction Rich had indicated. Turning back, she saw him huddled in the shadows that gathered in her wake. "I'll come back," she repeated, and hoped she was speaking the truth even as the words left her mouth.

She found the heavy, iron-bound door very quickly. She twisted its large latch and pulled hard. A gust of rain-filled wind hit her as the door flew open. She stepped through it and yanked it shut after her, then peered through the storm to get her bearings. A flash of lightning showed her that she stood on a tiny cupola on Holly Place's roof; thunder nearly deafened her a split second later. She stayed well clear of the iron railing that surrounded the platform. She had to find a way down before she got hit.

The thunder boomed and echoed as it rolled up the Palisades and on past Storm King Mountain and Breakneck Ridge. Hundred-foot maples and oaks danced wildly in the wind, their leaves sighing and twigs clattering. After the silent darkness through which she had been traveling for so long, the storm overwhelmed Cathy with its fury and noise.

The stone egg still glowed—just barely—and by its light, she saw that there was one good thing about the cold, pouring rain. It sluiced the cave slime off her arms as if she were under a pressure washer. She squinted through the gloom, looking for a way down. She didn't see anything—no convenient rope or ladder. Should she go back through the door in the hopes that it led to the attic this time? She fumbled with its handle, but it had locked shut somehow. *Great.*

The cupola cut into the exact middle of the back roof of the house. Looking to her left, she saw that the branches of a huge, white-limbed sycamore tree extended out over the corner of the roof. If she could get there, she might be able to climb onto one of them and eventually down to the ground. She already felt as if she'd done quite enough tree climbing during this whole, hellish adventure, but she didn't see any alternative.

She crouched under the door's lintel as lightning struck a weather vane on one of Holly Place's chimneys. *Get a grip,* she told herself. She could do this. She'd just have to make sure she didn't fall the way she had in her tapestry dream, since she was reasonably sure she was awake this time. As the thunder boomed, she quickly climbed over the cupola's railing and leaned her whole body against the flat, slippery tiles of the steep slate roof.

The copper rain gutter creaked and strained as she inched her feet along it. Cathy prayed that it would bear her weight. Slipping sideways, she dislodged several roof tiles, which slid past her and down through the air to shatter into bits on the stone terrace far below. Her eyes followed as one tile fell, and she quickly screwed them shut and brought her head back up as dizziness engulfed her. The ground looked much too far away for comfort. She concentrated on getting toward the corner of the house.

Finally, she made it there and grasped one of the substantial sycamore branches. She straddled it and settled on it experimentally.

Would it hold her? She knew that lightning could strike this tree at any moment. She had to get down as quickly as possible. She gripped the branch with her knees and crept along it, forcing herself to focus on getting to the tree's trunk.

Once she did, she found it relatively easy to get to the ground, hugging the massive trunk and using the irregular branches to step down until she reached the lowest one. Cathy dropped from it to the ground and leaned back against the trunk to rest. Her raw hands throbbed. She trembled, soaked to the skin and exhausted. She peered out from under the sycamore's dense foliage. The condition of Holly Place shocked her. Every window had been shattered, and ragged bits of curtain flapped wetly from their frames in the wind. The buttery limestone walls now looked diseased, streaks of mold and decay running down from under the house's eaves. What had Zared done?

She couldn't afford to sit and wonder, she realized. Her father had said that Blake's body was in serious danger. She had to get to the hospital as quickly as possible. After retying her sneakers, she set out through the rain at a jog. As she rounded the house and started down the path, the storm lessened almost immediately. By the time she had reached the end of the grassy, sycamore-lined walk, the rain and wind had stopped. She looked back at the house in the gray light of dawn. The storm's fury still assaulted it. It must have to do with Zared. She turned back to her path.

As she did so, she halted, nearly falling over with sudden vertigo. Ahead of her, two equally vivid realities superimposed themselves over one another. One was the rutted dirt path she had always taken to and from Lake Road. The other was a trackless, trash-heaped mess bordered by a high, razor-wire-topped, chain link fence.

"The dump," she breathed. She remembered what Januarye had said about walking between the worlds. Would doing so allow her access through such a barrier? She turned her attention to the dirt path and willed it to dominate the other scene. She summoned her faith and ran forward, insisting to herself that there was no fence blocking her path.

And then she was through. When she got to Route 403, the double vision continued to plague her. This time, she focused on the modern asphalt and concrete instead of the twisted deer track that ran through dense undergrowth into the distance. When she got to town, she turned left at Kashkawan's one traffic light and headed toward the hospital. After she veered into its driveway toward the glass double doors of the emergency room, she stopped abruptly. Dozens of wekufe clustered as thickly as vultures around the various entrances to the hospitals. As one, they turned their dark, hungry gaze upon her. Meanwhile, humans walked past her in either direction as if she—and they—were not there.

"They can't hurt you," she whispered to herself. She stood as tall as she could and clutched the egg in her fist. One tall, rangy wekufe glanced at her hand and shrunk back, hissing a warning at his peers. Cathy faked courage she did not have and strode up to him.

"Where is Zared?" she demanded.

The wekufe opened his mouth and cawed like a crow. Words slithered into Cathy's mind as he did so.

Inside. Near the body that will not be his for long.

The others hissed their agreement. Cathy suppressed a shudder as she hurried past them into the hospital. Inside, the staff didn't seem to notice her—Cathy guessed she was probably invisible as long as she stayed between the worlds. The wekufe thronging the corridors certainly noticed her, though. They glared at her but pulled away as she passed them. There were so many, and she guessed that each one pulsed with desperate hunger for a body to possess. She could see it in their tortured eyes and envious sneers.

Finding Blake's hospital room was easy. She simply followed the gathering wekufe to where the crowd was thickest. Gingerly, she sidled past them—she didn't know what it would feel like to touch one, and she didn't want to find out—and went inside.

Blake's body lay pale and inert on the hospital bed. Tubes and wires emerged from tape on both his arms, and more snaked up his nostrils and down his throat. A beeping, flashing array of monitors encircled the head of the bed. Malcolm slumped unconscious over the side of the gurney, one of Blake's hands clasped in his. How could he sleep with all that machinery going?

"He's worn out with worry."

Cathy turned to the far corner of the room, not surprised that her mother could read her thoughts. Athena arose from a chair by the window and held out her arms. Cathy ran into them and hugged her mother tightly.

"You'll never know how terrified I've been about you," said her mother.

What could she say in response? There was no point in trying to explain where she had been, or in making up more plausible lies. A bare-bones apology would have to do for now. "I'm so sorry, Mom."

"I'm just glad you're safe. We'll deal with the consequences of your actions some other day. I simply don't have the energy for that now."

"Fair enough." Cathy let go of her mother and looked back toward Blake's bed. Poor Malcolm. Remorse and pity filled her. However annoying she had once found her stepfather, she realized that she didn't want him to suffer like this. "What's going on?" she asked. "It looks like I've missed a lot."

"Your stepbrother overdosed on heroin two days ago. He's been in a coma ever since. Malcolm has not left his side for more than a moment," Athena said. The starkness of her words chilled Cathy.

"Was it an accident, or was it on purpose?"

"We don't know for sure. Malcolm has been in agony since it happened, trying to figure out where he went wrong as a father. He says he never would have suspected, though, and I certainly didn't see it coming."

Cathy gazed at her stepbrother's pale face and said nothing. Out of the corner of her eye, she saw her mother looking at her intently.

"You know, honey, I must say that I find it odd that you don't seem surprised at all. Did you know something about this?"

Cathy shifted from foot to foot uneasily. "I had my suspicions," she said at last. "And I saw Rich just a few minutes ago. That's how I knew to come here."

"Ah. Richard. He's been a good neighbor, hasn't he?"

Her words were too casual. Cathy glanced sideways at her mother, who kept a perfectly straight face. She knew or at least suspected something was up between Cathy and Rich. This is how she always acted when she was fishing for information. Cathy figured she owed her mother whatever honesty she could give her without ending up in a mental institution as a result.

"He's . . . I guess we're . . . going out." Cathy cringed at her own awkwardness. Why wasn't there an easy way to say that she had fallen in love with her best friend?

"Mmm."

Cathy chanced a look at her mother again. Her eyes crinkled at the corners. She had known. Cathy knew from experience, however, that Athena would not pursue the issue. Instead, she'd wait until Cathy brought it up again. Fine. Cathy was happy to let this issue lie for the moment. She had other things on her mind at the moment. And once again, her mother proved prescient.

"You said you'd had suspicions about Blake. As I said, Malcolm and I were completely in the dark. We're both still reeling from the shock, as you might imagine. What did we miss? What was it that made you wonder about him? It would really help me to know."

What should she say? Even if she was successful in restoring Bunny to his body, he would still have to deal with the consequences of Zared's actions. She had to do as much damage control as possible. That way, even if she failed, Malcolm and Athena would be shielded from the bulk of Zared's disgusting behavior. She made a mental note to wipe his computer drive if worst came to worst. Her family didn't need to see that side of the whole mess.

"It . . . was just a feeling I got a couple of times. He just seemed . . . a little too intense for the real world, you know?"

Her mother pressed her lips together. "I suppose," she said finally.

Malcolm stirred and moaned in his sleep. Athena went to his
side and laid her hand on the back of his neck. He quieted and resumed his soft snoring. "He needs to rest," she said quietly. "He has
a very difficult thing to do later this morning."

Cathy looked at the clock on the wall. It was nearly 7:00. Which
day? She had no idea. Blake had been in a coma for two days, but
how long had she been away before that had happened? She did her
best to suppress a yawn. Her desire to be resting in her own bed was
almost a physical ache.

Her mother came to her and smoothed her damp, matted hair
away from her forehead. "I don't know what you've been doing, but
you look awful. You need to rest. I'll run you home, and then I'll
come back here and stay with Malcolm."

"I can stay with you and keep you company," Cathy offered. She
was confused. Nothing was happening the way she thought it would.
Wasn't she supposed to do something here at the hospital?

Yes, she remembered after a few seconds of mental effort. She
had been expecting to find Bunny and Zared here in this room, not
her mother. What was going on?

"Oh, no. I don't think so, Cathy. That's very thoughtful, but I'm
sure the doctors wouldn't be happy to find practically the whole family camped out here when they come for rounds in a little while.
Come on. I'll drive you home so that you can get some sleep. We'll
catch up later today when you're feeling better."

Fatigue overwhelmed Cathy. Had relief at being with her mother drained all of the adrenaline from her system? If so, it didn't leave
her much to work with when it came to stamina. She could barely
keep her eyes open. She didn't know whether her nap in the rolled-
up tapestry had been an hour ago or a day ago—she couldn't keep
anything straight. Her mother's cool touch on her forehead felt so
good, so calming.

"You're asleep on your feet, sweetie," her mother whispered, taking her hand. "Let's go."

Cathy nodded numbly and followed her mother out the door.

The wekufe scattered like rats when they saw Cathy and Athena. *That's right, filth*, Cathy thought. *You think* I'm *bad? Don't mess with my mother.* The edge of her rubber sneaker caught on the linoleum floor, but her mother's strong hold on her arm kept her from tripping. "Sorry, Mom," she mumbled with a drowsy chuckle. "I don't know if I can even make it to the car."

"Maybe you're right." Her mother's voice sounded like it was coming down a long tunnel. "Let's just find somewhere quiet where you can lie down. Someplace where no one will bother you for a good, long while."

Cathy dimly felt Athena's arm go around her waist to keep her vertical. Her mother had always been so strong. She leaned against her shoulder and gave in to the immense weariness that pressed down on her mind. She was barely conscious as they backed through a swinging door into a room with colored glass windows and long, padded pews. She surrendered as her mother laid her on one of them. Athena pressed her cool palm against Cathy's forehead again, then bent down and placed a soft, lingering kiss on her cheek. "Just sleep now," she whispered. "When you wake up, everything will be so much better."

The last sound Cathy heard before she fell into a dark pool of oblivion was the soft *snick* of the door's lock turning.

CHAPTER THIRTY-ONE

A TRUSTY TREE

Rich sat in the dark and hummed. Januarye nestled in his arms, her frail body radiating feverish heat as she slept deeply. In an attempt to keep track of time and stay alert, he had sung through every Beatles song he could think of. Now his voice was hoarse, and he'd gone through "Blackbird" several times.

Blackbird singing in the dead of night

Take these broken wings and learn to fly

All your life

You were only waiting for this moment to arise

The words seemed like they had been written for exactly this situation, Rich mused.

"That one's my favorite," Cathy said. "I don't think I've ever heard you sing before." Bright light came from a camping lantern in her hand. She looked a lot cleaner—and more tired—than she had when she had left.

Rich looked up and smiled. "Hey," he said. "It's like you came out of nowhere. That was faster than I thought it would be, and nothing bad happened while you were gone. Nothing at all happened, actually. So—did you do it? Did you slay the dragon?"

Cathy nodded with a tired grin. "Our French homework awaits, my prince. Let's get out of here."

"What about Januarye?" He looked down at his charge. She didn't seem any better. Her skin stretched like yellow parchment across her small skull, and her hair was completely gone now. He frowned. He had hoped that once Cathy had done whatever she had to do to Zared, Januarye would heal instantly. That must not be how magic worked in the real world. This wasn't Oz, after all. Maybe Cathy had taken the last of Januarye's strength when she used that little egg. He looked up at Cathy again and frowned.

"Hey, what happened to that necklace that Januarye gave you? The one with the stone?" he asked.

Cathy raised her hand to her throat. "Oh. I used it up. When I fought with Zared. I guess it's gone now."

"Wow. I bet it was some battle. I hope you'll give me every detail." Rich shifted his legs so that he was on his knees and then carefully stood up. "Anyway, you didn't answer my other question. What can we do for her?" he said, nodding at Januarye.

Cathy pursed her lips. "I'm not sure. Now that we don't need her or the house anymore, I'm guessing we can just leave them behind. They'll probably heal with time. Let's take her someplace where she can be comfortable and leave her to rest."

Cathy's casual tone surprised Rich. She must be exhausted, he realized, and she was probably suffering from shock after everything she'd endured. He assumed she must know what she was talking about, though. "Okay, let's go then," he said. "Where now?"

"Here, trade me first." She held out her arms. "You take the light, and I'll carry her. Your arms must be worn out."

"No, that's okay. You know me. My legs are useless—usually— but I've got biceps of steel. You lead the way. You know this house better than I do."

Cathy stared at him for a long moment. There was a hardness in her eyes that Rich had never seen before. "All right," she said finally. "If you insist. Just let me talk to her for a second, though." She set the lantern down on the floor and stepped closer. She laid her hands on Januarye's cheeks very gently. Rich resisted the impulse to lean in and kiss her as she gazed down at the unconscious child.

"Can you hear me, little one?" Cathy whispered. "I hope you can. Because I want you to know that I've won."

With that, she twisted Januarye's skull sharply to the side until the bones in her neck shattered. Rich gasped, too shocked to cry out. The girl's body turned to dust in his arms and sifted to the floor. Agony compounded Rich's horror as pain shot through his legs. He buckled and fell on his face into the gritty filth that had once been a living being. He felt the awful, familiar twists in his bones return, and every muscle in the lower half of his body cramped and spasmed in response.

Standing over him, Cathy laughed. She picked up the lantern. Rich felt the ground heave and tremble. He shielded his head as rocks and pebbles began falling from the cavern's low ceiling.

"Goodbye, Richard," Cathy sang out as she walked away from him through what seemed like a major earthquake. He was in the dark once more.

CHAPTER THIRTY-TWO

FROM THE STRETCH

A CUFF ON HER WRIST zapped Cathy with a jolt of electricity. She startled awake and nearly fell off the narrow pew on which she lay. She looked at her arm. What encircled it was not a cuff, but Bunny's hand.

"Sorry," he said, and let go of her. "I couldn't wake you up, even when I yelled. For a minute, I thought you were dead."

Cathy looked around in confusion at the stained glass windows, white walls, and soft lighting. She rubbed her wrist where he had touched her until the tingling dissipated. "Where are we?"

"The sign in the hall says that this is the hospital's chapel. I snuck in after Zared brought you here. He locked the doors from the outside, though. I don't know how you're going to get out."

Cathy sat up and rubbed her eyes. "Zared brought me here? That's impossible. I haven't even seen him. The last thing I remember, I was talking to my mother. She was going to drive me home."

"That wasn't your mother; it was Zared. I've been hiding under the bed in the room where my body is ever since it was brought here. It seems like Zared hasn't been able to sense my presence ever since he had to leave my body, so as long as he doesn't see me, I'm safe.

"But he's learned something new. He can change the way he appears to people—and he can touch them, too. I couldn't understand why you were even speaking to him until you called him 'Mom.'" He looked the same as he always does to me, but I guess he didn't look that way to you.

"And he did exactly the same thing to my father a little while ago, except he pretended to be my mother. I wanted to jump out of my hiding place and punch him when he did that."

What? Cathy felt like she might throw up. Zared had fooled her completely—again. She had been so relieved to see her mother; how had she not noticed? She had been so real, so familiar. She had even smelled like Chanel, the way she always did. Cathy shuddered as she remembered hugging that . . . thing. It hadn't shocked her to touch him the way it did when she touched Bunny. If he could be that convincing at taking on someone else's appearance, how was she ever going to get rid of him? And why was he still hanging around, anyway?

"If Zared is out of your body now, why can't you just get back in?"

Bunny hung his head. "I tried every way I could think of. He's blocked me somehow. I can't even get close enough to my body to touch it. It burns me when I try. I told you—he's more powerful now than he ever has been before."

Cathy didn't understand how anything could burn Bunny when he wasn't connected to his nerves at the moment. Maybe he still had some kind of nervous system, though. After all, he could see and hear. Maybe the spiritual body was exactly like the physical body— just made out of different material.

Well, there wasn't time to sit and ponder. She stood and went to the chapel's double doors. The deadbolt had been turned and could be opened only with a key. She shook the doorknobs in frustration. She had to find a way out. "How long was I asleep?"

"Only a couple of minutes. Zared left the building after he put you in here. I don't know where he went, or when he'll be back. I feel like we'd better hurry, though."

Cathy checked the windows. They did not open, and she suspected they weren't windows at all, just sheets of colored glass with lights behind them. What now? Even if she managed to get out of here, how would she know who anyone truly was? She turned back to Bunny.

"I saw my dad a while ago, while I was still in Holly Place," she said. "He said that Zared was going to kill your body if he could. Do you know how he plans to do that?"

"Based on what the doctors have told him, my dad has decided that he's going to disconnect me from life support. Zared encouraged him to do that when he was pretending to be my mother. I don't know how to stop him."

That was the "difficult thing" her mother—no, Zared—had mentioned. Cathy's desperation mounted. "Can't you touch your dad and make him see you? Why am I the only one you can zap?"

"You're not the only one. It works on your sisters, too—at least the little one."

"Mae? When did you see her?"

"Zared had trapped me in your house in an invisible box, and I didn't think I'd ever get out. But Mae got me free as if the barrier wasn't even there. Whatever gifts you have—she has them, too."

Gifts—gifts that ran in the family. Cathy remembered the last things Januarye had told her. Could she do as Januarye had directed and walk between worlds again to get out of here? The double vision that had come upon her outside Holly Place had gotten her through a chain link fence. She had relaxed and let the world snap back into focus once she had gotten to Blake's hospital room, though. She had to find a way to get the double vision back.

Bunny. He lived in the unseen world of the wekufe; maybe she could use him as a fulcrum. She stared at him and let everything around him shift out of focus. *Yes.* It took a few seconds, but she could feel something within her moving even though she stood perfectly still. Out of the corners of her field of vision, she could see two realities once more—like looking at a 3D movie without special glasses.

"Follow me," she said. Keeping her eyes unfocused, she walked *through* the chapel doors and into the hallway. Bunny trotted at her side, shrinking closer to her as they passed the mobs of wekufe. Zared's appearance had scattered them, she dimly remembered, but now they seemed to be creeping back to surround Blake's hospital door once again.

Cathy stayed between worlds and walked into Blake's room. With her double focus, she could see the snare that Zared had set around Blake's body. It surrounded him with burning red lines like an intricate cat's cradle. She moved closer to the bed, and noticed that her stone egg's glow intensified as she did so. Januarye had told her to use it; maybe it had some power to cut through this web and free the body. She lifted up the stone and moved it toward one of the burning strands. The little egg shone brighter than a flash bulb for a second, then dimmed, turned gray, and crumbled to ash between her fingers.

Cathy gasped in horror. What had she done? That egg had been part of Januarye's essence. She hadn't realized it was so fragile. Had the snare poisoned it somehow?

"What happened?" cried Bunny.

Cathy couldn't bring herself to answer. Zared's snare remained intact. She had failed.

CHAPTER THIRTY-THREE

RAW MATERIAL

"*BRAVISSIMA.*"

Cathy whirled. Zared stood in the doorway with a broad grin on his pale face, appearing in his wekufe form for the first time.

"Your witch friend is dead, and her power is gone," he sneered, indicating the pile of dust that had once been the stone egg. "Meaning that you are now helpless."

"Bunny, run. Fly," she whispered, and the ghost boy vanished faster than thought.

Zared started after him but then seemed to think better of it. Instead, he sauntered around to the other side of the hospital bed. He reached through the snare and caressed Blake's cheek, his hollow eyes boring into Cathy's all the while.

"What do you mean, 'the witch is dead?'" she demanded.

"Your little companion with the magic house. All gone now. Oh—and so is your boyfriend, that pathetic cripple." The wekufe leered at her, revealing sharp, yellow teeth.

Cathy's heart plummeted. He had found Januarye and Rich.

Or had he? He'd lied convincingly to her so often before. Maybe this was another one of his traps.

"I don't believe you," she said.

"Let me paint a picture for you. A boy huddles in the dirt holding the dying shell of a being that has no business meddling in this realm. I find them together and put them out of their misery—her, by twisting her tiny neck until it snaps like a wishbone. Him? I merely leave him alone as his body returns to its mangled form, and that house and its weak magic collapse all around him. Have I convinced you?" He watched her avidly, clearly hoping to get a rise out of her. It worked.

"Why are you still here?" she shouted. "You blew it. You've ruined any chance you had of keeping Blake's body for yourself, so why don't you move on and go ruin someone else's life?"

Zared chuckled. "I might ask you exactly the same question."

"I'm just trying to help my brother."

"How altruistic. How misguided. Well—I'm just trying to enjoy a little revenge." He nodded at Malcolm, who still slept heavily at the side of the bed. "I can't wait to savor the pain on his face as he watches his precious boy die."

"Revenge for what? Malcolm has loved you and given you everything for years."

Zared's face twisted. "Revenge for all the mind-numbing idiocy I've had to endure from him. The hugs and the fatherly chats and the oppressive worry and the constant interfering."

"You're a real piece of work," Cathy said. "You stole a life, and you have the gall to complain about it? You've had it pretty good for a long time, it seems to me. But that's over now."

Zared leaned over Blake's body and hissed, "Your preaching is fascinating, but you can save your breath. I'm going now. I'm going to hunt down that little eidolon you seem to love so much and crush him out of existence. Then I'm going to come back here and watch his body die. I thought about destroying you first, but I think it will be more fun to let you watch, too." He laughed, and Malcolm whimpered in his sleep.

"I'm not going to let that happen," Cathy said through gritted teeth. She reached out and grabbed several strands of the snare with both hands. Hideous pain seared her skin, but she hung on and began pulling them apart.

"Stop!" roared Zared. He vaulted over the bed and tried to drag her away. When she wouldn't let go, he growled and started savagely biting her shoulders and arms while yanking all the while on her torso.

Cathy screamed and kicked at the wekufe. The snare felt like red-hot wires in her hands, but she kept heaving on them. At the far end of one of them, just where it went under the other side of Blake's body, she saw a thick knot. She realized in an instant that it must be the key to unraveling the snare. Ignoring the feeling of acid dripping into her skin where Zared bit her, she threw herself forward so that she could get to the knot.

She went through the bed and part way through Blake's body as well. She had managed to stay between the worlds, even without help from the egg. Januarye had said that Cathy's chances of defeating Zared were slim without her help, but that didn't mean they were nonexistent. She would keep fighting, no matter what.

She reached the knot. Zared howled when he saw what she was doing and redoubled his attack on her. The strands of the knot felt slippery and alive somehow, like little snakes. She fought back nausea at the thought and kept working. The pain in her hands increased as she fumbled with the knot, trying to find a way to untangle it. As she slid her fingers through a loop, Zared got his hands around her throat and started squeezing. Gagging and choking, she kept picking at the tangle. Green spots danced before her eyes and her stomach roiled.

Just as she was about to black out, she found a distended, pulsing bump on one of the twisted strands. There. That was the crux of the snare, she knew it. She made a fist and squeezed the bump until it popped like a boil. Zared bellowed and let go of her neck, diving forward and grasping at the unraveling strands. He got no purchase; the snare whipped and snapped as it fell apart, then disappeared. Cathy staggered back, retching as she gasped for air. The wekufe turned on her and bared his teeth. He grabbed her by the hair and barked an unpronounceable word. Cathy shrieked as the world imploded.

CHAPTER THIRTY-FOUR

OUTWARD ILLS

SHE STARES NUMBLY *into her bathroom mirror, the dim lights above it stuttering. Her stepbrother stands behind her, nuzzling the nape of her neck and running his hands up and down her back. It tickles when he does that, but not in a good way. Not at all.*

"What do you see?" he murmurs in her ear.

She shakes her head slightly, noticing the way her hair swings as she does so. She has no words to answer him; her mind is completely vacant. They are alone in this place, and they always will be. There has never been anything but this scrap of awful timelessness.

Except.

Beyond her stepbrother's reflection, she glimpses the faintest shadow of a face in the mirror. Its eyes look so familiar to her; she should recognize it, but she cannot. She half closed her eyes to bring it into focus, but it fades into obscurity before she can see it clearly. She wants to lean closer to the mirror's surface so that she can peer after it, but she does not dare. She is careful not to make any sign that something has broken the stasis of the moment. She understands that she must not betray any emotion at all.

Because with the help of that glimpse, she has found fear beyond her numbness. It is so bitter that her insides twist, but it is better than nothing. All the while perfectly motionless as she endures the repulsive touch of her stepbrother's hands, she latches onto the fear, sucks it dry, and digests it. After she has done so, something floats to the top of the black pool where her memory used to be.

The ghost boy.

She fumbles with that idea even as it frays and dissolves. She snatches at the last bit of it as it sinks below the surface of her consciousness and is rewarded with a name.

Bunny.

Everything comes back to her in a rush, and she forces herself not to stagger under the weight of it all. She sees now that the thing standing behind her is not her stepbrother; it is a shadow, a simulacrum. Zared. She tears her eyes away from the mirror and pivots to face her captor.

The wekufe is not there. As Cathy looks around, she sees that the bathroom is no longer there, either. That illusion has vanished with the return of her memory. She now stands amidst a dark, featureless fog with no idea where she truly is or how she can find her way out of it. The sheer nothingness of it terrifies her, but more powerful than her fear is the urgency she feels. If she remains here, Zared will find what he hunts, and she cannot let that happen.

How will she make her way out of this place? She wanders for a while until she decides that this place has no dimension. However Zared has trapped her, physical movement will solve nothing.

The sun. Where is it? It is the only thing she can think of that can be more powerful than a thick fog like this. She tries to remember the last time she saw it, and the memory of her tree dream comes to her.

She wonders whether she is trapped in a dream now, and whether she can find her way to that sunny field if that is the case. She remembers the intensity of that golden light, calls forth the feeling of it as fully as she can—

—And she found herself there, standing in the waving grain under a blue dome of sky with a brazen sun in the exact center of it. Only, looking around, she didn't see the tree. Why would the place she assumed that her imagination had created change on its own? It was as if her dream had come to life independent of her.

The breeze kicked up and grew in intensity until it became a strong wind. Black storm clouds filled the sky, and hail poured down as lightning crashed around her and thunder roared. She put her hands up to her face to protect her eyes as dirt and chaff blew through the air. A sound like a million angry bees grew from a whisper to a shriek—a cyclone. It appeared in the distance and rushed closer to her with freakish speed.

Zared must be aware that Cathy had escaped from her bathroom prison. He was coming after her. She cowered on the ground and tried desperately to come up with a way to escape this place. She thought of Holly Place; this field had originally been in a tapestry in one of its cellars. Had she found her way back? She pictured the house's grand front hall with its many-paned windows, twin staircases, and paneled wainscoting. She thought of the chandelier, blazing with a hundred lit candles—

—And realized she was sitting surrounded by its smoking ruin on a broken stone floor. Shattered glass, scraps of wallpaper, and splintered wood lay everywhere around her. *Hulsthuys* had been destroyed. Its limestone walls had tumbled to the ground. One staircase still leaned crazily up toward the sickly greenish-tinted heavens, its wrecked banister askew and its carpet runner flapping in the wind. Everything else lay scattered, as if the cyclone in the dream field had touched down here and left an indelible mark.

A howl broke the silence. Cathy looked beyond the mansion's wreckage to the trees that encircled Holly Place's lawn. In a line just beyond the edge of the grass stood several hundred wekufe, all with ravenous eyes fixed on her. The howl sounded again, and Cathy saw the wekufe who had uttered it—a lanky female with red hair that fluttered like ragged ribbons behind her. The next demon cawed like a crow; Cathy recognized him from the hospital's front door. The rest of the wekufe joined in, hooting and moaning until Cathy covered her ears with her hands to muffle the din. She lowered them when the sound cut off as abruptly as if someone had hit the power switch on a radio. The demons stood silently, and that was almost worse.

Footsteps crunched through glass and plaster to her right. She looked toward where the dreaming room had once been and saw Zared walking toward her.

"Here you are, Cathy," he spat. "You don't seem to want to stay put, do you? No matter. I can forgo the pleasure of having you witness Blake's death, especially since killing you slowly right here will be so sweet. I'll let your spirit out of your body a little at a time. When I do, those creatures out there will become so frenzied at the idea of assuming your physical form that they'll rip you to tatters and finish the job for me."

Zared towered over her now, gloating. Cathy tried to scoot away from him, but hissed in pain as a large shard of glass slit her right palm open. She looked around for something to stanch the flow of blood and saw a velvet curtain just to her left. She snatched it up and pressed it to her hand.

The wekufe growled and yipped again, and Zared laughed. "They smell your blood and your fear, little Cathy. They know it won't take much now for you to slip from your pretty little body, and they want that badly. Sit there and bleed a bit more. Let's make the bait even sweeter." He danced on the tips of his toes, circling around and taking in his audience.

Cathy bit back a sob. She was not going to give Zared the satisfaction of seeing her break down. Blood had soaked the part of the curtain she had pressed to her palm. She pulled more of it into her lap, dragging its heavy brass rod across the stone floor. Something tumbled along with it. Cathy squinted at it in the gloom. It was the book that Januarye had brought out of the window seat.

Cathy wrapped her hand up tightly in swaths of green velvet, then picked up the old leather book and clutched it to her chest. She took comfort from it, like Mae with her bedraggled stuffed elephant. It was all that remained intact of a place that had been filled with dreams and memory and grace. She rested her chin on its closed pages and watched Zared caper around her, cackling and taunting his fellow demons.

Throb.

The book pulsed against her breastbone in the house's old, familiar rhythm.

How was that possible? Was it trying to speak to her? Cathy stole a glance at Zared, who still preened in front of his envious audience, before surreptitiously opening the book to a page marked with a faded ribbon. The flowing handwriting on the yellowed pages was the same. This time, however, Cathy found she could read the Dutch as easily as if it were English.

She read with a growing recognition that felt like hope. It was the story that Januarye had mentioned to her, about the girl who had fought a monster to rescue her stepbrother. It was about her and Bunny, she realized, even though it looked like it had been written decades, even centuries ago. She began to read aloud, her voice gaining strength as she went.

"... *en het meisje verhoogde het boek en riep* ... and the girl raised the book in her hand and cried, 'Begone, thou Desolate. I name thee Forsaken, and cast thee to thine own.'"

A scream ripped through the air at her words. Cathy looked up to see Zared lunging toward her with bared teeth. She just barely got out of his way. *Aha.* Those words meant something to him.

"Give me that," he snarled as he turned. He charged at her again, and before she could dodge him, his hand snaked out and gave her an enormous shove. She stumbled backward and fell, knocking the side of her head against a chunk of limestone. Warmth flooded her ear and trickled down her neck. Lying amidst the debris, she blinked her eyes. Dizziness and nausea surged through her. She tried to push herself up from the ground, but her arms and legs would no longer obey her.

Zared squatted beside her and leered. He traced his long, bony fingers down her cheek, then put them in his mouth and sucked the blood off of them. The watching wekufe screeched with lust and envy. He closed his eyes in ecstasy. "You taste so good," he murmured. He laid his palm flat on her sternum, pushing slightly—

—and his hand went through Cathy's skin as if she were made out of clay. He wiggled his fingers as he pressed down, searching for something. His eyes burned into hers as he moved within her. *There.* He had latched onto something vital, something unspeakably intimate. It was her core, the real Cathy—everything that she was or hoped to be—and he grasped it in his hand and pulled.

It felt like rape as he pulled her spirit out of her body a little at a time. She screamed as the edges of her soul tore away from her flesh. She willed her limbs to move so that she could fight back, but she was paralyzed, whether from her fall or from Zared's violation of her. She gazed up at his face helplessly, feeling like a butterfly pierced alive by a pin.

"Do keep fighting, Cathy," Zared urged her softly. "It makes this so much better for me." He laughed and wiggled his fingers again before forming a fist. Spasms of scorching agony radiated from Cathy's chest throughout her whole being.

The horrible racket of the other wekufe reached a frenzied peak. The world reeled and careened around Cathy, going in and out of focus—and changing as it did so. She struggled to hold onto her grasp of the between-worlds place. As she tried to orient herself, she noticed that the book still pulsed in her hand, matching its rhythm to the throbbing in her wounded palm.

The book. Januarye had told Cathy it would help her. There must be a reason that she had found it. She clutched it tightly. She tried to repeat the words she had read aloud before, but the words gurgled in her throat. Tears leaked out of her eyes and down the sides of her face. She felt herself going numb all over, and her vision seemed to be darkening from the edges inward.

No. She would not let this happen. She had fought so hard; she couldn't give up now. She ground her teeth together and pulled back against Zared's grip on her spirit. Her stomach heaved at the agony. She gagged back a surge of vomit, her eyes rolling back in her head and her legs flailing as she choked.

Her legs! She had moved them. She could do this. Her hope renewed, she yanked back even harder against Zared until she twisted free of his fingers with a jolt. He was out. Adrenaline coursed through her at the pure relief of it, and with a yell, she butted him in the face with her forehead. As he reeled back, she scrambled up from the ground and kicked him in the gut.

Now. He was down. She had to finish reading what she had started. That was why he had attacked her in the first place—he had known that the book held power over him. She flipped it open, trying not to smear blood on its crumbling pages.

"Voort, gij Verlaten. Ik noem u Verlaten, en werpt u tot uw eigen!"

A beam of white-hot light burst from the pages of the book and shot out at Zared. It enveloped him with a sizzling sound and blasted him out beyond the lawn into the woods and the grasp of the waiting wekufe. Roaring and slavering, they fell upon him and tore him limb from limb until nothing remained of him. Cathy staggered back and looked away from their frenzy. After a few seconds, the wekufe quieted and turned as one back to face Cathy, appetites clearly whetted. She brandished the book at them and they slunk quickly into the shadows.

Cathy looked after them, her legs shaking and her stomach heaving. Blackness encroached on the borders of her vision, and she sat down and put her head on her knees in the hopes that she wouldn't faint. She couldn't stop now. She had to get back to the hospital and find Bunny.

With Zared destroyed, would Bunny know that it was safe to return to his body? Cathy couldn't be sure, and wanted to be there to see him restored. She could tell that she was in shock, her body rebelling against all the demands she had placed upon it. She would just rest here for a few minutes until she felt well enough to make her way back into town. Curling up against what remained of the front porch, she slid into unconsciousness.

CHAPTER THIRTY-FIVE

AS AT THE FIRST

HIGH UP ON THE ROOF of the hospital, Blake sits on the condenser of an air conditioner and gazes at the sky. The day is beautiful, a gentle breeze ruffling leaves that are just beginning to turn yellow and red. The pull of his body has lessened since Zared overdosed, so much so that it is almost comfortable to sit here so far away from it. The connection seems even fainter just now, which he finds is a relief. He basks in the sun, enjoying the faint heat his spirit self is able to feel.

"Blake."

He turns with joy. It does not matter that he has not heard that voice in fifteen years; he recognizes it instantly. His mother sits beside him, her sea-blue eyes smiling into his own. He throws his arms around her and buries his face in her shoulder.

"Mama. I thought I'd never see you again."

She lays her cheek on the top of his head and pats his back. "We've been separated for longer than I would have liked, but now we never will be again. It's time to go."

Blake pulls back. "I can go with you?" He can't believe it. Finally.

His mother smiles and nods.

"Okay!" He jumps off the condenser and somersaults in the air with glee. He stops short, though, as the full import of her assent hits him.

"My body will die," he says.

"Yes."

"But I've been working so hard to get back to myself. And Cathy—my stepsister. She's done all these amazing things to try to help me. It doesn't seem fair."

Blake's mother holds out her hand to him. He goes to her and takes it. "What we can see in the mortal world often seems unfair," she says. "You'll have a different perspective soon, and when you do, you'll realize that there is wisdom even in the most hurtful of situations." She stands up. "Shall we go?"

Blake drops her hand and turns away, afraid that what he wants most in this moment will not be possible. "I want to, but I can't, not yet. I have to say goodbye. Can't I?"

His mother turns her lovely face toward the sun as if listening for something. Then she smiles back at him. "You must be quick. I will come with you."

He is a tall boy, nearly coming up to his mother's shoulder, but she picks him up and cradles him as if he were a baby. In a blink, they are in the hospital room where his body rests. The machines keeping it alive still chitter and chirp like busy squirrels. His father slumps over the bed, but he no longer sleeps. His eyes are screwed shut in concentration and his lips move; he is praying. Blake jumps out of his mother's arms, runs to his father, and throws his arms around him. His father sits up, eyes snapping open in shock. He returns the hug, and Blake is relieved to see that his touch does not seem to bother his father.

He pulls back and stares into his father's tear-filled eyes. He finds he does not have words to express what is in his heart, so he presses a kiss to his father's stubbled cheek and lets go. His father's eyes move from Blake's face to the body on the bed. Then he sees Blake's mother standing at the window and inhales sharply. "Gail," he whispers. Blake hugs his father again and runs to take his mother's hand. She raises her other hand in farewell to his father, and they blink out of the room again.

In the hospital parking lot, Athena and her two younger daughters are getting out of their car. "Bunny!" Mae cries, and Fawn looks over and sees him standing on the pavement, too. He smiles and waves at them both before soaring up and away with his mother at his side. "Did you see a rabbit?" Blake hears Athena ask Mae as he goes.

They fly over the village and the surrounding forest and past the houses on Turley Lane. Blake waves at the house he had hoped to call home. He finds he does not regret that he will spend no more time there. His mother and he are heading toward *Hulsthuys*, Blake realizes, except that the house that was such a haven to him is no longer there. In its place, vast heaps of trash lie baking in the bright sunlight. They alight atop one of them and Blake looks around.

"Why are we here?" he asks his mother, and she points down the junk-studded hill to a pile of fabric that lies jumbled at its base.

Only it's not a pile of fabric; it's Cathy, wrapped in a dirty green velvet cloth. She does not appear to be conscious. He flies down to her at once and puts his hand on her grimy cheek. At his touch, her eyelids flutter open. After a few seconds, she squints up at him.

"Bunny? Is that you?" she asks, her voice hoarse and rough.

He smiles and nods, delighted to see her one last time.

She sits up and looks around, then focuses on Blake again, looking at him more carefully. "You're not back in your body," she cries. "I don't understand. What are you doing here? Why doesn't it hurt when you touch me?"

Blake senses that his mother is at his side once more. "The quality of his existence has changed," she says.

Cathy's mouth drops open at the sight of her. "You're Blake's mother," she says. "How did Bunny finally find you?"

"With your help," his mother replies. "You are very brave and have used your gifts well."

"But Bunny's not . . . back together again," Cathy says. "I failed." She puts her head down on her knees and sobs. Blake's mother puts her arms around the girl and embraces her tightly.

"No," she murmurs. "You succeeded. You have freed my son from an unnatural prison. Because of the wekufe, his time here extended far beyond what was meant for him. But through your efforts, Blake can move on. You succeeded." Gail repeats. She releases Cathy and stands.

"We need to go now, Blake," she says and extends her arms to him.

Blake hugs Cathy quickly. "Thank you," he murmurs into her shoulder. He releases her and goes to his mother's side. "Take care of my dad? I know he's not your favorite person, but you and your sisters and your mom are all he has now."

Cathy nods, a quavering smile on her lips. "Yeah, of course. I think I've gotten over myself when it comes to him. He's a good person. He'll be okay."

Blake grins. He looks up at his mother, and everything around them vanishes into a haze of glorious light.

CHAPTER THIRTY-SIX

UNTIED

CATHY CLOSED HER EYES against the blinding flash. When she opened them again, she stood alone amongst the stinking heaps of the Philipse County Landfill. Tears streamed down her face as she thought about Bunny leaving. He had looked so different—not as thin, and his face had lost that haggard, haunted look. His giant T-shirt and old jeans had disappeared as well. What had he been wearing? It had looked as if he had been clothed in light. There was no other way to explain his transformation.

Gail, too, had been radiant. Cathy had seen her in photographs, and she had been a beautiful woman in life, but just now—

"'Angelic' seems apt," she mused. She untangled herself from the curtain. She winced as she peeled the blood-stiff fabric away from her cut hand, but the scab held even as it pounded with pain. The curtain appeared to be the only thing in the dump that remained of Holly Place's ruins.

No, that wasn't true. Cathy spied the leather book wrapped in the velvet folds as she stepped free of the material. She picked up the book and then stood as she scanned the horizon for the best way out of this mess. She made her way across garbage bags, piles of appliances, and construction materials. She stopped after a few minutes, shading her eyes with one hand and looking around to get her bearings. The sun was high in the sky, and she didn't feel sure she was going in the right direction.

Just ahead of her, a small pile of trash shifted. A few black plastic bags tumbled down from the top of it and burst when they reached bottom. *Ugh*—there must be rats in there, digging for something.

The stench grew worse as the bags split and spilt their contents. Cathy wouldn't have believed that the smell could get stronger, but it did. She buried her nose in the inside of her elbow and worked hard at not gagging.

Then she dropped her arm in shock, the reek forgotten. A hand was working its way out of the moving pile. She ran forward and pushed as much refuse aside as she could, then grabbed the hand and pulled with all her strength.

"Richard," she cried, and he came free all of a sudden. They tumbled backward together and landed on an old piece of plywood. Lying on her back, Cathy gazed up into the tilting blue eyes she loved so well.

"It's really you this time," he said. "For a while I thought you had turned into an evil demon."

"And I thought *you* were dead," she said, her voice breaking. She could feel tears running down the sides of her eyes and into her ears.

"I thought I was, too. But are you sure we're not? Because this place smells about as hellish as I can imagine." Rich brushed her hair back from her forehead and smiled.

"Oh, no. I've been to hell recently," Cathy assured him. "It's nothing like this." She reached up, put her filthy, sore hand on the back of his neck, and brought his lips to hers. The long, slow kiss lit a delicious fire in Cathy's core, but didn't do anything to disperse the dump's fetid reek.

Rich rolled off of her, braced himself on his elbow, and looked around. "Whew. Back to reality. The last I remember, I was in Holly Place's basement getting buried in an avalanche of rock. I guess the house really did sit exactly where you said it did. What happened to it?"

"I'm not sure." Cathy sat up. "Zared told me he killed Januarye, and I think she was . . . part of the house somehow."

Rich nodded, his lips set in a grim line. "Yeah. It was the worst thing I've ever seen. And I was helpless against him. I let you down in every way possible. I am so sorry."

Cathy looked up at the gorgeous blue sky, trying to put all the puzzle pieces of her ordeal together in her mind. "No," she said after a few minutes. "I think Januarye had to die. I think this was all part of her plan. Everything happened the way it was supposed to."

"So Blake is . . . ?"

"Blake is dead, too," Cathy said, her voice trembling.

"And that's what was supposed to happen?"

Cathy nodded. "Yeah. I still haven't come to grips with it, but he's not in this world anymore. I just saw him. He's with his mother now, which is what he wanted in the first place." She swallowed the lump in her throat and looked at her bloodstained shirt, searching for a spot she could use to wipe her eyes. After a few seconds, she gave up. "We've got to get ourselves out of here," she said. "I can give you all the gory details of the dragon slaying once we're home, cleaned up, and I'm released from grounding—probably when I turn eighteen in December."

"Right." Rich winced. "Real world fallout from otherworld-ly battles. Not pretty." He looked all around. "I don't suppose you stopped by the library and brought my crutches with you, did you?"

"The library?"

"Never mind. I'll see your gory details and raise you one miracle at some point in the distant future. Do you have any brilliant solutions to our situation? We're going to add sunburn to our woes if we don't figure something out soon."

Cathy stood up. She had gotten out of this dump before; she had to be able to do it again. She didn't have Holly Place or Bunny as a focal point this time, though. Could she find a way to walk between the worlds without one? She closed her eyes and thought about Januarye. A snippet of melody floated into her mind and stirred her memory. She chanted the odd skipping rope rhyme the girl had sung at their first meeting—

God guard me from those thoughts men think

In the mind alone;

He that sings a lasting song

Thinks in a marrow-bone

—then repeated it twice more.

The smell of the dump faded. She opened her eyes and saw that she stood between worlds again. In one, Rich lay at her feet on a rotting pile of garbage. In the other, a pristine green meadow extended in front of her, a double row of ancient sycamores holding back the wild woods beyond.

She gasped and whirled. Holly Place rose whole and unspotted before her, its smooth stone walls and tall windows intact, its serene beauty restored. A tall woman in a rose-colored gown stood on the top step of its porch, a gleaming white stone on a golden chain around her neck.

"Januarye?" Cathy couldn't believe what she saw. She turned to Rich and crouched down in front of him. "I'm going to carry you piggy-back," she said.

"You can't lift me out of here by yourself," Rich protested.

"I don't think I'll have to. Just do it—trust me."

Rich looked at her, thinking for a moment. "I guess I shouldn't ever doubt you again," he said finally. He scrambled onto his knees and levered himself onto Cathy's back. Grunting with effort, Cathy hoisted him up and faced Holly Place again.

"Look," she directed. "Can you see it?"

"See what, the rusty bicycle, or the old washing machine?"

Cathy narrowed her eyes, forcing the world of the dump to recede, until only Holly Place remained. Rich's resulting cry of amazement felt very satisfying, and she laughed out loud. Then she moved forward across the lawn slowly.

"You're really heavy, no matter what realm we're in," she panted.

"Let me down. I can walk."

Cathy looked down at Rich's knees, that she supported with her bent elbows. His twisted limbs had straightened themselves out again.

"Nothing stays out of true here," Januarye said. Now that she appeared as an adult, she looked and sounded just like Athena, Cathy marveled.

"It's good to see you again," she said.

The woman inclined her head in her direction. "Who are you?" she asked.

Cathy frowned. "I'm Ca—" she caught herself. "That depends," she responded a moment later. Out of the corner of her eye, she saw Rich look at her quizzically.

The woman gazed at her, seemingly bemused. "Yes. It depends on what you need."

"I need—we need to get home."

The woman nodded, satisfied. "Then I am Catalyntje," she said, curtsying deeply. "And you are a true Voorhees, Cathy Wright. Be welcome to *Hulsthuys*, both you and your friend." She motioned for them to approach. "I will take you where you need to go. Come with me."

Cathy and Rich climbed the porch stairs and followed Catalyntje, who now stood to the left of the massive front door. Cathy placed her hand on the lintel and felt the house's pulse.

"Go through the door," said Catalyntje.

Cathy turned the knob and pushed the door open, but did not recognize the room before her. Instead of Holly Place's front hall, she saw a room filled with bookshelves and old, comfortable-looking chairs.

"The Reference Room," Rich breathed. "This is where I found Januarye." He pointed to the floor near a wooden display case. "My crutches are right where I left them."

Cathy looked at Catalyntje, a lump back in her throat. "Will I ever see you again?"

The beautiful woman smiled. "If there is a need . . . or perhaps a want."

Cathy nodded, looked around the porch once more, and stepped through the door. Rich followed her, walking easily until he came to his crutches. With a sigh, he picked them up and fitted them to his arms. In an instant, he resumed his regular form. He looked at Cathy with grief in his eyes.

"It was . . . fantastic while it lasted. But, hey," he added, glancing down at himself. "At least we don't look—or smell—like we've been camping in the dump anymore."

Cathy looked down. It was true: she was clean, her clothes appeared freshly laundered, and the gash in her hand had completely healed. She sighed as she flexed her fingers. One less thing to explain—that was a mercy.

Rich moved to the door and took a key off a little hook on the wall next to it. "I need to return this. Are you coming?"

"Yeah." Cathy glanced at the display case and did a double take as she saw the engraving of *Hulsthuys* within it. "Goodbye," she whispered, touching her fingers to the glass for a second. She followed her friend into the main part of the library.

The librarian took the key from Rich without a word, but her watery blue eyes glinted as she put it in her desk drawer.

Outside on the sidewalk, Rich looked at Cathy. "Where to?" he asked as they walked.

"I'll go to the hospital. I'm betting Malcolm is still there with Blake's body, and my mother is probably there, too. I don't even know how long I've been gone, or how I'll explain all this, but maybe it will be forgotten for now. We've got a funeral to plan, and all."

Cathy's mixed emotions threatened to overwhelm her. She felt happy for Blake, but knew that Malcolm and Athena must be devastated by what they knew of the circumstances of his death. She knew they would need her more than ever now. She remembered that she needed to erase Blake's hard drive the minute she got home, and she'd have to find a way to sneak a look through all his stuff before his father started sorting through it.

How would her sisters deal with another death? Bunny had made contact with Mae, at least. Maybe she and Fawn would have an easier time understanding all of this than she might have thought.

Inside the hospital's main doors, she turned to Rich and threw her arms around him. "I don't know what I would have done without you," she murmured into his ear. "I love you, and I feel so lucky to know you."

He squeezed her with one arm. "I love you, too." He kissed her then, his lips so tender against hers that she wished time could stop so that she could savor the moment forever.

"I'll stay here and wait for you," he said when it was over. He smiled at her before swinging himself over to a row of plastic chairs in the waiting room. "Good luck," he called as he sat down.

She rolled her eyes. She would need it.

Outside Blake's hospital room, Cathy paused. She didn't feel ready for this. "The only way out is through," she reminded herself, and pushed open the door. Her family stood with heads bowed around Blake's bed, the myriad machines now silent. Cathy put her hand on her mother's shoulder and looked at her stepbrother's lifeless body.

"I'm back," she said.

Author's Acknowledgments

I am deeply indebted to the following:

Jump Rope Rhymer Extraordinaire: William Butler Yeats

Peerless Editor: Stephen Carter

The FabuBabes: Anne Eliason, Dianne Freestone, Jana Winters Parkin, and Kimberly VanderHorst

The Rough Writers: Jennifer McBride, Frank Morin, Stephen Nelson, and Lee Ann Setzer

Critique Angels: Christine Edwards Allred, L. T. Elliot, Jennifer Haines, Josi Kilpack, and Annette Lyon

Dutch Consultant: Ellen Cornelis

Chief Muse and Head Cheerleader: Patrick Perkins

Raisons d'Etre: Christian, James, Hope, Tess, Daniel, and Anne Perkins

About the Cover

Jana Winters Parkin came up with the book's genius title. Cali Gorevic took the magnificent photograph of Ireland's Moore Hall. Jason Robinson created the gorgeous cover. Thanks to you all. I know that potential readers will judge this book more kindly due to your incredible talents.

CPSIA information can be obtained at www.ICGtesting.com
Printed in the USA
LVOW102006220113

316782LV00033B/1511/P